EDGE

EDGE: Book Three of The Golden Trilogy
Copyright © 2018 by K.M. Robinson.

Published by Crescent Sea Publishing.
www.crescentseapublishing.com

Cover designed by Reading Transforms.
Image copyright © K.M. Robinson Photography.
Interior graphics by Millennium Genesis.

EDGE

K.M. ROBINSON

Crescent Sea
PUBLISHING

DEDICATION

One spark can light your entire universe on fire. One choice, one action, one word can give permission to change the way a life is lived.

To those of you who are unintentional world changers-spark the world for good.

My story ends like this:

Having been discovered, Goldilocks is forced to fight for her life, clawing her way away from the enemy. With her new family by her side, she runs into the war to free her people, but not everyone will survive. As she discovers that every choice she makes, she will be held accountable for, she must do everything in her power to survive the consequences of her actions.

But the stories of Goldilocks and the Three Baers never mentioned just how deadly my story really was. No one ever said I would lose people on both sides of the war. They always forget to mention that I would have to do horrifying things just to survive and protect the people that I love.

My name is Auluria, but the world knows me as Goldilocks, and I won't stop until the entire Society has heard my name and taken a stand...one way or another. The Society will fall.

Chapter 1

My fingers failed me, tangling in my hair. Everything was muffled as I struggled to hide myself. Voices echoed inside my head, but I couldn't make out what they were saying.

Suddenly, I was snapped forward, jolted back to reality. Fixing my hood no longer mattered. Anetta tried to support me as I crashed into her. I came alive, realizing that we were under attack.

The Society men lunged toward us in the foyer of the mansion. I was suddenly grateful Canton had been led away before the soldiers realized who I was. Justin had good timing.

The noise of the fight dulled over the loud tearing of fabric. A red tapestry boasted a long tear, threatening to topple from its place on the wall. The ripping cloth drew my attention when it shouldn't have, making me involuntarily turn. A rough hand on my shoulder forced me to reach for the knife resting on my hip, its jagged edges begging to be used.

I sliced the man's arm, silently hoping that it was the worst damage I would have to do. Blood bubbled up on his skin as his eyes grew narrow and fiery. The man's nails dug into me in what I assumed would end in yet another scar on my body which was already marred by so many tales.

Gregory took the man down just as I drew back to attack once more. He nodded at me solemnly; the first time I'd ever seen him anything less than flirtatious.

"Behind you," he nodded.

I spun on my heels to confront whatever waited for me, my hair splaying out with my movements. Instead of being confronted with an attack, I found Shadoe grappling with a soldier.

"Here," I announced just loudly enough for my former handler to hear me.

I stepped beside him, taking a defensive position. Before I could help, Shadoe leaped forward and snapped the man's neck. Shock waved over me in the two seconds between the dead man hitting the floor and another soldier rolling over my shoulder as I ducked, tossing him effortlessly as he attacked.

Shadoe looked impressed as I stood back up, having felt the man's approach and flipped him over. I turned away from Shadoe to see where else I could help and was immediately confronted with Dov's eyes, ten feet away. They were wide and surprised, but that same brilliant shade of deep blue.

I smiled to let him know I wasn't hurt, but it immediately faded as a soldier approached him. I jerked my head to the side to give him warning before I raised my hands, using my left arm to steady myself, and released my knife at the soldier. It embedded itself in the man just before Dov attacked.

"Auluria!" Silas shouted a warning, looking beyond me. "*Anetta.*"

I followed his gaze to where Anetta was fighting off two soldiers and failing. One grabbed her around the waist, attempting to lift her off the ground. Eden launched herself at the second man, kicking him so hard in the hip that I thought I heard it crunch. He toppled into a man beside him, taking them both to the ground. Shadoe and Locust appeared out of nowhere, slicing the soldiers' throats.

I ran to Anetta as she kicked in the air. She bit down on the man's hand, making him shriek and swear. I pulled an extra knife from my boot, plunging it into her captor's arm. The blond fell to the floor, bouncing up as soon as she hit the stone. Pulling her own knife, she drove it into the soldier's leg. His boot helped to protect him from her attack. He grabbed Anetta's hair, ripping it out from under the hood that only partially covered her head.

Locust—having finished off the men Eden had kicked down—stood up and took three wide steps forward. His hand dug into the soldier's wrist as he held him in place. His grip forced the man to release Anetta. He pulled back, preparing to hit the man as I turned.

"Fancy seeing you here." The low voice sent tingles up my spine.

The knife glistened in his hand as it moved toward me. The blood had been wiped off, though only so much could be removed from the strange, jagged blade without a proper cleaning. My sight traveled up the length of his arm to his face.

"Your knife, my lady." Dov smiled before growing serious. "Are you okay, Auluria?"

I took the blade from him, heat exploding through my hand when our skin touched. Tucking my backup weapon away in my boot, I opted to keep the knife Shadoe had provided for us.

"So far," I replied. "You?"

"Yeah," he mumbled before another soldier moved toward us.

I moved behind him, taking a position to cover his back. Hearing Dov fighting without being able to see him made me slow as I focused on what *he* was doing. I forced myself to block him out of my thoughts in order to protect him.

I kicked a soldier causing a sharp pain to crawl up my ankle where I had injured it before the attack on the mansion. I sucked in a deep breath, trying to control the burn creeping through my leg.

The soldier came at me again, yelling something I blocked out. I lowered my stance just enough to get a secure footing, putting as much weight as I could on my uninjured leg without throwing myself off balance. When he moved, I elbowed him in the nose. Blood gushed down his face.

He stepped forward again, undeterred by my hit. I prepared to strike, but suddenly, he fell at my feet. Silas lowered his weapon, having used it to hit the man in the head, knocking him out.

"Miss me?" he asked as he turned our two-person team into a trio.

"Nice to see you haven't died," I could hear the grin in Dov's voice as he called over his shoulder.

"Reinforcements are here," Silas informed us.

I glanced around, noticing that most of our team was in the foyer. Berwyn had made his way to Eden and Anetta, who appeared to have formed a partnership during the fight. Ben and Carter must have finished securing Wallace's men if they were available to join the combat, leaving us one less thing to worry about during the battle.

"You all okay?" Raselin yelled from a few feet away as he fought with a soldier.

I stepped ahead, darting my good leg out to sweep the Society man's feet out from under him. He crashed forward, nearly taking Raselin down with him. A tooth bounced across the ground, looking like a horrifying white bug skittering across the forest floor. I heard every ding and scrape it made as it moved.

Raselin nodded and shrugged when the man didn't get up.

"Works for me," he added.

"Shadoe!" Dov warned loudly.

"Shadoe, no!" I echoed when I saw that my former fiancé was doing as much damage as he had when he threatened Canton in the weapons room. Bodies littered the floor. "We need them."

Nikko took out another Society soldier before looking to Shadoe for direction. I searched for Ella but didn't see her in the room. I tried not to think about what mission Shadoe had sent her on that would have prevented her from joining the fight.

Shadoe nodded, knowing he had to play by the rules in a room filled with people who would not tolerate his deadly behavior. Berwyn's people and Raselin's group would work together to outnumber Shadoe's team if anything were to happen.

"Give up now and you won't get hurt." Berwyn's voice filled the room, giving the remaining Society men an option.

Most of the soldiers relented and stopped fighting, knowing they were outnumbered. One man rushed forward, refusing to back down. He launched himself at Devin. I leaped forward, despite knowing I would not be able to reach him in enough time to help. Devin tossed the man over his shoulder, protecting his newly-healed arm. He kicked the man's arm, making him cringe into himself. Carter stooped down to bind the man's wrists behind him.

I found Silas and Dov giving me questioning looks when I turned back to them, having only made it a few feet forward to help Devin.

"You didn't actually think you were going to help that situation, did you?" Eden scoffed from behind me.

"I was going to try," I growled back at her, knowing she wasn't being malicious, but also not caring of her intentions.

"Get these men taken care of," Berwyn announced. "Quickly. We still have to handle the men outside."

"This isn't over yet," Raselin added.

We quickly scrambled to determine who was awake, unconscious, or dead. The men who gave themselves up were bound and taken to the cells. I walked a man down the dark corridors with Eden and her charge as Dov and Silas carried an unconscious man behind us.

The cells were as bad as I remembered. The chill seeped into my bones as the hollow silence filled every space in my body. The last time I was there, I was meant to die, and my cousin, Lowell, had been the one to sentence me. The walls held the memory of my last conversation with my cousin.

Eden tensed next to me, her gait becoming stiff. She pushed the soldier forward with sharp fingers to his back between his shoulder blades. I forbade my muscles from tightening around my captive's hands; he didn't need to know my terror.

Dov and Silas looked less concerned about being in the space. I assumed they had been down here since our arrival. Dov had spent so much time in the mansion during his captivity that it was practically his second home. It didn't seem to affect them to be back in the cells... or they hid it well.

"Right," Dov instructed as we neared the end of the hall.

We turned, finding another series of hallways.

"Take the first one," Silas said, his voice strained under

the weight of the unconscious man he was helping to carry.

We steered our charges down the walkway and found ourselves in an entirely new wing of cells.

"I didn't realize this was down here," Eden mumbled.

The man in front of me started to say something. My nails dug into his wrists silencing him before he could start.

We locked the men up, keeping them bound to prevent them from helping each other inside the cells. Dov and Silas checked all the locks on the prison doors before we left.

"We didn't either until we explored once we got in," Silas explained, "once we were away from the Society men."

"*I* didn't even see all of this," Dov commented as I slipped an arm around his waist, tucking myself under his arm as we walked through the muted gray lights of the cell passageways.

Shadoe and Raselin walked toward us, carrying another unconscious man. I expected Shadoe to try to talk to me, but instead, he locked eyes with Dov. They held each other's gaze until we passed, continuing to the foyer to see if we needed to move more Society bodies.

Several of our people filed past us, moving the Society prisoners to their new living quarters deep below the magistrate's mansion. I watched for my friends as we moved.

"You okay?" Dov whispered quietly in my ear, his lips tangling in my hair.

I nodded, not trusting myself to answer out loud. His hand tightened against my hip, pulling me closer. I leaned toward him, resting my head on his shoulder for a moment before stepping into the foyer.

Berwyn noticed us as we stepped into the light, motioning us to join him. Eden hurried to take her spot by her husband. His fingers slipped around her hand quietly at their sides so that only our tight circle could see.

"We have control of the mansion again, but we're going to need to handle the soldiers outside," Berwyn guided the conversation, his angry tone ever-present. "We're going to have to use Canton to deal with the courtyard."

"Can we trust him?" Eden asked before I could open my mouth to speak.

"Where is he?" I followed up.

"Justin is still guarding him. Apparently, he got Canton to a cell and kept him ready in case we needed to use him to end the fight down here." Berwyn grimaced at the thought of coming so far only to play our hand before we were ready. "He's still with him...I'm assuming because he's thinking what we're all thinking—Shadoe will do something reckless."

"No surprise there." Silas and Dov murmured at the same time.

"What's the plan?" I asked, knowing I probably wouldn't like it. I wasn't fond of not knowing the next step. It reminded me too much of my time with Lowell.

"We're going to have to take Canton out and have him calm the courtyard." Dov took my hand, mirroring Berwyn and Eden. "And, once we've done that, we have to get a stronghold in the towns."

Dov glanced at Berwyn.

"One of us is going to have to go out and tell the people what is going on. They'll side with us, but right now, they have no idea what's going on here. Once we do that, then we can start to use Canton against the Society."

"And who is going to go out into the towns to do that?" I asked.

Dov's eyes shifted to me.

"No," I forbade it. "You are not going out there. Someone else can go."

"It has to be one of us," Dov tried to persuade me. "Berwyn can't go. He needs to stay here and lead everyone. If it can't be him, it has to be me."

"What if *I* go?" I insist, trying to find another way.

"No offense, Auluria," Silas interjected. "But even though people have heard about you, you still worked for

Lowell, and Lowell is dead. They might not know which side you are on."

"Despite the fact that you did all this, babe, the famous Goldilocks is still not as well-known as the sons of Griz Baer." Dov grinned, teasing me.

"That's not fair."

"We can't all be famous, Auluria." Dov's eyes sparkled as much as they did the time we sat on the floor of his house, mending socks and fantasizing about taking on the Society soldiers.

"*Auluria* might not be famous, but Necesta has been awfully quick to start spreading tales of *Goldilocks*," Raselin said, sidling up to the group, running his fingers through his dark brown hair. "Don't underestimate her... she knows what she's doing."

"Which one?" Silas smirked.

"Both." Raselin leveled a glare at him, removing Silas's joking grin.

"The point is," Berwyn growled, "That we need to handle making Canton cooperate first."

"Are we considering letting Shadoe handle this?" Raselin asked with concern. "He seems to be the one the Magistrate fears, but do we really want to let him oversee Canton?"

"Do we have a choice?" I asked. I trusted him more than the others did, but I still didn't like what Shadoe was turning into.

"Can Justin handle it? He did well before the fight." Silas suggested.

"He can handle it," Dov, Raselin, and I all said in unison.

"The better question is whether we can afford to have Justin be Canton's handler and lose him for everything else."

"Would it be better to let Shadoe oversee Canton and let Justin help with the missions we're running?" Eden added, tucking a lock of hair back over her shoulder. It caught on the hood of her uniform as it lay on her back, leaving the strand of hair at a strange angle.

The group took a collective breath, puzzling out the best choice for the good of the team. It was quickly interrupted as Talley walked up.

"Whatever we're planning on doing, we need to do it now. The Society men outside are not going to wait any longer," she announced. "What's the strategy?"

The tall woman glanced at me, then to Raselin, looking for an answer. When we didn't speak, she turned to Berwyn.

"Well?" she prompted.

"Do we have a plan yet?" Devin bounded up next to his sister, looking out of breath.

"Are you okay?" I asked as he leaned forward to calm his rapid breathing.

"Yeah, I just ran from Justin to find out what's going on."

"Is he okay up there with Canton?" Talley asked, concern filling her voice.

"He's fine. Canton is behaving. But Shadoe is up there, so we'd better get moving if you weren't the ones to send him."

Everyone turned, sprinting toward the flight of stairs. Deep red carpet covered the stair, so soft it felt like layers of moss piled on top of each other.

"Time to vote," Berwyn said. "Who do we leave in charge of Canton?"

"Justin." Eden cast her vote first.

"Justin," Talley added, assuming her vote counted as part of the leadership vote.

"Justin," Devin echoed a vote for his brother.

"Shadoe." I shocked the Hersh siblings into looking at me. "We need Justin elsewhere and this will give Shadoe something less destructive to do. Plus, Canton is already under his thumb. He's terrified of him."

"She makes a good point," Raselin nodded. "Shadoe."

"Shadoe." Silas grimaced.

Dov only sighed and nodded once.

"Shadoe," Berwyn finished the count.

"You're not moving him." Justin's voice rang out as we approached the room Canton was being held in.

"Get out of the way, Hersh. We don't have time for this." Shadoe threatened.

"You're not taking him until I have confirmation that he is really supposed to be moved," Justin argued.

"Are you really going to take me on?" Shadoe's strong voice filled the hallway.

"Enough," I shouted, still far enough away that I wouldn't be able to step between the men, even if I wanted to.

I rounded the corner to find Shadoe and Justin facing off, chest puffed out and standing at full height. Canton leaned against the corner as I peeked over Berwyn's tall shoulder. The magistrate looked defeated as he slumped against the wall, eyes bouncing back and forth between his captors. He perked up when he saw the top of my head peering at him from behind Berwyn.

"Stand down," Raselin said from alongside Berwyn. "Shadoe, we need you to handle the magistrate's announcement. Justin, you're working with these three."

He nodded to me, indicating Justin should follow us. My friend's eyes bounced from Raselin, to me, to his siblings, and back to me. I nodded, hoping he would cooperate.

Reluctantly, he stepped aside, moving toward the door. Shadoe turned toward Canton.

"Up," Shadoe commanded.

Canton scrambled to his feet, locking eyes with Shadoe, ready to obey.

"Excuse me," Justin said quietly, slipping through the door once Berwyn and Raselin had stepped inside to give Canton directions.

Devin and Justin traded a look. Talley looked unimpressed with her brother's decision to take on Shadoe.

"What's the plan?" Justin asked.

"You and Dov are leaving. Now," Eden said before anyone else could speak. "They're handling Canton and quelling the soldiers outside. You two are sneaking out while the men are distracted by the announcement and you're going to rally the townspeople. We need them on our side."

Justin nodded.

"And the rest of you?"

"We have things to do here. There really isn't time to explain. You need to go." Eden reached out and put a hand on his arm, pulling him into motion. Dov followed quickly behind.

It took everything inside of me to force myself not to argue. Dov needed to do this—it was the only rational way. I had to stay and keep Shadoe in check. I was the only one that could.

"We'll be back in a few hours," Dov whispered quietly. "I'm not that easy to get rid of."

He grinned before surprising me with a quick kiss.

"Don't let this get out of hand." He took my hand and placed it on his chest when we reached the door.

"I'll watch him," I assured him.

"Don't get caught," Talley said a few feet away. She patted her brother on the shoulder.

"Come on," Justin said, nodding to Dov. "Let's get moving before the announcement starts."

The two men slipped out the door into the bright light of day. The white light bounced off the mansion floor. The light colors reflected the white light harshly, temporarily adding a green haze to my vision as I watched the people I cared about disappear into the world.

"They'll be fine," Talley acted as the voice of reason. "They're both very good at this."

"Justin will watch out for Dov." I murmured, knowing that he would.

"He knows to watch for Dov's injuries. He's not quite back to himself yet. Besides, unlike the rest of you, Justin isn't well-known. He can blend in and watch, where Dov will likely be recognized. They'll make a good team."

"Auluria," Eden's voice echoed from the stairway. "Get up here!"

Chapter 2

"Happy?" Shadoe asked sarcastically.

"Yes," I responded as he came to a stop in front of me. He squared his feet with his shoulders and glared at me from behind crossed arms.

He watched me as if hoping I could guess what he wanted me to say. I didn't care enough to try.

Shadoe had forced Canton onto a balcony overlooking his soldiers. He quietly stood just behind the magistrate's shoulder, off to the side, acting as his personal guard. Every word was precisely spoken to planned perfection as the man convinced his minions to do his bidding. In the aftermath of his announcement, he cowered in the next room over under Devin's watch.

"What?" I shouted, demanding my handler say something as I looked up from the map I was studying.

He continued to stare for a moment before storming off. I considered going after him, but after everything that had happened that day, I needed a few minutes to myself.

The paper crinkled under my fingers as I gazed at it. My eyes traced the town lines. I followed the length of the Wall surrounding the Society, marking each place I thought we should begin the teardown process once we had defeated the Society. Liberating Raselin's country to the northeast would be the next thing we needed to do.

"Learning anything important?" Silas's voice frightened me.

Two deep breaths and I banished my shock, returning my shoulders to their normal position after gasping. Anetta smirked as she took a seat across from me at the table.

"We need to free the camps." I redirected.

"I know," Silas agreed.

Anetta shifted her focus to the window on the side of the room. Her eyes bounced slightly as she focused on something. I turned to glance outside. In the dark, small green lights flickered on and off.

"Didn't you see enough of those with Lowell?" I teased.

"I like fireflies." She shrugged.

Silas moved his chair closer to mine, leaning into my space to look at the map.

"Here," he pointed. "This is the route Dov would have taken. He's starting here, then here, and here."

His fingers traced along the towns, showing me where my boyfriend would be completing his mission. My gaze moved outward to the other towns. We needed a plan to reach them.

"The first step," Silas said as if reading my mind, "is to get control of the justices in these towns. If we can gain control there, we've got a shot."

"Once we handle that, we should be able to get at least two of the other magistrates," I added.

"And if we can get them, we've got them all. We know, we know." Anetta rolled her eyes, turning back from the scene outside the window. "But how do we get them?"

"Once we have the towns and the camps with us, it shouldn't be hard to do exactly what we did here." Silas looked up from the map briefly to address her.

"This one," I said, pointing at the piece of paper, making it crinkle again. "We need this one."

Silas inspected it.

"You're right," he said, making me grateful for Shadoe's training. "We need that one first. We have the best chance of getting in there unnoticed."

"But we also need the rest of them."

"Or at least most of them." Silas nodded. "We'll have to send out multiple teams."

"What are we going to do about Marjorie?" Anetta interrupted, demanding answers.

We both looked up, slightly surprised at her outburst.

"She'll stay locked up in the cells," I answered, "For now, anyway."

"But she *will* answer for this?" she pressed.

"She will. Just not today." I felt Silas's leg tense next to mine as he spoke. I bumped his foot with mine, assuring him he didn't need to prepare to stop Anetta from running down to the cells and taking her revenge on her former best friend.

"Just how do you plan on breaking into the camps?" She changed the topic.

"We have a few ideas," Silas said, glancing at me, telling me he and Dov already had a plan. "You probably won't like them."

It was light when I woke up, still early, but not early enough to be up before visibility entered the room. I moved the covers off my body, remaining warm for only a moment before the rush of air beat against my skin.

I looked back, the pillow re-inflated, erasing the dip

where my head had been resting. I brought the covers back up over the top of the bed, something I hadn't had to do since fleeing the Baer's cabin. I paused, wondering what had become of their family home.

I moved to the curtains, drawing them back just enough to see outside. It was quiet out. A few Society soldiers stood at their posts, but nothing concerning. I half expected a war to be raging three floors below me as I looked past the curtains.

Turning back, the bed caught my attention. As a child, I had slept in a small bed at my aunt's house, though nothing like ones in the Magistrate's mansion. My aunt's house had been small and safe. The mansion was bigger than anything I had ever seen. All of the comforts of this life invaded the space, cloaked in deep reds. I wondered if red was the color of all of the magistrates or if Canton just had a thing for that hue.

I crept to the door, still cautious to stay quiet. I paused, listening at the door. After a moment, I turned the handle, peering into the hallway.

"Morning, Goldilocks," Nian said as he stepped into the hallway from the landing.

I raised an eyebrow.

"You should go downstairs," he waved his hand toward the door. In his signature move, he reached up and brushed back his bangs. "There's food down there, and we've got a long day."

"Thanks," I answered, walking past him to the stairs.

The marble was cool against my hand as it glided over the banister. I pulled my hand away and raked it through my hair, trying to untangle it before I reached the bottom of the stairs.

I heard Dov and Silas talking before I walked into the dining room. They were seated at one end of the table, plates of food in front of them. Maps sat beyond the plates, toward the center of the far end of the table. Dov had a knife in his hand, slicing the apple that rested in his other palm.

They both looked up when I entered, Dov jumping to his feet. He grinned.

"Told you I'd be back."

"Yeah, yeah." I brushed him off with the wave of a hand, taking a seat next to him.

"I brought you a present." He handed a slice of apple to me.

"Just what I always wanted," I grinned as I bit into the slice.

"The present brought *herself*, thank you," a voice said behind me.

"Reyla!" I unintentionally yelped when I realized to whom the voice belonged.

"Sit," she commanded before I could rush to her. She slipped into the seat next to me. "The girls are with me.

Dov figured we'd need some reinforcements for storming the camps."

I glanced at Dov, giving him a pleased look.

"It's less about needing our help getting in, of course," she teased, "and more about having other females to comfort those poor girls in the camps once we break them out."

"Good point," I said, accepting another apple slice from Dov. He leaned closer.

"The boys pretty much have everything covered," she added.

"Did you expect anything less from these two?" Katarina swayed into the room, making her way to the opposite side of the table. She took a seat by Silas as I beamed. The whole team was coming back together.

"Well, good morning, Sleeping Beauty," Justin walked in and caught sight of me. His head swung around taking in the sight of the newcomers. "Well, well. If it isn't the prettiest ladies from the Baer clan."

Grabbing an apple off the table, he rubbed it against his shirt as if to clean it. Katarina noticed appreciatively while Reyla bit back her smirk. Silas gave him a strange look as he sat next to Katarina. Justin eyed the maps. He turned to Dov, waiting for an explanation.

"Camps," Dov said by way of an explanation.

"I get to go too, right?" Justin prompted.

"Yes," Dov nodded. "And your brother and Talley, too, if they want. Fitch is coming as well."

"Shadoe?" I asked, risking a look up at Dov.

"That's up to him, I suppose." Dov shrugged. "He's going to have to decide what is more important."

"Does he know about this yet?"

"Yes, he found us on the way in."

Reyla leaned toward me, adding quietly, "You might want to go help him with that little decision."

Her eyes told me more than her words. I needed to go see Shadoe. I ducked my head, mumbling confirmation that I would help him work out what he needed to do behind the veil of my hair, blocking my face from the others.

Berwyn ambled into the room, eyeing the food we were all picking at.

"Nice that Canton had so much ready for us."

"He had a lot of people to feed," Silas replied.

"Don't forget, now *we* have to take care of all those people," Eden said, following Berwyn into the room. "Speaking of...has anyone checked on our visitors in the cells today?"

"Raselin is down there now. He took Arin and Fitch with him, so I'm assuming they're looking for information," Justin answered, leaning back in his chair. "I think Talley was on her way to check on them when I passed her in the hall."

"We need to leave quickly," Dov reminded us. "Not all of the teams can leave at once. The ones going to the camps on the edge of the Society need to leave immediately so we can strike at the same time."

"Berwyn and I worked out a list of the teams last night," Silas offered.

I glanced at him. It must have been after I had fallen asleep.

"Once Arin and Raslin are done with the interrogations downstairs, hopefully, we'll have a little more information about how to get into the camps. The only thing left is to talk to Canton." Berwyn's response sounded more like he was grumbling.

Dov subtly shifted closer to me. I liked having him back.

"We're going to the Wall," he whispered.

I nodded quietly, trying not to draw too much attention from the other people seated around the table. I picked up a piece of food and popped it into my mouth, not taking the time to taste it. I was pleased that I had confirmation that I wouldn't be held back to watch over Shadoe, should he end up remaining in the mansion to keep Canton under control.

We finished eating as Berwyn, Dov, and Silas ran over details of the mission. They'd have to do it again for the larger groups, but they used this time to work out the details with the inner circle. I found my hand in Dov's by the end of the meeting, resting against his knee under the table. I had to force myself to not lean my head against his shoulder.

Raselin, Talley, and Arin joined us, revealing what they had learned about the camps. The Society soldiers had proved helpful enough, giving us locations and details we needed to make decisions.

"Hello, Goldilocks," a voice crooned in my ear, making me jump. "Your friend needs to see you."

Necesta pulled back, taking a few strands of my hair along with her. They didn't detach from her sweater until I turned to face her, pulling them away.

"You too, Charming," she nodded that Dov should follow.

We stood, excusing ourselves from the meeting and followed Necesta out into the hallway. I noticed how strong she looked now that she wasn't trying to deceive her own community into thinking she was frail and helpless. She still walked with the weight of her maturity, but she acted at least ten years younger than the appearance she had projected when I had first met her. Even her posture was straighter than I had ever seen her stand on her side of the Wall.

"Your young friend has a choice to make, and I don't think he's making it well," Necesta explained. "You need to go talk some sense into him."

She glanced at Dov, looking him up and down.

"And she shouldn't be doing the convincing alone."

"Do you have a preference on whether he stays or goes?" I tried to withhold my smirk at Necesta's oversight on the matter.

"Whichever is best, dearie," she shrugged. "You know more about this situation than I do. I just don't want him to meltdown before a decision is even made. He looks like he's about to burn so hot that he will melt right into a puddle on the floor."

"Well, that can't be good," I mumbled, picking up the pace.

Ella glared at me as we approached. She was leaning against the doorframe, arms crossed harshly over her chest. Her hair sliced into the line of her arm, falling halfway between her shoulder and elbow in a vicious straight line. I had no doubt if she whipped her hair toward an oncoming enemy, it would decapitate them where they stood.

"Where is Shadoe?" I tried to keep the edge from my voice.

"With Nikko and Sherman," she huffed.

Refusing to let her try to intimidate me, I raised my eyebrow at her, mirroring her glare. She relented after a moment, nodding across and down the hall. Necesta paused to engage the girl in conversation while Dov followed me to the door.

The handle felt cold in my hand, threatening to send

a tingling chill through my spine. I forced it down and swung the door open. All three men looked up, scowling at the sight of me, then looking downright murderous when Dov followed me into the room.

"Have you made a decision?" I asked.

"I get a choice?" Shadoe's voice teetered between anger and shock.

"Of course," Dov said. "You're a leader here too, Shadoe. We're all working together on this."

"You're just going to support me, whichever way I choose?" Shadoe challenged.

"On this, we are," Dov put his hand on the small of my back, creating a united front. I hoped it didn't set Shadoe off. "There are benefits and downfalls to both staying and going. You need to be the one to make this choice. Do you think you will help the group better if you stay and control Canton or if you come with us to help free the camps? It's up to you."

Shadoe stayed quiet for a moment, collecting his thoughts.

"I'm not sure yet."

Sherman looked like he wanted to say something, but out of loyalty to Shadoe, he remained quiet. I took that as my cue.

"Yes, you are," I softly prompted. "You know what you need to do...you just don't like it."

Shadoe flushed a shade of red.

"Shadoe, where do you need to be?" I took a step forward, hoping to show him that I was on his team with this. "What is the best strategy here?"

"I need to stay," he said reluctantly. "I need to stay here and control Canton because if anything goes wrong at the camps, the other justices and magistrates are going to need answers, and Canton needs to be the one to give them to them. I have to be here to oversee him."

"Okay," I confirmed his plan.

"Our men need to go," Shadoe insisted hurriedly. "They need to go and bring down the camps. Even if I have to stay, our people need to go."

"Okay," I agreed to his terms.

"I want a say on who goes," he pushed.

"Okay," Dov nodded.

"I want to help plan the attacks."

"Okay." I was starting to get annoyed. "Shadoe, we're not cutting you out of this. You can be involved in everything. Berwyn and Silas were working on a strategy last night, and Raselin and Arin interrogated the soldiers in the cells this morning. You can go to them right now and help plan."

"Well, there is one thing we need you to do first," Dov halted the conversation.

"Canton," Shadoe snarled.

"Ready?" Fitch asked, ambling up beside me, his wife trailing behind him.

"We have to be."

I glanced up at the top of the staircase to where my former handler stood. The moonlight filtered in from the high circular window, cascading just to the left of where Shadoe stood. Dust floated in the air, spinning at odd angles in the light.

Shadoe glared at my boots, asking without words if I had extra weapons with me. I tapped the toe of my boot once, letting him know I was annoyed he was asking such an amateur question.

He shifted his gaze, locking onto Nikko as he stood a few feet to my left. Shadoe didn't look at me again. He had left oversight of Lowell's team in my hands... assuming Nikko was unavailable.

Reyla used her hip to bump into me, reminding me not to roll my eyes. The last thing we needed was to upset Shadoe before we left him behind.

A cool breeze filled the room as the door opened. The changing weather took away any hope of warmth in the evenings, sending even the crickets into hiding. I stepped into the pale night.

Through Canton, Shadoe had commanded the rest of

the Society men into cells, adding another full wing of men to the confined rooms below the mansion. Our own people patrolled the courtyard, nodding as we made our escape into the night.

Fifty men and women from three different groups converged together to form one rescue party as we set out for the camps near the Wall where Dov and I had once said goodbye. We had control of the area, but were still cautious, wearing Society uniforms and breaking into small groups to travel, with intervals in between our departures. We set up several checkpoints along the way, but we each had to find our own path to the same destination.

"I still don't understand how you tolerate these things," Katarina grumbled before branching off with Henry and Carter's group. She glared at the trousers she was wearing.

"She'll never get used to them," Reyla smirked under her breath. "They aren't *terrible*, but they wouldn't be my first choice."

"I know," I cast her a sympathetic look.

"This is where we split up," Fitch announced, looking around at the group. "See you all tomorrow at the checkpoint."

He nodded to the group surrounding him and they took off, jogging out of sight. Twenty minutes later, it was our turn to follow. Reyla stayed by my side as we moved out, Dov keeping a watchful eye on us.

The stars sparkled in the sky, darting in and out of the wispy gray clouds trailing our steps. Like shadows in the sky, they moved along with us. The warmth of Dov's hand in mine kept me focused on the journey and not the heavens above.

"It's nicer when we aren't running, isn't it?" Dov leaned toward me an hour into our journey.

"Can you tell in the dark?" I questioned, giggling. "Oh, that's right. I forgot...owls can function in the dark."

"Still not an owl," I smirked, running his free hand the length of my arm.

"Lovebirds," Silas coughed harshly, sending Reyla into a fit of giggles. She looped her arm through his.

"We should probably start taking bets on this," she motioned to us.

"On what?" I asked.

"We should," Silas ducked his head toward her conspiratorially. Together, they examined us.

"Looking for a show?" Dov stopped walking. He pulled me close, wrapping his arm around my waist.

"Oh, gross," Silas teased as Dov kissed me.

Reyla laughed, her voice only catching on the last note of her melodic giggle. She was probably thinking about Peter, the love she lost in a Society attack. I pulled back, wanting to spare her feelings. I swirled my thumb over Dov's hip twice to let him know I wasn't pulling back because of him. He flawlessly bounced back into step, hand falling to intertwine with mine.

"Jealous." I saw Dov mouth the word to Silas, mercifully keeping quiet in front of Reyla. He must have noticed too.

Silas glared at him before rolling his eyes and shaking his head. I would find out what girl he liked if it was the death of me.

"So, you all ran all this way?" Reyla started up a conversation. "That must have been awful."

"Well, it wasn't fun," I remarked.

"It certainly wasn't," Dov agreed. "Speaking of which, we should check in on Barone if we can. I'd like to make sure he's okay. I heard rumors about a man being hurt for helping us, but I never knew if it was true or if it was some device Canton was using to try to break me."

"Let's hope it was a ruse." I realized I hadn't even had time to think about the man who had helped us escape since I returned from the other side of the Wall. "Hopefully, he'll be safe in his home and we can rest there for an hour and tell him what's going on."

"I'm excited to meet him. He sounds lovely," Reyla chirped cheerfully, echoing the first bird of morning in the distance.

"We should probably pick up the pace if we're going to make it to the checkpoint before it gets too bright out,"

Silas reminded us. We broke into a jog down the main street of a sleeping town.

Twenty minutes later, we slowed, pausing our steps by the side of the road. The trees hung out over the street. Silas and Dov jumped, trying to reach the apples on the lower branches. My eyes darted to Reyla before sprinting to the tree trunk. Taking a running start, I threw myself at the bark, praying my foot would give me enough resistance against it to propel myself to a branch. I clawed in the air, miraculously grasping onto the rough bough. Scrambling up, I moved onto the branch.

I inched my way out on the thick arm of the tree as the boys managed to rip off an apple.

"Heads up," I said before releasing two apples above them.

Dov and Silas caught them, tossing them quickly to Reyla.

"Get enough to take for the others," Dov quietly shouted up to me.

I heard Reyla shuffling things around in the bag she had brought, transferring the contents to Silas' bag. Each apple I dropped smacked into waiting hands, only to be transferred with a thud into the sack.

"That's all we can fit, babe," Dov stopped me. I pulled four more apples and dropped them below for us to eat on the way. "Do you need a hand?"

"No, just step back," I cautioned, preparing to drop down out of the tree.

I positioned myself to sit on the branch, suddenly grateful I wasn't in a skirt that could get tangled in my descent. Inhaling, I kicked my feet out, pushing myself off the branch, only catching my body with a hand wrapped around my former seat. My body jarred to a stop as my grip prevented me from falling. My feet swung with the momentum of the sudden movements, and I paused long enough to glance down to make sure I wouldn't hit anyone when I let go.

I landed on the ground, surprisingly avoiding hurting my ankle. Suddenly I thought of Eden and was exceptionally thankful I wouldn't be hobbling to the Wall like she had the last time we went there. Everyone looked impressed that I had remained upright. I had been prepared to fall and roll and felt like a part of myself was missing when I didn't complete that part of my self-assigned mission.

I held my hand out for my apple, realizing they had cleared out Dov's bag as well to make room for more food. The more we gathered like this, the less we had to acquire from the towns and cities we passed through.

My teeth broke into the skin of the apple. A sharp, sweetness raced over my tongue and lanced into my ears, painful for just the first second as the taste exploded against my lips. My tongue recoiled against my back teeth, attempting to quell the unexpected feeling. The second bite was gentler.

"These are really good," Silas commented.

"The checkpoint should be just a few streets that way." Dov pointed to the left, apple still in his hand.

When we rounded the corner, my hair bristled. One street to go and something was wrong.

"Stop!" the voice behind us commanded.

Chapter 3

I clenched the apple core in my hand, wishing I hadn't eaten it so quickly. Even with my non-dominate hand, I was certain my aim would be true if I needed to throw it at the soldier's face.

We turned to find a group of men standing behind us. Their clothes were worn, covered in dirt. One man had a tear in his shirt. They held brooms and shovels that I had no doubt were meant to give a plausible reason for having a weapon at the ready.

"Who are you?" the same voice asked.

"Who are *you*?" Dov said authoritatively.

We hadn't expected townspeople to stop us.

"Wait," the man studied us. "I know you."

His eyes flitted from Dov to me, locking onto my hair.

"You're Barone's friends," he loosened his grip on his shovel.

"You know Barone?" Silas asked cautiously, aware that Barone was still a town over.

"You're Griz's kid," the man continued.

The entire group of men relaxed. Ordinarily, I would assume it was a trap—a clever way of getting us to let our guard down—but the feeling that normally resided in my chest when bad things were about to happen refused to make an appearance.

"Who are you?" I asked.

"Name's Chester. We're on your side. Word has been going around that you're rallying troops," he paused when my eyes grew wide. "Worry not, miss; it's all being kept very quiet. We all want this to end as badly as you do. We're ready to help."

He motioned to the group as they all nodded.

"Barone and I are cousins. You can trust me," he placed a hand over his heart. Leaning forward, he added, "He told me you stayed with him once."

He looked us over before nodding to each of us.

"You, and you, and you." He identified us as the people Barone had described to him before assessing Reyla. "You look a bit young to be—"

"She's not," Dov, Silas, and I answered, confirming that she wasn't Eden.

"Ah," he recovered. "Well, he told me most of you

stayed with him. Your father was kind to him back in the day."

Dov nodded, relaxing beside me. *Another ally.*

"Where do you need to go?" Chester asked.

"We're meeting our team," Dov explained.

"And you're going to the camps?" Chester questioned. "We'll go with you. You're going to need all the help you can get. How many people do you have with you?"

"Fifty," Silas confirmed. "We'll never turn down help, though."

"Good, I'd hate to have to argue with you. Come on," he said, pushing by us. His men followed.

At the end of the street, they let us take the lead, not wanting to frighten our team.

"Everyone safe?" Fitch asked, greeting us.

"We're all here," Dov confirmed. "Did the other groups make it?"

"Almost, just waiting on Nian's group to show."

Dov explained about the recruits we had picked up along the way. Several of the new men raced home to tell their families what they were doing. They would catch up along the way.

Reyla and I passed out the apples we had collected to the team.

"Well, isn't this sweet?" Justin grinned.

"The apple or Auluria?" Reyla questioned as she transferred the contents of her bag back into her sack.

"The apple, but Goldilocks too, I guess," he teased.

"Is there a particular reason you're here, sunshine?" I asked, throwing out the first nickname I could think of.

"Food," he replied, crunching into the apple.

"Where are your siblings?" I pretended to snap with a grin.

"Devin is over there," he nodded. "Talley is...somewhere. I don't know. She's fine."

"Talley is probably the most capable of you Hersh kids anyway," I commented, watching his eyes spark, ready to challenge me.

"Just be glad you aren't one of us...you'd never hack it," he smiled triumphantly.

"I'm pretty sure she could give you a beat down, baby brother," Talley joined us, slinging her arm around Justin's shoulders.

"Which is why I like *her* best of all," I taunted.

"I'm wounded," Justin flailed around like I had stabbed him in the heart.

"What, did she tell you that you're not pretty enough, baby bro?" Devin grabbed his brother's chin and shook it playfully while dropping his insult in a baby voice.

"Oh no," Talley said in a deadpan voice. "Don't tell him he's not pretty."

She glanced sideways at her youngest brother. Justin gaped at her, shocked that she had gone there.

"Why do I talk to you all?" he yelped playfully.

"Well, I think you talk to Auluria because she's pretty." Reyla sounded like Katarina. "I have no idea why you talk to your siblings."

She shrugged, slinging the pack over her shoulder.

"Awww, it's okay, big guy," I chattered. "You're still prettier than me."

I patted his shoulder, attempting to stifle a giggle.

"Do I need to be worried?" Dov asked, joining the group.

"Oh, be careful, Auluria," Reyla leaned in and whispered loud enough for just the small group to hear. "Gloria is over there. You don't want her swooping in on your man."

Dov looked more affronted than I did, making Justin and Devin burst into laughter.

"Relax, I think she's finally given up," Reyla said apologetically.

"Don't you give me that look, Dov Baer. I distinctly remember you flirting with her the night you took me on that raid," I chastised.

"*Reallocation project*," Dov corrected with a smirk. "Besides, she couldn't win me over even if she tried."

He stepped forward and drew me into his arms as the rest of the group hassled us. His arms felt extra warm around my waist as I pulled him closer.

"It's a good thing you came first, Baer, or we'd have to beat you up for doing that," Justin added.

"Really," Devin said as if we made him gag.

"I think they're cute," Talley interjected, bumping Reyla with her shoulder as if they were on the same team.

"I guess I can see it," Devin relented.

"Fine, whatever," Justin sighed, rolling his eyes. "But seriously, enough with the kissy face."

"Oh, leave them alone, Justin," Katarina waltzed over. She moved quickly to Justin's side and looped her arm through his to lead him away as Henry paled. "If they want to kiss, I say we let them. None of us get much of a chance to do that these days."

"Shame," Justin said grinning wickedly at her.

Suddenly, as if propelled by some unseen force, Henry darted forward and latched on to Katarina's arm. He whipped her back so quickly that she collided with him, nearly sending them both crashing to the ground.

Everyone froze, watching the scene unfold.

He stared at her in his arms as she blinked quickly at him. Her face melted out of her shock and into a radiant smile.

"About time, Henry," she said in a low, quiet voice.

He kissed her and Reyla and I accidentally cheered out loud. It didn't deter them one bit. Devin and Justin joined in, clapping enthusiastically.

"You kids can thank me later," Justin joked.

"Who knew you were the key to solving everyone's relationship problems, Justin?" Devin clapped his brother on the back. "You hang out with Katarina, and she gets together with Henry. You hang out with Auluria, and she gets back together with Dov—"

"Hey, now! To be clear, she was getting back together with Dov long before I came along."

"And for the record, he never tried to steal her," Talley quickly interjected, wanting to make sure her brothers didn't inadvertently get themselves in trouble with their leader.

"Never thought he did," Dov said confidentially. "But even if she had, my girl never would have fallen for it."

He winked at me.

"They're here…" Silas trailed off as he jogged over to the group. "What did I miss?"

We all nodded toward the newly official couple. Katarina snuggled into Henry's chest as he held her protectively. Silas beamed.

"About time, buddy. Well done," he turned back to Dov. "They're here. Time to move out. I think Fitch is done grilling Chester, by the way."

"I assume he cleared?" Dov said, turning to follow Silas as he nodded.

"There's something you need to know, Baer," Chester said, meeting him halfway.

Dov waited quietly for Chester to proceed.

"We're going to Barone's next, right?" he asked

cautiously. "You should know that he isn't quite the same as when you left him."

"What do you mean?" I asked, stepping alongside of Dov.

"Once you left, you see," he said as he wrung his hands nervously, "Magistrate Canton wanted information. He sent soldiers looking for anyone who might have seen you. Someone must have figured it out because they came for him."

"Oh no." My face fell.

"He withstood the beating, but..."

"But what?" Dov asked somberly.

"He's missing a few pieces, that's all," Chester replied, looking down at his hands again.

"What do you mean?" Silas stared.

"He means that there are always consequences, Silas," Fitch interceded. "We've all learned that the hard way over the years."

"No one gets out unscathed," I murmured, catching Dov's attention. It was something my aunt used to say, more as a warning than anything else.

"You lot will come with me to see him," Chester informed us. He nodded toward Raselin. "He thought it would be best if we didn't overwhelm Barone."

"The rest of us will go on as planned and you'll meet us at the next location," Fitch concluded. "Raselin will be joining you."

Lowell's voice in my head argued that we didn't have time for a side trip, that we were wasting valuable time. Basic humanity quickly won out, elbowing my cousin out of my head. He was dead, and his vicious agenda should be too.

I was grateful Raselin would be joining us. He would keep us on track—it would be far too easy for us to get distracted. Reyla might not have met Barone, but she would react the same way we would, wanting to stay and fix the problem we had created. Raselin would have to act as our clear head.

Dov nodded as Fitch glanced over my shoulder.

"Time to head out," he murmured.

"We should go, too," Chester echoed quietly. He turned on his heels and started out.

"Time to go," I muttered to Reyla as we fell into step.

"I'm going." Barone raised his voice.

"I don't think that's a good idea, cousin," Chester pleaded with him.

"We finally have a chance to do something about those camps, and you expect me to sit here and do nothing?" the older man argued.

"Barone," Chester's voice retreated to a whimper.

"I'm going," he said, placing his stump of a hand on the table. He lifted himself off the bench with great effort. It scraped across the floor, echoing loudly in the silent room.

I saw Dov take a deep breath, preparing to engage in the battle to convince Barone to stay. Barone's foot hung limply as he held his weight on his good leg, bracing himself with his arms against the table. He was in no shape to travel.

"Barone," Raselin interjected, directing the man's attention away from his fight. "Chester said you had information for us..."

"Yes," he said, shifting more weight onto his hands. He looked to Dov before continuing. "I know the guard schedule."

"What?" Silas tipped his head.

"At the camps, boy," Barone leaned forward, shifting his weight again. He needed to sit down. "I know when the guards come and go."

Realization crept over Dov, Silas, and Raselin's faces. Barone wanted to come along, and he might withhold information to do so. I stepped forward, taking a seat on the bench across the table from him as he eyed me. Placing a hand on the table, I tried to draw his attention in enough to quietly convince him to sit.

"Barone, how did you find this information out?" I asked quietly.

From the corner of my eye, I could see Dov and Silas visibly relax as I took control of the situation. Lowell would have been thrilled that I was putting my training to good use.

"How did you find out?" I repeated as the older man watched me with hesitation. I patted the table, inviting him to take a seat and join me in conversation.

Slowly, he lowered himself to sit, leaving his remaining hand on the table. Three fingers stared back at me. Searing pain crept into my own fingers just looking at the mutilation the Society had caused. When we returned, I would be having a conversation with Magistrate Canton on behalf of Barone's missing pieces.

"I watched them," he started, leaning forward sadly. "After I lost my family, I started watching the soldiers. I watched the camps, looking for an opportunity, but I never had the manpower to do anything.

"That day you stumbled into my house... I had just returned from another mission to scout the soldiers who were on their way to the camps. I haven't been able to go, but a few of my people have been watching it. It hasn't changed in all these years.

"The Society is arrogant. They think no one can overtake them—and so far, they've been right. None of us have been able to get the upper hand. But now.... Now we stand a chance. Now that we're all working together, now that we have more people," he paused to nod to Raselin, "Now we can fight and win.

"But they don't know that. The Society has no clue that we can stand against them. Their imperiousness has left them with a false sense of security, and they've become apathetic. Their systems haven't changed in years. We know their game, and now we can win it."

"It hasn't changed at all in years?" I asked. "Not even after we escaped Canton?"

"Not even then." Barone forced a smile that looked more like a grimace. He swallowed hard.

"Your people have confirmed this?" I confirmed.

"They have," he nodded, finding a less painful smile. "We can get you in."

"Barone," I said as I placed a hand on his. He flinched in surprise, his remaining fingers flexing instinctually under mine. "I know you want to help, but do you think you can really make it all the way to the camps? I see the way you're shifting your weight when you stand. Your leg is injured."

"I'll be fine," he grumbled but didn't shift away from me.

"May I look at it?" I asked. "There was a woman I met, a friend of ours, who helped to take care of me when I was hurt. She taught me a few things."

Barone suddenly looked concerned when he heard I had been injured, a fatherly look slipping over his face.

"What happened?" he demanded.

"May I look at your leg?" I asked again, hoping to keep him on track.

"What happened?" he repeated, looking to Dov.

Dov nodded to his leg, indicating that we would fill him in as I examined him. He acquiesced and pushed the bench back. A pebble dug into my knee when I knelt on the floor to the side of the table. I brushed it away, adjusting my position in an attempt not to wince. I worried about adding validity to Dov's account of my injuries as he filled the man in on what had happened.

Necesta's training offered me little help. I could tell something was clearly wrong, but I didn't have the skills to properly assess the damage. I glanced at Reyla. She was watching me examine the leg, well aware that I was clueless. The best I could do was to offer some peace from the pain.

"Here," I said taking a small vial from my pouch. "I don't know enough to really help—I'm sorry—but this should make it a little less uncomfortable."

"What is it?"

"It's for pain," I responded, unsure of how to answer. "We've all used it, and it's been a great help."

Dov, Silas, and Reyla nodded in response.

Barone nodded sharply and opened the vial, quickly swallowing its contents without argument. He set the container on the table.

"You're not going to let me go, are you?"

"No," I said quietly, looking down.

He sighed.

"It's time we had a talk."

Dov tucked the maps inside his uniform, shielding them from unwanted eyes. Each paper contained small marks, a code that they had developed in case the papers fell into the wrong hands. The marks spelled out everything we needed to remember to find the right locations to break in once we arrived.

Walking away from Barone was nearly as difficult as walking away from my aunt's home with Lowell when he took me in after her death. He leaned against the door, watching us go, knowing there was nothing he could do to help us. The Society had taken everything from him, including the ability to fight back. I had no doubt that wouldn't stop him from hindering the Society's efforts on a more local level though.

"We have to get the timing right," Silas said, talking to Dov about how to split up our forces. "If we hit all at once, they won't be able to get their feet under them in time to stop us."

"I want to verify this first," Dov replied, hand slipping

to his chest where the papers were hidden inside his pocket. "We need to watch them just to confirm."

"Agreed," Silas nodded.

"I think we need to split up," Dov directed the conversation.

"I think we need to split up *intentionally*," Silas glanced meaningfully at him, indicating that Dov and I shouldn't be in a position to be a distraction to each other.

"I'd say there is some merit in that for *everyone*," Raselin mused. I wondered if he knew something I didn't. The secrets were starting to frustrate me.

"Look," I glared at them, "I know you two have issues being separated, but I think you can manage one mission apart. I promise I'll take good care of Dov."

"And I'll take care of Silas," Reyla grinned, reaching up to grab his chin like she was talking to a child. "We won't let either of you do anything foolish that will get you killed and ruin your friendship."

"That's not—" Silas tried to interject, making a face.

"Oh, but it is," Reyla stopped him. "That's exactly what you meant because we know you *of all people* weren't trying to say Dov and Auluria are too emotionally invested to work together."

Raselin opened his mouth to say something, but Dov and Silas cut him off, making him suppress a grin. The brunette shook his head, refusing to give anything away, when I squinted at him, silently begging for more information.

"We'll be fine," Dov said definitively.

"I don't think it's a good idea," Silas countered. "Auluria and I work well together; I think we should partner up."

Reyla looked down at the ground, deciding to stay out of it as we walked

"We could each lead our own team if that's what it's going to come to..." I supplied.

"Do you honestly think we need so many teams?" Dov asked, raising an eyebrow at me.

"Four isn't bad," I insisted. "Reyla and I can lead a team. We'll be fine."

"I believe in true love," Reyla jumped back into the conversation, "but I'm also totally fine with working with Auluria."

"Aww, did we just turn into these two?" I asked, pointing at our leader and his right hand.

"I think we did," Reyla nodded seriously.

"Well, you can't break up the team, now can you, boys?" I asked, challenging them.

"I don't think it's a bad idea," Raselin said as we slipped off the road, entering the forest. He ducked under a branch that nearly snapped back and hit Silas in the face.

He caught it, holding it up for Reyla to duck under while I walked around it.

"I still don't think we need an extra division," Silas added.

"I agree. I'd rather have Auluria and Reyla supporting us."

"Fine, but I'm working with Dov," I respond. "I'm tired of being separated."

"Me too," Dov said softly.

"Silas and I have always worked well together, so I guess that's settled." Reyla finalized our plans.

We stayed near the edge of the woods, watching the town, as the wind tugged at our uniforms. I reached back to adjust my hood, attempting to make it lay more comfortably. Hoods and long hair did not mix when the goal was to hide the hair. A gust of wind knocked into the side of my head making the fabric grate harshly against my ear.

"Well, maybe the noise from the wind will cover up our approach," Silas smirked.

"Can anything keep you from being noticed, Silas?" Reyla teased.

Before I could jump in, Raselin's step faltered.

"There they are."

On the horizon, sitting on a fallen tree, were Justin and Talley. They perked up when they saw us, Talley raising her hand in greeting as Justin jumped to his feet.

"I see you made it," Talley welcomed us. "They're all waiting over there."

She pointed deeper into the woods where everyone was setting up camp for the night, far out of sight. Justin stared directly at me until I gave him a small smile, letting him know I had survived seeing Barone in such a shattered state.

We changed course, walking further into the cover we had become so familiar with over the years. Leaves rattled on the trees as the wind slammed into them, growing softer as we continued forward, only to spring back up as we let our guard down against it.

"You good?" Justin sidled up next to me, bumping his arm against mine.

"Yeah, I'm good. Where's Devin?"

"He's at the camp."

"Didn't want to spend too much time with you, huh?" I grinned.

"Nope." Talley came up behind us, pushing her brother's head forward good-naturedly. "So I got stuck with him."

"Barone had some interesting information for us," I added once I finished rolling my eyes at their antics. "He knew the guard schedule at the camps. We know when and where to hit to get in."

"That's great," Talley said somberly.

"We're dividing into three main groups, and we'll take

on the camp from there," Dov instructed. "One from the front, one from the back, and the last group will follow once we're in to help with any resistance we encounter."

"Sounds like a smart plan," Justin nodded.

"Have you figured out the teams yet?" Talley asked, reaching up to push back her hair.

"Yes, on our way here," Dov nodded. "You're all together with Auluria and me."

"I can work with that," Talley agreed. "Justin?"

"Works for me," he concurred. "What about you, Rey?"

"I'm with Silas' team on this one," Reyla smiled. "We're taking the opposite side of the camp from you."

"My team will be the follow-up," Raselin added. "We'll be taking point on the girls' camp, though."

Ahead, I could begin to see signs of our team. The quiet murmur of voices was momentarily carried to us on the breeze, mixed with the scent of smoke. A colorful leaf chased after it, landing at my feet. I stepped around it, not wanting to crush the pretty thing.

"You're back. Everything okay?" Carter called down from a tree, making Reyla startle.

"We're good," Dov tipped his head up to see his friend through the leaves. "Everything look okay up there?"

"Yes, sir. We're good," Carter nodded, shifting on the branch where he was perched, legs stretched out and crossed at the ankle. He leaned casually against the trunk of the tree, hands folded on his lap, but he was clearly alert and watching for signs of intruders.

We continued walking toward the campsite, eerily feeling like I was stepping back into my transient life with my cousin before he had sent me to the Baers. We paused to nod as we walked by more of our scouts, hidden quietly in the trees.

"Hey, *Goldilocks*," Gregory said slyly as we passed.

"Probably a good thing you're up in that tree, Gregory," Dov taunted, nodding toward me. "I don't think you'd fair well if you were within arm-range."

He chuckled, grinning at me.

"I'm sure you're right, Dov. That's why I'm doing it from up here!" Gregory laughed hard enough to nearly knock himself off balance. He quickly reached down, grabbing onto the branch to steady himself.

"You know, I don't actually feel bad about that," Dov laughed, raising his hand to wave as we continued.

"Would have served him right," Reyla giggled.

"Oh please, you would have been the first one by his side had he fallen," Silas teased.

"Are you really insinuating that I'm faster than Auluria is?" her eyes sparkled.

"That...is a good point," Silas bowed his head in defeat. "I don't think anyone could outdo the legend of Goldilocks at this point."

"Really? It's come to this?" I mocked, rolling my eyes.

"I think you're just going to have to accept this, Auluria," Dov wrapped his arm around me, pulling me close.

"Necesta has done me no favors with this," I muttered.

"She kept you safe and built you a name," Dov replied quietly. "And even if you don't think it's helped you, it's helped us. People have heard about Goldilocks. They've heard about the Baers. We have a reputation, and that's definitely helping this situation."

"What if it gets us killed?" I posed the darker side.

"Auluria, we were going to die anyway," Dov grinned. "Need I remind you of our little tangle with the noose not too terribly long ago? The Society knew who we were long before your name was ever known, and they've known about the three of us Baers for longer than that. But now the *people* know too. It doesn't change our fate either way, so why not live the glory?"

"I guess that's a decent point," I relented "Speaking of points and legacies, you and I still need to find time to talk."

"We will, I promise," Dov assured me, running his fingers down my arm as we walked. I fought against the shiver that movement made course through my body.

"Welcome back," Fitch greeted us as we walked into the space littered with campfires and supplies. The people resting looked up to see us, some raising a hand in greeting. "What did you find?"

"Answers," Raselin slapped his friend on the back. "We found answers."

"Come with us," a sharp whisper hissed in my ear as a hand latched onto my arm.

Ella tugged me away, nearly causing me to trip. I waved Reyla off as she started to follow me, wide-eyed. The girl dragged me away from the crowd, beyond the fires, to a quieter location, Locust in tow.

"What do you want, Ella?" I demanded, yanking my arm from her piercing grip. When I looked down, I saw the nail marks on my forearm.

Ella stepped back, glaring at me as Locust took the lead.

"We're going to have a little conversation, *Goldilocks*." He grinned lecherously at me now that we were away from the others.

Ella rolled her eyes. Crossing her arms, she kicked her hip out to the side, placing all her weight on her left leg, locking her knees to hold her pose. Her eyes traveled the length of my body, judging me. Dissatisfied with what she saw, she sneered at me, wrinkling her nose.

"You need to see Brittella," he informed me.

"What?" I asked in surprise.

"Brittella," Locust snapped. "You remember her, don't you? She trained you back in the day."

"Of course, I remember Brittella," I snapped accidentally.

"Shadoe said she's here, in the town. You need to go find her and bring her into this," he insisted. "She's stayed neutral all these years, but we don't have time for that anymore. You know her better than the rest of us, and we need her on our team. So, go get her."

"And do what?" I barked. "Just what is she supposed to do to help us?"

"You know exactly what Brittella is capable of," Ella reentered the conversation, growling. "And she has contacts that we need. Go get her and get her to work with us."

"We don't have time to waste," Locust grabbed my arm, turning me back to face him. "Get her here before we move out. She won't stay long. She hasn't stayed in one place for longer than a few days in a long time."

"She's not staying at her house?" I asked, trying to piece together a new picture of the woman I once knew.

I tried shaking him off, creating enough of a disturbance that people noticed. In the distance, I saw Reyla stretch up to see what was happening before turning away to point us out to Dov and Silas. They cautiously started to approach, giving me space to handle the situation before rushing to my aid.

"No, even Brittella knows when to get out. She may own half the people she comes in contact with, but she's smart enough to know when things are no longer safe." Ella answered.

"So then, how do we know she's here?" I challenged. "If she's on the move, why would she be here?"

"Shadoe has informants everywhere," Locust replied, "maybe he knows one of her people. Who knows? It doesn't really matter. Shadoe said you're going to do this, so you're going to do this."

Ella looked at me skeptically, waiting for me to step out of line so she could put me in my place. I owed Shadoe, and although I didn't understand his reasoning or know where his information came from, I knew I needed to play along. Having Brittella wouldn't hurt anything, and she *was* a master at manipulation and getting her way. I was willing to give this one to Shadoe and avoid a fight with his people—*our* people.

"Do you know where she is located?" I asked, backing them down as my friends drew closer, watching the scene.

"Locust," Ella warned when she noticed the approach.

He glanced sideways, noting my boyfriend. I could see his eyes twitch as he decided his next move. For a moment, I thought he would try to swear me to secrecy, but I judged wrong.

"Besides," he said, stepping back from me in a grand sweeping motion. "Your boyfriend needs to thank her. After all, it's the entire reason you're together."

He grinned at me, swaggering away. Ella pushed away

from her post, still angrily crossing her arms over her chest. She turned when she reached his side, eyeing me once again.

"You really owe Brittella for everything she taught you," Locust continued. "You'd probably be dead by now if you weren't able to seduce all those people like that to get out of all of those situations...or into them."

"Better hurry, Lur. We have a lot to accomplish," Ella grinned smugly before turning her sights on Dov.

The two walked away, leaving me to deal with the fallout.

"You'll know where to find her," Locust shouted over his shoulder as he slinked away.

"That was...interesting," Dov turned to me, waiting for an answer.

"They want me to find Brittella. She was one of the people who trained me before I was sent to you," I responded, annoyed.

"Trained you to do what?" Silas asked in horror, having heard their comments.

"Umm, to read people and respond to them in a way that would get them to do what I needed to do," I said carefully.

"She trained you to seduce Dov?" Reyla leaned in, whispering quickly in my ear so the boys couldn't hear.

"No," I yelped sharply. "Kind of...maybe. I guess. But not just that."

Dov patiently waited for me to finish panicking.

"She taught me persuasion tactics," I tried again.

"When was this?" Dov asked.

"Before you," I answered, hoping he wouldn't press for more. I clamped my teeth together, hoping to control the red flush tingling in my cheeks.

"And how did you meet this woman?"

"Lowell sent me to work with her." My entire body flushed with embarrassment.

"She worked with Lowell?" he asked skeptically.

"No," I quickly looked up. "She didn't work with him. He knew her, but she didn't work with him."

"Then what was it?"

I paused, unsure of how to answer.

"She was a woman he knew who had many talents and would occasionally train people. I'm not sure how many people Lowell sent to her, but I think the two of them were more like informants for each other. My cousin had information she wanted, and she had information he wanted."

"Interesting," Dov mused. "Just how often do you find yourself using what she taught you?"

"I..." I faltered. "She taught me how to get information out of people, so, I guess I use it enough."

"And who have you used this on?"

I searched his eyes, trying to figure out what he was asking.

"Just when I need information. She taught me to identify what a person wants or needs and use that to my advantage."

"As a female who could bat her eyelashes and get what she wants?" Silas offered, making me turn red again.

"Sometimes, yes."

"She was pretty good in practice," Locust yelled, making me whip around to look. I hadn't realized he stayed close by.

"I *never* did any of that *anywhere near* you!" I shouted angrily, making him smirk.

"But you did practice, didn't you?" Dov said a little sadly.

"No. Only with Brittella listening but not directly with anyone, and never that." I quickly said.

"No? So how did you get so good when it came to me?" Dov stepped closer, flirtatiously putting his hand on my hip. I hoped Locust saw and felt like it was a punch to the gut.

"I wasn't very good," I commented.

"Well, if *that's* what '*not very good*' is like, Auluria, I *can't wait* to see how you handle yourself with a bit more practice." He ducked his forehead to mine, lips a mere inch away. "You can practice on *me any*time."

Silas snorted, trying to keep in his laughter while Reyla swooned.

"Stop it, Silas," she hissed, "That was the most

gorgeous thing I've ever heard a man say and if you ruin this moment for them, I'll...do something horrible to make you regret it."

He laughed as her threat petered out. Silas let Reyla slip her hand through his arm as she guided him away. She peeked back over her shoulder, winking at me.

"You're willing to be my test subject?" I asked, locking eyes with him.

"If you really need one, I think I can help out," he grinned.

He tipped his head just slightly before pulling back.

"You didn't kiss him, did you?" He nodded toward the onlookers just enough so that I could see it, but not enough that they could.

"*Him?*" I gasped, horrified. "No. Never."

"Shadoe?" he asked sadly.

"No, never him either," I assured him. I unintentionally gripped his arms tighter.

"But you..."

"I kissed him, but never for that." I couldn't help the disgusted face I was making. "Even Brittella knew that."

"So, we have to go...what, rescue her?" He redirected.

"No, she's fine. She will *always* be fine," I answered. "She's Brittella. She's the only one of us who can pick either side and actually end up as the right-hand to the person in power without ever changing her allegiances. I don't know what it is about her, but she has the power."

"Then we are...?"

"We are asking her to join us. Apparently, she's in town."

"To what end?" Dov questioned. I reached up and tucked back a piece of his dark hair.

"She'll be an asset to us. She understands people more than any of us do." I let my fingers fall to his collarbone, grasping the edge of his uniform fabric. "I don't know why Shadoe wants her, but if nothing else, she'll be able to help us convince the people from the camps to join us. She's really good at convincing people to do things, but never takes away their free choice. She's kind of magical to watch."

I gave him a small smile. I respected the woman, though I didn't always like her tactics. I *certainly* didn't like her hold over my cousin...or maybe I did. It was nice to see him so out of sorts with her.

"Well, I guess we have to go see a woman about a membership to the club." He grinned. "But first..."

He leaned forward, closing the space between us.

Reaching up my back, he pulled me closer, tangling his hands in my hair. My tresses shifted, tickling the back of my neck, adding to the sensation of his hand searing into the skin between my shoulders and my head.

I pulled on his collar the way I had the day he kissed me after the fire. For an instant, I could smell the smoke from that day, but quickly realized it was a more present scent, directed to us by the wind as it carried the campfire smoke to us. It was mixed with the smell of cooking food, and Dov's lips crashed into mine faster, as if he were starving.

I waited, letting him dictate our moves, before making my own. Knowing we were very much in the open, I allowed myself one small moment to use some of the tricks my mentor had taught me on the man kissing me. He responded by grinning and playing into my every move.

"Well, that's more like it, Goldilocks." His eyes lingered on my lips as he slowly pulled away. "Any chance we can try more of that?"

"Are you going to keep calling me Goldilocks?" I taunted him.

He grunted with a nod before leaning back in to kiss me.

When we finally looked up, Silas was elbowing Reyla from where they had chased away Locust and Ella. They grinned at us, happy to see Dov and me back to a bit of normalcy.

"We should go," Dov said, brushing his nose against my hair.

"We should," I agree, standing there.

He smiled and sighed, pulling me into motion.

"Always making me do the hard work, huh?" he teased.

"Hey now," I challenged. "I recall a certain one of us pulling the other up a cliff once."

"And *throwing herself off a cliff once...*" he continued to tease.

I slapped his arm good-naturedly, using the other to pull him closer.

"Glad to see you two back to normal," Silas grinned.

"Should I even ask if you set that up, Silas?"

"No, Auluria, you should not," he started to walk away. "But for the record, I did no such thing. And quite honestly, I don't think it should be *me* that you're asking."

He glanced at Reyla, making her sputter.

"I would never!" she exclaimed.

"Would never meddle?" Silas threw a look at her. "No, of course not."

"Says the one overseeing everything!" Reyla spit back.

"Wait, what is this?" I asked, realizing there was more than met the eye.

"Nothing," Silas insisted.

"Nothing but a plan to get you two to a *happily ever after* like you were headed to before," Reyla informed us. "Don't you think for a second he hasn't been working behind the scenes on this."

"We, my dear, have been working on this," he said, "Credit where credit is due."

"Fine, thank you both," I said, shocking them.

"You're not going to fight us on this?" Silas asked.

"No," I leaned over and kissed Dov's shoulder as we walked.

"That was unexpected," Silas breathed. With a shrug, he added, "I'll take it."

"You two want to come with us to go find this Brittella?" Dov asked, glancing over at his friends.

"Actually, I think Reyla and I should go alone," I interrupted.

"Why?" Dov looked at me, concerned.

"Just trust me on this one."

"I'm in," Reyla smirked. "I like a good girls' mission."

"We'll be fine, you just wait for us by the edge of town," I said, grabbing Reyla's arm, darting away from Dov and Silas.

"By the edge of the town!" Dov shouted after us, mandating that we be there. I could feel him restraining himself from running after us.

"Edge of the town!" I confirmed, not looking back.

Chapter 4

Brittella was perched against a booth, her hip leaning against the edge of the counter. She leaned forward, speaking quietly to the man on the opposite side. The woman reached out and stroked the man's arm as she talked. He nearly swooned under her gaze.

"Really?" Reyla murmured as she noticed the woman commanding attention from every man within a twenty-foot radius.

She looked closer, watching Brittella maneuver the conversation.

"How does she do that?" Reyla turned to look at me. "Wait, can *you* do that?"

"I have no idea, I've never tried," I admitted.

"But she taught you how to do that?" Reyla pushed.

"She did."

"I'm not sure if I should be impressed or concerned," Reyla added.

"I'm not either," I sighed. "We should go get her."

"How do you propose we do that?"

"Wait here; she'll come to me when she sees me."

Reyla nodded, allowing me to go without protest.

I slipped around a few stands, ignoring the meager goods for sale and trade. Something spicy hit my nose, and for a moment, I thought about looking for food. My hand trailed along the booth as I left the thought behind.

Angling myself, I wandered into Brittella's line of sight. I turned, enough so she could see me, but not far enough to make it obvious. I would make her come to me.

She took a slightly longer breath when she noticed me, just enough to be noticed by someone watching for a shift in demeanor, but not enough to concern her entourage. Brittella swayed back, still engaged in conversation. I could hear the final strains of her laughter as it filtered over the crowd. She swayed again, and the crowd of men moved with her, mirroring her every move. Pulling back into herself, she ducked her chin to her shoulder, petting her dark mane as it fell across her chest.

She detached herself from the group skillfully, leaving them wanting more of her attention. They finally wandered off when she waved them away. The woman made her way through the tables, finding her way slowly to a place where she had easier access to me.

"Auluria," she purred, looking down at a table. Her fingers traced over a string of decorative beads, similar to the ones she was wearing. "Where *have* you been all this time, my dear?"

"Shadoe sent me." I ignored her question.

"Ah," she moved closer. "Your young man has stepped up since Lowell's passing."

"You know?" I confirmed with her.

"I know everything, Auluria." She smiled softly, a wistful look on her face. "The benefit of being me. Now, I asked you a question."

"I've been on Lowell's little mission," I tried not to sneer.

"Still?"

"New mission," I answered.

"With the Baers?" She picked up the beads, leaving a coin on the table. The owner kept his distance, allowing us to talk.

"And others, yes," I said cautiously.

"Why are you here?" She purred again.

"Shadoe sent me to find you."

"But why?" She finally turned, making eye contact with me.

"He would like you to work with us. Here is not the place to talk." I waited for her to respond.

"So, you and your friend have come to take me where?" She glanced at Reyla who was still waiting where I left her. "She's very pretty by the way. Have you trained her?"

"No," I frowned, wishing she would cooperate.

"Well, I've always loved a good conversation. Let's get on with it." She motioned that we should walk.

We walked together past the tables. She nodded to a few people as we moved through the area to the main road where Reyla joined us after I signaled her. Brittella had clearly been there long enough for them to become familiar with her, though I guessed not long enough to truly know anything about her. She was good at making friends and better at making contacts.

"Reyla, this is Brittella," I started.

"Reyla..." Brittella interrupted me, looking my friend up and down. "Beautiful name. I'm pleased to meet you."

She turned to me, an aware smile crossing her lips.

"This one has seen love," she nodded to her other side where Reyla walked. "I see you have too. Quite the change."

Reyla's eyes widened, but she said nothing.

"Who is he?" my former mentor asked. "Not that boy you were sent after?"

"His name is Dov."

"So, the rumors are true," she said lightly. "You're

working with the Baers. You're the famous Goldilocks. How quaint. Lowell would have some thoughts on this."

"Lowell is dead," I reminded her.

"Yes," she paused. "Shame."

She ran her hand through her hair, letting it fall in front of her.

"Do we like this new man?"

"We do."

"We *really* do," Reyla added with a smile. Brittella glanced at her.

"I suppose I'll get to meet this man?" she asked.

"Sooner than you think," Reyla muttered, stepping around a stone in the road.

"Ah, we're going to meet him," Brittella reflected. "How delightful. I look forward to meeting the young man who persuaded you away from your loyalties. I admire that, mind you. You took care of yourself. That's what I taught you to do."

"You did," I agreed. "And now I'm Goldilocks."

"The most well-known woman in the Society, I'd wager." She surprised me when she put her hand on my back. "At least that's the way I've heard it in my travels."

"Why did you leave, Brittella?" I had planned to wait to ask, but I took the opportunity. "What made you walk away?"

"Safety, Auluria. Alliances are shifting, as you well know. Lowell's men and the Baers working together? A warrior girl rising up in gold? All signs that it was time to manage my situation. I can tell when it's time to change allegiances, my dear. I've lived on my own, taken care of myself for so long, but I got comfortable, and comfort leads to carelessness. I couldn't have that.

"I knew I'd need new resources, new people to count on in times of war. War is coming, Auluria, but you know that. Safety is in the unexpected. Moving, changing, presenting myself to new people and disappearing...it's all unexpected. I'll survive this and so will the two of you. I'll help you."

"You'll help the two of us, or you'll help all of us?" I suddenly noticed every stone, every pebble, every piece of dirt in the street as I waited.

"I will help you," she said cautiously. "You're working against the Society, and right now, they are my only enemy—or at least my most important enemy. I'll help however you need me to. What is your plan?"

We quieted, moving as quickly as we could without raising suspicion. It felt strange to be in a dress again after so many days of wearing the Society uniform. The hem of my dark skirt brushed against my ankles softly. We would need to change back into our uniforms soon, but for the moment I relished it.

The two women and I neared the edge of the town, making our way to a silent street away from the crowds.

Once we were far enough away, I told Brittella about our plan to overtake the camps.

"I see," she followed my reasoning, responding quietly. "And I'm going to help convince them to join you, I take it?"

"I had hoped so, yes."

"You think you can't do that on your own?"

"Oh, I know she can," Reyla interjected, "but it never hurts to have more help. Auluria can't be everywhere at once. She also can't stay."

"You expect me to stay?" Brittella asked, surprised.

"No, just perhaps a little longer than we'll be staying," I replied.

"You're bringing me there and then leaving?" the tall woman remarked. "What could Shadoe possibly want me for then?

"We'll see when you return. I wasn't notified of this plan until a few hours ago."

"He's running his own strategy, then?" she bowed her head in thought. "That doesn't seem very productive, nor does it seem particularly helpful to your mission.

"Auluria, I've studied you for a long time. Even when you were younger, Lowell would tell me about you. I've also studied your friend. If I was a betting woman—and I have been, just not with the stakes most men lean on—my beautiful jewels wouldn't be placed on his plan.

"He's calculating, that's a given, but his strategy is

single-minded. He has an objective, and he takes the straightest, most true path. It's quicker, perhaps, but messier and more treacherous.

"His plan isn't your plan, nor is it the Baer's plan. I can tell."

"I don't know his plan," I admitted.

"I can tell that too. But he's still allowing you to be a part of it, whatever it is. There are pieces I'm missing though. I can't form a clear picture.

"Is he here?" she inquired about Shadoe's whereabouts.

"No, he's not." Reyla supplied.

"We have control of Magistrate Canton. He's watching over him."

"He's controlling him, you mean," Brittella corrected. "A man like Canton requires fear. Fear must be brought in a way Canton doesn't think he can escape and only Lowell's man can provide that level of insurance."

She grinned at the slight shock that crept into my face.

"You forget that I knew your cousin well, Auluria. Who do you think helped him with his little schemes? I may not have been one of his fold, but I certainly understood his game, and I knew how his people operated. You were the wildcard, my dear. You were the only unknown in his little enterprise. The rest of them all fit into a neat little box.

"Auluria, is that your man?" Brittella abruptly changed the topic, surprising me.

I looked up to find Dov and Silas standing above the tall grass at the side of the road. It waved around their waists like a river of light brown fuzz as the wind kicked up.

"Yes, that's Dov and our friend, Silas."

"Charming." Her purr was back.

She pulled her shoulders down and forward, making her collarbone pop out sharply as she held her upper arms taut against her body. Dipping her chin, she prepared to meet the boys—something she did every time she wanted to appear demure and fragile.

As we approached, I saw their eyes grow wide. My stomach dropped, worried it would be Lowell all over again. I couldn't bear the thought of my men following Brittella around like lost puppies.

"Hello," Brittella dropped her voice. As she neared, she held out her hand, waiting for them to take it.

Dov and Silas remembered themselves, adjusting their faces into a smile.

"You must be Brittella," Dov said, reaching politely for her hand.

"You must be the one she practiced on," Brittella said flirtatiously. Dov faltered, sneaking a glance at me. "It's easy enough to see, young one; she didn't have to tell me. It's nice to meet you, Mr. Baer."

"And this is Silas," I supplied, relieving Dov of responsibility of talking.

"Ma'am," Silas extended his hand for hers as well.

"Hmmm," she raised her eyebrows, staring at him intentionally until he squirmed. Only then did she release him from her hold. "Interesting. We should be on our way, gentlemen."

Her abrupt change in tone threw the boys, but they recovered quickly and led us deeper into the woods. They explained the plan as we returned to the camp, giving her only as many main details as were essential.

Once again, we were greeted by the scent of smoke on the wind long before reaching the site. A few crickets gathered, the last that remained so late in the year.

Locust was waiting by the edge of the camp. He disappeared into the darkness once he confirmed Brittella was with us, pausing for only a moment to leer at Reyla and I standing in our dresses. I made a note to change into our uniforms immediately.

The camp was bathed in an orange glow, and twisted gray smoke climbed into the sky. A fire sparked, dropping orange flecks to the ground as we made our way to where Raselin and Fitch were waiting. Lydia sat by her husband, clinging on to his arm that was nearly as wide as she was. She smiled when she saw us approach.

Raselin turned when Fitch nodded toward us,

glancing over his shoulder. When he saw us, he leaped to his feet.

"Brittella?" His jaw fell.

"Raselin," the woman faltered. I had never seen Brittella so out of sorts.

"They told me they were picking up a contact..." Raselin trailed off.

"It's been far too long," Brittella recovered gracefully, rearranging her face into a gracious smile. "I see you made it back."

"I did." Raselin returned her grin as Fitch's eyebrows shot up behind him in the background.

"I always wondered what had happened to you," Brittella murmured. "Shall we sit?"

Raselin suddenly backed up, making room for her to sit next to him on the log near the fire. He gestured for her to join him as Britella gracefully swooped in to take a seat. She reached out her hand, allowing him to steady her descent.

"We'll let you talk," Reed said, standing. He nodded to Nian who joined him.

"After you," Dov murmured, guiding me to a seat near Brittella. Reyla and Silas settled opposite us as I gazed across the flames.

Heat enveloped me, and I realized how cold I had been.

"How have you been, Raselin, darling?" Brittella took his hands in hers, patting the top of them.

"We've come to free us from the Society," he told her as if she didn't already know.

"So I see," she smiled pleasantly at him. "And you brought reinforcements, how lovely."

"I take it that you'll be helping us?" Raselin asked. "Is that the plan?"

He leaned forward, looking around Brittella to me.

"It is."

"Tomorrow we'll be entering the boys' camp," he settled back, speaking to Brittella again. "We have a plan for getting inside."

"So I've heard," she purred. I didn't realize humans could sound so much like cats.

She removed her top hand, bringing it back to her shoulder where she stroked her hair, dipping her body backward with a swaying motion for a moment. She was good.

My eyes grew wide as Fitch and Lydia caught on to Brittella's flirtation. Horror raced through my body, knowing they'd figure out I had been trained to do that as well. I relaxed when Lydia stifled a giggle.

"How have you been, Brittella?" Raselin lowered his voice.

I clamped down on my back teeth, willing my face to remain calm. I tried as hard as Lydia did not to laugh at the scene. Maybe bringing Brittella with us was a good thing after all, and, *perhaps* Raselin had the ability to control her a bit. Lowell certainly hadn't.

The two fell into discussion, catching each other up on the missing years. Reyla and Silas talked quietly, giving them space. I attempted to listen in, letting Dov murmur quietly to me, knowing I was spying. Brittella was too smart for that and kept her voice low.

When we finally separated for the night, arranging our bags on the ground to sleep, she slipped off with Reyla and me to change into a Society uniform.

"I like him," she whispered into my ear loud enough for Reyla to also hear.

"Raselin?" I questioned.

"Dov." She drew out his name slowly. "I like him."

She slipped her dress over her head and dropped it next to her, picking up the uniform we had provided her. Brittella made a face mixed with judgment and disgust.

"Unlike Shadoe," she continued, "he's better for you."

"We know," Reyla said, winking at me.

"And then there's *you*," Brittella turned her attention to Reyla as she shrugged on the uniform, pulling her hair out from between her shoulder and the sleeves.

Reyla shifted to a nervous posture. I knew she wouldn't want to talk about losing Peter, so I commandeered the conversation.

"How long have you known Raselin?" I asked.

"Since long before he went over the Wall."

"You were friends?" I hinted, hoping she'd give us more information.

"We were," she smiled, settling her hair back in place, cascading down the front of her chest. "I suppose I won't be able to keep this down."

I shook my head.

"Ah, well," she sighed, tucking her mane behind her. She popped the hood over her head to try it, grimacing. Brittella glanced at us, likely wondering how we could be so comfortable in pants.

"You'll get used to it," I assured her.

"Lowell did a number on *you*, Auluria," she shook her head. "I should have taken you away while I had the chance."

"Well, I for one, am glad you didn't," Reyla jumped in. "I like having her around, and if Lowell hadn't messed her up, we wouldn't have her. And Dov would be very lonely."

"What do you really anticipate me doing tomorrow, ladies?" She asked, tucking a piece of hair back inside her hood. "I don't fight. I can't imagine I'll need to do much sweet-talking. After all, the soldiers will be under your control by the time I'm brought in and the boys will likely side with you.

"Besides," she continued, "they're much more likely to follow along after a rousing speech from you and Dov, don't you think? You're closer to their age, my dear, and you're the ones leading them to victory and freedom."

"What are you proposing?"

"I think I should work with the women, my dear. They're going to need me more than you will. I can train them when the time comes."

Reyla glanced over at me to see what I thought. I nodded softly, considering her words. It made sense, though I wondered how helpful she might be with Magistrate Canton and his friends.

"Don't give me that look, young lady. I want nothing to do with that man," she chided.

"Who?" Reyla asked.

"Canton." I assumed Brittella knew everything I was thinking all of the time.

Brittella looked Reyla over yet again. "I could teach you a thing or two, you know. Come see me after tomorrow and we'll talk."

She grinned wickedly, tipping her head to the side.

"Oh, I don't know—"

"I'm really not sure—"

"Auluria, please. If you haven't figured it out by now —" Brittella snapped at me before being cut off.

"Everything okay?" Lydia asked, walking around the group of trees we were using as cover. "The boys were wondering where you ladies ran off to. It seems you were taking long enough that they thought you might have become lost."

"Not quite, Lydia," I smiled.

She quirked her lips up, smiling back at me before extending her hands to Brittella.

"We haven't had a chance to talk yet. May I walk back with you?" She slipped her arm through Brittella's and they walked together, chatting like old friends.

"Will that be us someday?" Reyla giggled, looping her arm through mine.

"You really think we'll both live through this?" I asked with a teasing grin. "One of us, maybe, but do you honestly think I'm going to make it?"

Reyla slapped my arm.

"Yes! I'm expecting little Dov and Auluria nieces and nephews, my friend. Don't you deny me becoming an aunt!" Reyla pointed an accusatory finger at me, feigning shock.

"Reyla!" I yelped loud enough to cause Lydia and Brittella to turn around to look at us.

She cast me a look, daring me to protest again. With a deep breath, I relented and turned to step forward.

"I mean it, Auluria. Babies. When this is all over, I want a big, lavish wedding, followed by nieces and nephews, preferably living next door."

"Wouldn't you get bored living next to me?"

"Have you seen the way you live, Auluria? I doubt any

of us will *ever* be bored," she smirked. "I'm just hoping you calm Dov down and he calms you down. All this nonsense involving you running into burning buildings and escaping the hangman's noose is getting old.

"I want you settled and happy," she finished.

"Fine, but only if you're happy too," I said, making it a condition in the agreement.

"Having nieces and nephews will make me very happy," she informed me. "Maybe we can get Katarina and Henry on that too once this is all over and done with. You'll obviously be getting married first, but your kids can play together."

"That's assuming they get to that point," I reminded her.

"Trust me, I've known them a lot longer than you have," she replied, "They will."

I reached over and took her hand. I knew she wouldn't be ready to move on from Peter for a long time, but I desperately wanted her to find someone to be happy with. One day, when she was ready, I would make her my new mission.

She smiled and patted my hand, knowing.

"It will be fine," she reminded me. "Speaking of gorgeous men..."

She nodded toward the fire where everyone was preparing to rest.

"Let's just hope we all make it out tomorrow," I sighed,

taking in the image of the people I cared about resting around the golden flames before finding a place to rest.

"Ready?" Dov asked, taking a deep breath.

"Ready," I confirmed, turning to signal our people.

Justin and Devin winked at me at the same time, their hands mirroring each other as they pushed off their knees to stand. I slowly rose in front of them.

The youngest Baer brother led the way as I quickly rallied behind him. A moment later, Justin and Devin followed behind us. Quietly, we moved forward, allowing the rest of our team to slip in behind us. We kept a safe distance between us, giving us space should anything happen.

We waited for the guard to round the corner, then slipped along the cold edges of the building. It was cold in the shadows, but I was grateful it masked our movements. The sun might have kept us from shivering, but it also exposed us in its deep orange glow.

I paused behind Dov, waiting for his signal to move forward. I kept my sight trained over his shoulder, looking where he wasn't. I tapped his shoulder, indicating that it was clear.

He risked a glance back at me before turning around,

his back to the wall, weapon ready. I mimicked him, ready to protect Justin as he stepped between us, preparing to break into the entrance to the camp. Devin carried a second tool to help break in. Together, they quietly tried to break in, a harsh, metallic sound filling the air. I held my breath.

Talley sidled up next to me, a third layer of protection for her brothers. Her jaw was set in a harsh line, her eyes furrowed. She forced a breath out of her nose, the rush of air making a small snorting noise as a form of communication with me. I did it back, confirming it was all clear.

A loud bang sounded. My eyes darted around, checking for signs of guards.

"We're in," Devin whispered. He moved next to Talley, taking my place as Dov and I stepped backward, ready to lead the raid into the compound.

Justin took a place to my right as we stepped inside. It felt bitterly cold inside the building; worse than the wind outside. We hurried down the hall, finding places to wait. Any empty pocket, recess, or room was occupied by as many of our people as could fit.

Dov and I took the last place, tucking ourselves away in a dark corner hidden around a closed off room. His fingers found their way to mine as we waited. We stood, chest to chest, waiting in the silence.

For a long time, he watched me, staring into my eyes. Finally, the smallest of smiles crept onto his lips. His deep blue eyes wrinkled just enough to notice that he was restraining his grin.

I rolled my eyes, making him smirk.

My breath caught as someone entered the hallway.

A second set of footsteps joined the first, padding down the hallway. They talked quietly, mumbling as they went. My eyes bore into the ground to my left, watching for them to pass. Society uniforms flashed by, safely passing us. I waited for them to reach the end of the hall, praying they didn't notice any of our people lurking just an arm's length away.

The door to the outside world shut with a soft click halfway down the hall. They hadn't gone far enough to notice our entry point.

Impulsively, Dov leaned forward and brushed a kiss against my lips. I looked away, grinning, trying to remain focused. When I looked back, he was stifling his own smile.

He was going to get us all killed.

I shook my head, looking at him. Darting forward, I surprised him, brushing my lips against his. When I pulled back, he stared so intently at me, I knew he was forgetting where we were. The voices dragged us back to reality.

Multiple footsteps sounded, filling the hall with a soft padding noise. A row of men shuffled past us in drab grey clothing. The boys.

We waited for them to pass, attempting to count how many filed through. Once it was quiet again, we held our positions long enough to feel like it was safe.

Dov was the first to venture out, stepping cautiously into the walkway. He held my hand, letting his linger behind the wall. When it was clear, he tugged me forward. Crossing my path, he guided me toward the door, while he moved deeper into the building, pulling our people out of hiding. If we were caught, it was all over.

Once everyone was in the hall, we moved en mass toward the door. Silas and his team would be on the other side of the building, waiting to exit as well.

Talley placed her hand on the door, waiting for Dov's signal. Outside, the boys were training, as they did every day. We nodded to Talley to open the door just enough to see outside. Waiting, we watched as she peeked out, counting the guards and waiting for the patrolling Society man to pass by.

She held up her fingers, counting down. On cue, she threw her arm back, yanking the door open as she crushed herself against the wall to get out of our way.

Without wasting time, Dov walked through the door, into the sunlight which was now much higher in the sky. We calmly walked into the yard, the boys barely taking notice. Unlike the captives, the guards took note of the intrusion.

"Surrender now, and we won't hurt you," Dov announced.

Our people spread out, surrounding the front building. Confusion broke out among the Society men, trying to decipher who we were and why we were there. One man finally activated the rest, spurring them into action.

They shouted to their captives as they ran drills, forcing them to turn their weapons on us. The boys carefully stepped toward us, reluctant to go into battle as their trainers launched an attack, leaving the boys with their training weapons as their only defense.

"My name is Dov Baer, I am the son of Griz Baer. My father died fighting to free this country. Join us and help us overthrow the Society," Dov addressed them, standing tall.

"Dov?" a voice in the crowd carried to us.

Dov searched the crowd, looking for the source.

"We can trust him," the voice cried.

"He's Society!" screamed another. "Look at him. It's a training tactic."

The voice muscled his way forward.

"He's with us."

"We're here to free you. Our people are at all the camps as we speak, starting the first wave of assaults," he said, neglecting to tell them that we also had the upper hand with Canton and the magistrates.

"Lur?" another voice pierced the noise of the training yard.

I knocked my hood off, exposing my hair. Dov had given himself up, so why not me? It fell around my waist in a wave of gold.

"I know her," he said. He was young. Lowell didn't usually let such young people join; perhaps it had something to do with Shadoe.

"You know us. If not personally, you know our people...our families. We're just like you; the Society is willing to throw us all away to get what they want," I said. "But we have a plan to free the camps and rise up against the magistrates and take back our country!"

A guard ran at us, coming from my side. I stepped toward him, blocking him from Dov, allowing him to continue to talk. The blade Shadoe had given me tore into the man's forearm, forcing him to drop the knife he attempted to plunge into my chest. Blood quietly dripped to the ground, like the beginning of a rainstorm, one small, intentional drop at a time.

"We promise to tell you everything once we, together, have taken control of the camp away from the Society," Dov yelled over the screaming guards, "and we promise you a free choice in whether or not you join us, but for now, we ask you to help us in this fight—right here—and bring this camp to its knees."

Four boys stepped forward, running at their captors.

Another half a dozen followed behind, engaging in battle against the men who whipped them when they stepped out of line. The rest of the young men being trained against their will stepped forward, encouraged by our bravado.

Glancing around, I took stock of the scene.

I registered Dov shouting to tie the men up as I watched two men brawl. One was young; still a teenager. His opponent was tall with dark hair covering his face.

I ran at them, determined to take the knife from the man. My foot lashed out, striking him in the hip, turning him over as he toppled from where he straddled the boy.

"Nope," I muttered under my breath as I reached for his hand. He grappled with me, trying to get the knife back.

The man cursed at me, attempting to claw at my face. I kicked at his arm, trying to block him. His bone shattered. The man wrenched over in pain, shrieking in agony. My eyes grew wide. I didn't realize I had put that much force into my kick.

"Auluria?" Dov called.

"Not me," I answered back. The knife sat in my hand as I darted away. I was surprised I had scooped it up from the ground without realizing it. Shadoe would be proud.

The young boys worked together, taking on their trainers. More men joined from inside the building, but the boys outnumbered the men who were overseeing them. Without time to plan, their efforts were disjointed.

A metallic scent filled the air as blood pooled on the ground. I hated the carnage. The boys held at the camp had been taught to succeed in battle. Their skills were focused on causing destruction. Their aim was to defend their battleground and take down as many opponents as possible. The Society had planned to quell any uprising from inside the camp long before it started, and end any intruders before they entered. They hadn't planned for rebels to get inside and start a coup.

"Lur!" a voice shouted, causing me to duck.

A large man tripped over me. I lifted my shoulders as he collided against my side, dropping him on the ground beyond. The boy was by my side—knife in hand—ready to slit the man's throat.

"No!" I yelped, blocking his arm. It crashed into mine as I gritted my teeth against the immediate pain. "I know Lowell's mission was less careful about life, but he doesn't need to die."

The man groaned on the dirt, shifting. I reached down, clamping my fingers around his thick wrist. I started to instruct the boy to tie him up when he looked at me, annoyance written across his face. He grunted but turned the knife in his hand so that the blade faced away. With a quick movement, he brought the hilt down on the man's temple, knocking him out.

"I can live with that," I nodded. "But tie him up."

The boy nodded back.

"What happened to you?" he asked, working quickly as chaos continued to erupt around us.

"When did they catch you, before or after Lowell?"

"Lowell is dead?" his eyes widened.

"Yes, Shadoe and I are in charge now." I made sure he knew whom to respect. "We combined our forces with two other groups: the Baers and a faction from beyond the Wall.

"Can you get the other boys to work with us?" I asked, hoping he had some influence.

He took a deep breath, studying me.

"What exactly is the plan?" he asked over the shouting. For a moment, the world quieted and it was just the two of us.

"We're bringing down the camps...all of them. We're shutting them down simultaneously and making it look like they're still functioning. We're going to move as many people inside the Society as possible." I decided to trust him, even though I shouldn't. "We have control of Canton. They won't even know what hit them."

The boy's eyes grew wide at Canton's name. He tipped his head, considering my words as someone grunted beside us.

"You okay there, Goldilocks?" Justin grinned as he grappled with a trainer. He pushed the man backward, but the Society guard got his feet under him and pushed back, moving Justin a few feet.

"Goldilocks?" the boy asked incredulously.

"It's a...thing." I shook my head, dismissing it. I turned to Justin. "Do you need help?"

Justin pushed forward again, this time shoving the man hard enough for him to lose his balance. Talley stepped up behind him, catching the pressure point on the man's neck between her fingers. He dropped to the ground.

"Nope," Justin shrugged. His grin fell as he eyed us. "What's this?"

"I'm one of her men," the boy straightened, addressing Justin like the loyal soldier Lowell or Shadoe had trained him to be before he was taken. He spun on his heels to face me. "I'll help you."

"Good, start getting these men organized." I glanced around, noting that we clearly had the upper hand. "I'm going around to the other side to check on Silas' group."

"I'll come with you," Justin announced, nodding to his sister to stay. She turned to see where she could help. "Come on."

The scream in the distance prompted us to run faster.

Chapter 5

"Go," I instructed, "Help her."

Justin split off from me, racing toward where Reyla held her ground. She was cornered, but not giving up.

I ran toward Henry and Katarina, throwing myself into the man rushing at them. He was more solid than I had anticipated, sending me rocking backward. A jolt of pain coursed through my body as I stumbled, catching myself after a few staggering paces.

I lashed out at him, using the knife Shadoe had procured for me. It sliced across his arm, only serving to anger him more. He stepped toward me menacingly. Perhaps I couldn't stop him.

I braced myself, waiting for him to lower his stance

and barrel at me. I gripped my knives tightly in my hands, hoping to be faster than he was.

"I always knew I'd be the one to save you," Gregory said, stepping up to my side. "Prince Charming, at your service."

The man's eyes widened as he continued to move toward us. His steps slowed for a moment before he toppled toward us. Henry stood with a bloody knife as Katarina lowered her foot. They had turned around to discover I had joined them and used the opportunity to take down the threat while we distracted the man.

Katarina grinned smugly, crossing her arms over her chest.

"I believe that's prince and *princess* to *you*." She pointed between herself and her boyfriend. She batted her eyelashes at Gregory to tease him.

Henry's face dropped suddenly.

"Look out!" he warned.

I whipped around, elbow ready to crash into any face I may find behind me. Gregory acted quickly, taking on the assault himself. When I was sure he had it under control, I maneuvered around to see where I could help.

The light shifted, moving from day to evening despite the early hour. The world seemed to mute as light and sound went dull. I had seen the switch before. I knew what it meant.

A moment later, without any time to react, the sky

opened up, dousing us in rain. It fell hard and fast, angled so strangely I almost thought it had to be a part of the Society's plan. The one thing they *couldn't* control was the weather...aside from us, anyway.

As if taking a collective breath, the entire training yard paused to glance up. A few men grimaced as raindrops hit their unprotected eyes. Just as quickly as everyone had stopped, they started again, growling and slashing at each other.

Nikko ran by me, happily taking on anyone who got in his way. Not far behind, Ella took her time picking off Society trainers until we had the upper hand.

"Auluria," Reyla said, announcing herself before she could frighten me as she approached from behind.

"Is everything okay out front?" Silas asked, following behind her.

"Yeah, I came around to check on your team," I replied, glad that the fight was dying down. "Have you secured the boys over here?"

"I think so," Silas said. "Reyla did a great job."

I grinned, nodding to my best friend.

The rain fell harder, soaking through my hair. Reyla wrinkled her nose as she tucked a stray piece of hair back into her hood. My fingers fumbled as I attempted to pull my own hood back up. Reyla reached over to help me as I fought to push all of my hair inside.

"Graceful," Silas commented, smirking before he took off to help Justin.

"He's just mad that he couldn't help you like Dov would have," Reyla teased.

"Oh?" I rolled my eyes. "And just how would that have been?"

"Very, very slowly, I imagine." She brushed her fingers down my arm and laughed. Reyla delighted in teasing me.

"We should move everyone inside," I commented, watching puddles grow on the ground.

"At least the rain will help hide all the blood," Reyla grew serious.

"Go get Justin and tell Silas we're going to clear the building," I instructed her.

I made my way to Henry and Katarina to explain the plan.

"Find Dov and tell him I'm taking a small team in to clear the building. If you can, send a few of his people in to help us," I pointed around the side of the building. "As soon as things are under control, get everyone to the same side of the building and move them inside."

"On it," Henry said. He pulled at Katarina's hand and guided her quickly along the building.

Reyla made her way over with Justin in tow. Silas waved from where he stood, directing his team to let me know he approved of the plan.

Locust appeared alongside Anetta, Reed, Gregory, and a few others. I quickly explained that we needed to clear the building and split the group up into pairs.

Justin and I took the lead, entering through the back entrance. We swept the bottom floor, quickly moving on to the second floor, as Gregory and Reyla did a more thorough search. Locust and Anetta branched off, looking for Society men to the left.

"Clear," Justin whispered, backing out of the room as I waited in the hallway.

"*Clear,*" Locust said harshly from down the hall. His voice echoed, making me cringe. I could almost feel Anetta's glare against my back.

I took the next room. Swinging the door open, I prepared for confrontation. The room was empty, a small set of shelves against the walls. Books sat at odd angles. A few maps were tucked away between books, an occasional page spilling out of a pile, cascading down over the shelf below it.

Once satisfied, I stepped back.

"Clear," I whispered.

Justin moved down to the next door, preparing to check it as I took my place behind him. I tapped his shoulder to let him know I was on my mark. The door opened, revealing a similar room to the one I had just swept.

Justin tensed. A man stood by the window inside. The

sky outside had brightened a little since we made our way inside the building. It illuminated him, wrapping light around his figure just enough to see his features. The backlight was harsh against the dark shadows that played across his face.

"I've been waiting for you," he said, sadly.

Justin rocked forward, waiting to make his move.

"I take it this means we lost," the man said. He placed a hand on the windowsill behind him. "You know the magistrates won't take kindly to that."

"I do believe that's the point," Justin replied dryly.

The man sighed.

"You realize I'm supposed to put up a fight..." His lips turned down as he spoke.

"Oh? Why is that?" Justin asked.

"Part of the job description," he tipped his head sideways, studying Justin. "I have a family and I'm sure the magistrates would take it out on them."

"What if we could help them?" I asked, stretching up to be seen over Justin's shoulder.

"You can't." He looked defeated.

"What if—" Justin tried to push.

"No, this is how it has to be."

The man lunged toward Justin, nearly tripping over himself as he crossed the room. Justin reacted, moving far enough back to move us both out of the way. He caught the man as he propelled forward. The man didn't stop.

Throwing his elbow back, he collided with Justin's shoulder, making my friend yell in pain. Locust and Anetta shuffled in the hall, coming to investigate. I latched onto the man's wrist, forcing his knife away from Justin.

The man was strong. As I clung to him, I had to use my full body weight to drag him down, and even then, it was a fight. Justin wrenched one hand behind the man's back. His kick to the man's leg was his undoing, sending him crashing to the ground. I was tugged along in his fall, forcing me to the ground. My knee slammed against the floor making me cry out.

Anetta burst through the door, eyes frantically searching the scene. She found us in a messy heap on the floor as Justin wrestled the man into submission. I clawed back his hand that I had managed to keep a hold on.

"Want me to kick him?" Anetta asked. She took a terrifying step toward us, preparing to slam her boot into the Society man's face.

"No!" I yelped, hoping she would drop back.

"Let her, Lur," Locust said over his shoulder as he watched the hallway. "We need to keep going and don't have time to deal with him conscious."

"No," I held a hand up to stop her.

She studied me, deciding between listening to Locust and her intuition, or me. She backed down, moving back toward the door.

"You better handle this," she said, giving me the space to deal with the situation.

Justin accepted responsibility, reaching forward to knock the man out. The man's head smacked against the floor. We held him for a moment longer to make sure he was really out.

"You okay?" Justin asked quietly, glancing at Anetta and Locust in the doorway.

"I'm fine," I answered. "Are you okay?"

"I'm good." He put his hands on the ground to push himself up. Once standing he added, "What are we going to do with him?"

He used the tip of his boot to push the man's leg, rolling it slightly. I shrugged, wondering if there was a safe place to tie him up.

"What if we put him in the room down the hall? We could block him in the closet." Justin suggested. "Put a chair in front of it and he won't be able to get it open even if he *does* wake up before we get back to him."

"Locust," I called. "I need you to help Justin move him to the room down the hall."

I traded places with him, temporarily partnering with Anetta. Justin and Locust lifted the man, dragging him out the door as we covered them in case anyone should unexpectedly appear in our path.

Inside the room, we maneuvered the Society trainer into the closet. Justin tried to position the man so that it wouldn't be too painful when he woke up, but there was only so much he could do. They tied the man's wrists under his knees where they bent to fit inside the small closet.

Closing the door, Justin waited for me to bring him the chair. He wedged it under the door handle, tipping the chair on its back legs.

"Good luck getting out of there, buddy."

"They're here," Anetta said from the doorway, relaxing her stance. She nodded inside the room.

A moment later, Dov stepped around her.

"Should I ask?"

"Creative jail?" Justin shrugged from the corner of the room, nodding to the barrier outside the door.

"I'm not going to ask," Dov looked amused. "Everyone okay?"

"We're good. Are they sweeping the rest of the building?" Justin joined our small circle.

"They are," Dov confirmed, wrapping his arms around my waist. "The good news is that the rooms where they keep the boys all lock from the outside, so we can lock the trainers in there. We've got the boys partnered with our people and they're overseeing the Society trainers.

"The bad news is that we definitely have a few bodies."

"Any of ours?" I asked.

"No," Raselin rounded the corner, expanding our group. "A few injuries, but no deaths, thankfully."

"Most of the bodies are from when the boys initially turned on the trainers before we talked them down," Dov said. "We need to talk to them."

"There's a dining room downstairs," I added. "We could hold a meeting there."

"That's a good idea," Dov agreed, flipping a piece of hair out of his eyes. "Let's get all of the boys down there. Fitch can oversee watching the prisoners."

"Good idea. We don't need everyone in the meeting," Raselin put his hand on Dov's shoulder. "Go get your people, Dov. We'll meet in fifteen minutes."

"We should work with them," the blond boy shouted from where he stood by his chair. "We've been trained to fight, and they need fighters. They're working against the Society, which is something we *all* want to do.

"Just look what the Society has done to us!" he bellowed, holding out his arms to expose the scars. "This is our chance to get them back for destroying our lives!"

"And our family's lives!" Another added, standing to his feet.

"But we could be free," a third boy argued.

I resisted the urge to find a wall to lean against as they talked within their group. The blond boy looked at me, begging for me to be as vicious as Lowell had me trained to be. Fire was one thing; destruction was another.

One hundred boys sat around the tables, hovering between revenge and freedom. They looked like scared mice ready to bolt at any moment. The blond kid looked to me again, trying to motivate me into action. Dov's hand on my back was the only thing that prompted me to speak.

"Our goal is for all of us to be free." I forced my hands to remain at my sides instead of crossing them over my chest. "But not just *you*. We want the entire country to be free of the Society.

"In theory, we now have control of all of the boys' camps. The next step is to free the girls. Right now, as we speak, our leaders have control of certain factions of the Society. We want to make it look like everything is business as usual around here, and then sneak most of you in with us."

Dov stepped up next to me. I hadn't realized I had moved forward while speaking to the boys.

"By the time the Society realizes we hold all the power, it will be too late. They won't be able to recover," Dov smiled convincingly. "We're going to arrest the people who are working against us."

He held up a hand before the boys protested and chuckled.

"I know that seems counterproductive. We need these men alive though. We need to question them. These men have been running the Society since long before any of us were born. They know everything about it, and more importantly, about what's going on outside of the Wall.

"You see, once we've freed ourselves from the magistrates' control, we still have to protect ourselves from the outside. This all started specifically because the outsiders came for us. Our leaders bent to their will in an effort to save us originally, but continued to bow to them in order to protect themselves."

The slight pressure on my hip indicated that it was my turn to jump in.

"That threat doesn't go away just because we take down the Society," I said, shifting my foot to touch Dov's. "Our immediate goal is to close down the camps and take power from the magistrates. We have leaders set in place to facilitate this—"

"I thought *you* were our leader," someone interrupted.

"We are part of the leadership, yes," I agreed. "We have leadership from the Baers, from my cousin, Lowell's, group, and from a faction from over the Wall."

I nodded to Dov, Raselin, and myself.

"We aren't the only ones. There are many of us. And before you ask, we are not keeping the power when this is all done. We're only overseeing things until we bring the Society down. We'll stay on after to bring down the Wall and end the threat from other countries if that helps, but after that, it will be up to the country to decide."

"No one is that *good*," someone said, "Certainly not *Lowell's* people. He wanted power."

Dov's hand tightened around me, ready to back the boy down for me.

"Yes, he did," I said before Dov could speak. "My cousin only wanted power, and he didn't care what he had to do to get it. But where is Lowell now?"

I shrugged, waiting for them to speak. When they didn't, I continued.

"Lowell is dead. His greed and deceit lead to his downfall. My cousin was willing to do anything to get power. He used me and threw me away when I was no longer useful. I watched him do it for years. He wouldn't hesitate to use each and every one of you right now and let you die to get him the power he wanted.

"We don't want to use you. We want you to stand with us, but even if you don't, we'll still fight for you." A few of the boys perked up, resonating with my words.

"You don't have to help us," Dov added. "You will get your freedom either way if we win."

He paused, tipping his head. "It would be a lot easier to win if you'd help."

The boy who remembered me from my time with

Lowell looked affronted. He must not have known me well even back then if he thought I would sweep into the compound and order a massacre of my enemies.

"We are not the Society. We don't need to be like them," I looked directly at the boy, hoping my words would mean something. "We want to be free of them, not bring in a new generation of them."

The group nodded all at once, surprising me.

"Okay," one boy murmured. The others followed, creating a soft echo.

"If you don't want to help, that's fine," Dov said, pulling his hand off my hip to emphasize his words. "We'll show you where to go to be safe until this is all over.

"If you *are* joining us, we're going to need a few of you to stay here to run the compound. You'll need to make it look like the camp is still operational and keep an eye on the trainers we have locked up. The rest of you will be coming with us."

Dov took a breath, preparing to direct people.

"If you don't want to stay, stand up now and move to the door. Silas is going to help you prepare to leave. He'll show you where to go and will give you some supplies to get you started."

He paused, allowing three boys to stand and make their way over to Silas. The rest remained seated. I grinned.

"I'm glad to see some of you want to stay and help." Dov shifted forward. "I know most of you probably want to take the fight to the Society, so I'm going to ask for volunteers to stay here and protect our cover."

"If you stay," I added, "you'll be responsible for handling your former trainers. You are not allowed to hurt them. Remember, we're going to need them once we have control of the magistrates. They'll all be held accountable for their crimes. If you stay here, we have to be able to trust you."

"Some of our men will be staying to help you. There's a plan in place for handling these trainers. They're also prepared to handle anyone who may show up unexpectedly." Dov nodded to one of the men who stood against the outside wall. "Who can we trust to stay and handle things here?"

Dov surveyed the room, waiting for volunteers. When no one stood, my heart stopped. I pressed my tongue against the back of my teeth to keep my worry in check. I didn't need my face betraying my confidence in the mission.

"I'll stay," the blond boy said, standing to his feet. He looked right at me. "If this is our mission, I'll stay."

He was a soldier through and through. Lowell would have been proud.

A dozen others stood, joining him. Progress.

"Good men," Dov praised them. "Come with me and I'll introduce you to your new leader."

Dov led the boys across the room, quietly explaining their new mission. They listened intently as he shifted their attention over to one of Berwyn's men that would be overseeing the camp.

I turned my attention back to the main group.

"Tomorrow we're going to the girls' camp. We need to break them out. The ones that can, will be joining us. Many of them will not be able to."

"Why?" one of the youngest boys asked. He couldn't have been more than twelve.

"Many of the girls will be carrying babies. They train you to fight and they took the girls so they could create new fighters. Did any of you come directly from a camp?" I asked, knowing I'd hate the answer.

Many of them nodded. They had been taken from their mothers; created and raised specifically to be added to the training camps. They had never known any other life.

"We're going to make sure they're all safe. We'll need some of you to stay there to help protect them if the Society figures out what we're doing. We'll need volunteers for that too."

Several of the boys jumped up, looking furious.

"I'll protect them," one of the boys who had just admitted to being raised in a camp said.

"My sister was taken to a camp," another proclaimed. "I'll stay with the girls."

"Good, we'll need everyone we can get," I smiled. "We'll set out for the camp tomorrow. Tonight, we need to get you all fed and ready to move out.

"I need you all to help us gather supplies."

The boys listened as I rattled off a list of things we'd need them to bring. I kept them seated as Dov returned.

"Meet back here in one hour. At that point, we'll share a meal together and go over the plan," Dov instructed.

They all filed out, ready to collect supplies. Dov and I watched them go, waiting until the room cleared.

"Time to talk," Dov said.

Chapter 6

Dov tugged at my hand, guiding me into the room. It was quiet despite the shuffling out in the hall. Brilliant orange lit the space, bits of gold adding pops of glitter as it glared through the window. The rain had ended.

"Took long enough," Silas smirked from the chair.

"Did you find anything?" Dov asked, taking the seat opposite his friend.

"The building plans for the girls' camp." Silas pushed a piece of paper across the study table.

"This seems too easy," Dov joked, shaking his head.

"Everything else has been incredibly hard, Dov," I reminded him as I perched on the arm of his plush chair. "Accept a moment of ease."

"Good point." He took my hand in his, bringing it to his lips.

The sunset glinted off their hair as I looked over from where I sat, highlighting them both beautifully. We'd been through so much together in the months we had known each other. I could barely remember my life before Dov and Silas. My world would be so empty without them...even without Berwyn and Eden.

I couldn't help myself when I reached out to touch Dov's hair when they finished discussing the papers in front of them. He ducked, not expecting my touch. Even Silas' eyes were wide when I giggled.

"I honestly don't know where I'd be without you two."

"Dead," Silas smirked.

"Still with your cousin," Dov suggested.

"Probably a killer," Silas offered with a shrug. "What, you know he would have pushed for that."

"Not my girl," Dov said, reaching up to tuck my hair back. It caught the orange glow, lighting it up like fire.

"You two really did save me," I commented, my voice laced with contentment.

"And you saved us," Silas said, making Dov grin. "Well, *him* at least...and the others. I totally had this, though."

"Give her a little credit, Silas." Dov's eyes sparkled mischievously. "She's not done yet. You know she's going to make it happen."

"Make what happen?" I sat up straighter.

"I know no such thing," Silas disagreed playfully.

"Make *what* happen?" I persisted.

Dov locked eyes with Silas, challenging him.

"*Don't*," Silas cautioned.

"I'm going to have to tell her sometime," Dov shrugged, leaning back in the chair. "Wouldn't hurt to be today."

"It would be a distraction," Silas corrected him with a glare. "We need everyone on top of their game."

Dov sighed dramatically, nearly knocking me off the chair arm. I scooted closer, wrapping my arms around the back of the chair.

"Fine," he teased. "But you really should stop putting it off."

"Oh, Silas," I shook my head. "You know I already know."

He studied me, trying to decide if I was bluffing. I raised an eyebrow at him, daring him to call me out.

"I really have no idea if you do or don't right now," Silas admitted, struggling to read me.

"Brittella trained you well," Dov turned to me, pride radiating across his face. "Speaking of..."

"Well if *that's* where this is headed, I'm out." Silas laughed, standing up. The dwindling orange light raced across his face, darting in and out of the shadows as he moved. "I'll check in with Raselin and Fitch."

He walked toward the door, turning back to add, "Don't be long, we have things to do."

"*Yes, Dad*," Dov teased as Silas closed the door behind him.

When the door clicked, Dov turned to me. His face was covered in dark shadows, making his skin almost blue. A bit of light bounced off my own skin, illuminating his eyes as he pursed his lips.

"I've been promising you a conversation," he spoke softly.

"You have," I agreed.

I reached out, tangling my fingers in his hair. He responded by reaching around my hips and roughly pulling me onto his lap. I managed to work my knees around his during the short fall so that I didn't get caught. My left hand left its spot on my thigh and wrapped around Dov's neck.

He leaned forward quickly, holding me to avoid throwing us off balance. He breathed in as he approached me. The sunset danced behind my eyelids as Dov kissed me.

His lips were warm against my skin as he trailed down my neck. I leaned into him, burying my face in his hair. A laugh bubbled up to his lips as I tickled his ear with my nose. Dov dragged me closer.

"Playing dirty, are we?" he growled as he pressed his fingers against my back.

"I was never trained to play fair." I dropped my voice as I ran my hand over a lock of hair that had fallen between us. "Take it or leave it."

"Oh, I'll take it." His voice rumbled deep in his chest.

I beat him this time, closing the distance between us. His fingers found their way to my chin, caressing my skin with each kiss. He tilted my face, anticipating each move so that we would fit perfectly together each time we touched. I tugged on his hair, encouraging him.

"Auluria," Dov breathed against my neck, his voice hitching.

I pulled my knees up, moving my feet from the floor as I let them fall on the chair next to Dov's hip, curling into myself. His arm wrapped around my legs, pulling me close. I leaned in, desperately wanting to be closer.

When I finally pulled back, the sun was perfectly aligned with the horizon outside, glaring in through the study window. It bathed Dov in a radiant golden light.

My eyes, tired from lack of oxygen, rested half-closed as I watched him. He stared at me like I was brand new to him.

"I love you, Auluria." He smiled, drawing small circles on my back.

I watched him for another moment before leaning in to brush our lips together.

"I loved you from the moment I first saw you, Dov Baer."

He tried to keep from smirking as he gave me a look, challenging my statement.

"Fine, maybe not the first moment," I said, thinking back to the time I crashed into him in the woods, "But definitely when you sat me down at your kitchen table."

"That's more believable," he grinned, "The *first* time you saw me, you threw things at me and hurt my feelings."

"Oh," I pretended to be sorry. "I should make up for that."

"You should," he nodded.

"But first," I added, shattering his plans, "that talk."

"Yeah," he sighed, "that."

"That." I traced his jaw with my finger, making him tip his lips to kiss it.

He watched me, trying to decide what to say.

"Dov, when you—"

The knock at the door scared me so much that I jumped, making Dov jump as well. He closed his eyes, sucking in a deep breath to steady himself. I threw myself to my feet as the doorknob twisted.

Brittella entered, giving me a knowing look as she locked eyes with me. She stepped aside, making way for the blond boy from earlier.

"Sorry to interrupt your meeting, my dears, but Eli wanted to say something," Brittella said, holding no remorse in her voice. She looked like she was enjoying the moment.

Eli's face was hard as he stepped forward. Dov stood from the chair, joining me near the table.

"I know who you are now," Eli started. He held Dov's gaze. "You saved my brother."

Dov squinted at him.

"What do you mean?"

"You pulled him out of a fire, and then you let him escape. Anyone else would have tortured him for information." His words implied that he meant Lowell would have tortured him. "Had it been Wallace, he might have killed him just for the fun of it. But you let him go.

"It took me awhile to make the connection, but they were talking about you downstairs. That was you, wasn't it?"

"The storehouse," I whispered, realizing it was the boy Dov had pulled from Shadoe's failed mission to attack the Baers' storehouse not long after I joined the Baers. It was right before Dov kissed me for the first time.

"I remember him," Dov confirmed. "Was he...okay?"

"Yes, he made it back," he looked down, kicking at an imaginary rock. "It wasn't long after he returned that I was captured and sent here."

Dov nodded, allowing him to continue.

"I owe you," the boy finally said.

"You don't owe me, Eli," Dov said gently. "I was happy to help your brother."

"He wouldn't have helped you," Eli finally looked up. "I wouldn't have either."

"You have a chance to change that now," Dov said, trying to encourage him. "You volunteered to help the girls, didn't you?"

"I did that because of Lur. She needed volunteers, and she's my leader now that Lowell is gone."

"So you're a good soldier," Dov said cautiously, "but you also have the opportunity to be a good person.

"Many of the girls we will free tomorrow won't be able to take care of themselves. Many of them will be with child or will have young children. Your job is to protect them if the Society comes for them, and to help them if they need anything while you're there."

"It may be your job, Eli, but it's also your choice," I added.

"I helped your brother when no one else could," Dov continued. "Now you can help people that no one else can. I have faith in you."

"I do too," I told him.

Eli's gaze shifted away as if lost in thought. Suddenly he turned back, straightening. He threw his shoulder back as if he were preparing to speak to Lowell or Shadoe.

"Thank you for helping my brother." He spun on his heels and exited the room.

Brittella took that as her cue. She sauntered across the room, batting her eyelashes.

"And what have we here?"

"Did you need something, Brittella?" I asked, trying to keep from sounding terse.

"A word," she purred before smiling at Dov. "Run along, Mr. Baer. I believe your friends are looking for you."

Dov eyed me but sidestepped around Brittella to make his way to the door. He closed the door over behind him.

"Have a seat, Auluria." She motioned with her hand as she took the chair Dov and I had just occupied. "I have one more thing to teach you."

With the recruits organized, supplies in order, and the camp trainers under heavy guard, it should have been easy to sleep. Reyla and I spent the entire night fighting to turn our minds off and rest.

"This isn't going well," Reyla whispered quietly after hearing me sigh in defeat.

"Nope," I whispered back. I propped myself up on an elbow before pushing myself to my feet. "Come on."

She quietly followed me out of the room, making our way to the hall. Sounds of snoring and soft breathing hit my ears as we passed by each open door. I shivered in the cold.

"Couldn't sleep?" Lydia asked as we walked into the study.

"You couldn't either?" I asked, lowering myself to the floor to the right of the window. I pulled my knees to my chest, securing them in place with my arms.

"I don't like being away from Fitch," she admitted, leaning back into the chair. "I've also never felt anything so luxurious in my life, so spending the night in this chair isn't the worst thing ever."

I smiled, giggling as she scrunched herself up in the chair.

"These are pretty wonderful," Reyla sighed. "What shall we talk about, ladies?"

"How do you think Canton is behaving? Do you think Shadoe is keeping him under control?" Lydia asked.

"If Shadoe can't, no one can," I replied. "I'm worried about what Canton might do when he gets around the other magistrates though."

"Have we found out how Raselin and Brittella know each other yet?" Reyla interrupted. We turned to her a little shocked. "Well, do we?"

Her persistence made us giggle.

"They grew up together from what I can tell," Lydia informed us with a knowing look. "No connections other than that as far as I can tell."

"Back to your matchmaking ways, Rey?" I smirked.

"I handled you and Dov, didn't I? I need a new project."

"I volunteer Jasleen," I offered.

"Auluria, she's five." Reyla rolled her eyes.

"Precisely, that should keep you away from everyone else's love lives for a while." I paused. "Actually, new assignment: Silas and Justin need girlfriends. They're your new projects."

"Hmm," she tapped her chin. "I can work with that."

"Talking about my brother?" Talley said sleepily, ducking into the room. Her hair stuck out on one side She noticed us looking and reached up to straighten it. "I saw you two slip out and got bored, so I decided to follow you."

"Join the party," Reyla said, stretching out her hand to wave her in.

Talley slid down the wall next to me, dropping her head on my shoulder. She mimicked my pose, wrapping her arms around her knees.

"I really don't have a preference on which girl you get to marry Justin, as long as you get him out of my hair," she teased. "While you're at it, Devin, too, please."

"Talley, I'm going to need your help tomorrow," I lowered my voice as Lydia and Reyla discussed possible girlfriends for Silas, Justin, and Devin. "We need to make sure the girls can handle themselves before we go bringing them into battle. Many of them will have been at the camps for a long time, and while I'm sure some of them can fight, we have to make sure their skills are still sharp enough that they won't get hurt when we take on the Society."

"I can help with that." Talley nodded, sending her hair tumbling over her ear where she tucked it and into her face. She let out a short, sharp breath and blew the strands back. "What do you want to do?"

"We need to see them work. If they feel like they can join us, we need to see them in action. I'm sure they'll feel better if they're fighting us than any of the guys. I'm also a little worried they might take their frustration out on the guys and we don't need any of them getting hurt before we take on the Society men."

"Assuming everything is going well at Canton's mansion, we should be able to get in without too many problems."

"Hopefully," I commented. "We'll have Dov, Silas, Reyla, and Fitch help us decide about the girls tomorrow. I have a feeling Lowell's former girls will opt to come with us because Lowell has always trained them to handle the mission first. We may actually have a fight on our hands with some of them if they can't come for some reason."

"You'll reason with them," Talley assured me.

"Auluria doesn't do reason," Reyla joined the conversation. "Auluria does impulsive."

"*Hey*!" I shouted.

"She has a point," Talley teased.

"Really, you're all turning against me?" I questioned, looking each of them in the eyes.

"Yes," they all chorused.

"Careful," I warned them, "I might just be inspired to leave you all to guard the girls' camp tomorrow."

They rolled their eyes, chuckling.

"Auluria," a small voice at the door made us all look up. Maylin and Katarina stepped in. "I want to stay tomorrow."

"You want to stay?" I questioned.

"Necesta has been teaching me," Maylin looked down as if she were embarrassed. "I don't know much, but I think I can help."

She glanced up, waiting for my permission. I studied her in the doorway. She was soft and sweet. Fighting was no place for a girl like Maylin, but Necesta knew that long before we left.

"I think you would be a great asset, Maylin. I imagine Necesta sent a few things with you?"

"She did." Maylin pulled her pack off her shoulders and gently set it at her feet. "I think she planned this."

"I have a feeling she did," Katarina agreed as she patted Maylin's shoulder.

"You have to agree to come back to us once this is all over though, Maylin," I instruct the girl. "We can give you up for a little while, but we can't have you leave us forever."

Maylin smiled. "Okay," she promised. "When it's all over and the girls are safe, and their babies are all okay, I'll come back."

"I'm just pointing out," Katarina swayed over to Reyla and sat on her armrest. "*I* wasn't the one who had to make that mandate."

She winked at Maylin.

"We'll all happily benefit from it though," Reyla added.

"Since you know what you're doing, Maylin, maybe now is a good time to teach us what we should be looking for tomorrow," I suggested.

Maylin glanced at the way Katarina was perched on the chair before confidently walking over to the edge of the table closest to the window. She sat on the edge, testing it cautiously as she put her hand back to guide herself. She walked us through what Necesta had shared with her before we all fell asleep for a few hours before we left for the camp.

"Can I get you anything?" I asked the girl. She rested in a bed, looking like she could give birth at any moment.

Raselin's team had breached the camp without needing any backup from the other groups. We quickly flooded the halls, letting the girls know what was happening.

"I'm fine, thank you," she smiled sweetly at me. "Could you send Katarina over when she has a moment?"

"Do you know her?" I asked, glancing across the room to where Katarina attended to another young girl.

"I did." Her nod was stiff against her pillow. It moved her hair behind her, causing it to stick up at a strange angle. "She hasn't seen me yet though...or maybe she doesn't recognize me."

She reached up, attempting to fix her hair. Once it was successfully tucked back under her head, she added, "I hope she remembers me."

I quietly slipped away and crossed the room. I tapped Katarina on the shoulder.

"You're needed over there," I tried to suppress my mischievous grin.

She gave me a curious look before walking away.

Katarina glanced over her shoulder, waiting for me to indicate that she was going in the right direction.

"Hannah!" she shrieked when she saw the girl.

Katarina raced the rest of the way, throwing herself onto the edge of the small bed. She burst into tears and the two talked incoherently.

"What's that about?" Reyla asked as she joined me, squinting to try to make out the scene.

"That would be a girl named Hannah," I replied, still watching the old friends reunite.

"Hannah?" Reyla gasped, nearly dropping the glass of water she was holding. She managed to shove it in my hands and mumble to get Silas and Dov before racing across the room.

It took a moment for me to return to my senses. I found the girl the water was meant for, and set out in search for Dov and Silas. They stood in the hallway, lecturing Ella for being too harsh with one of the girls.

"Gentlemen," I interrupted, "I was sent to find you."

Dov sent Ella off. I could feel her roll her eyes as soon as her back was turned.

"Ella," I lectured sharply. The girl froze for a moment. She plastered a smile on and turned over her shoulder enough for me to see. "Please tell Anetta I need to speak with her. It's no rush."

Ella bounced off as I dismissed her, brown hair swaying behind her.

"Any chance we can leave her here?" Silas complained.

"Haven't these poor girls suffered enough?" I joked, putting my hand on his elbow in mock sincerity.

"What did you need us for, Auluria?" Dov called us back to the mission.

"Oh," I shook my head to refocus. "Reyla told me to come get you. We found a girl I'm assuming used to be one of yours. Katarina and Reyla were both in tears, so I'm guessing that's a good thing. Her name is Hannah."

Neither Dov nor Silas looked like they were breathing. The moment stretched on so long that I began to worry.

"Hannah's alive?" Dov breathed before his slack face came back to life.

"She's alive?" Silas repeated, still in shock.

"Guys, who is Hannah?" I asked, feeling very left out.

"Sharone's sister. She went missing...years ago. We thought she had died." Dov informed me, still not moving.

"There was so much blood," Silas remembered.

"She's in there," I pointed down the hall. "She's very pregnant, but she seems to be in good spirits. Do you want to see her?"

They nodded but didn't move. I tugged on their wrists, guiding them toward the door. After a few steps, they moved quicker. I left them to check in on Sharone's sister while I looked in on the other girls.

"Auluria," Anetta stepped up behind me after a few minutes. "You wanted to see me?"

"I wanted to see how you were doing," I started, "I was wondering if you wanted to stay here or come with us tomorrow.

"I'm not done with the Society yet," she said, sounding slightly offended that I had asked. "I found some of Lowell's girls though. They'll probably want to see you. Ella's with them now."

"Of course she is," I muttered.

"Ella will get over herself soon enough," Anetta assured me. "Shadoe's not the only one in charge around here. She'll just have to deal with that."

"Have you found anyone who can fight with us yet?" I asked as she led me down the grey halls.

"I found the *children*." She wrinkled her nose as she spoke.

"Where are they?" I stopped walking.

"Downstairs. I'll show you in a minute. We're going to go annoy Ella first." I continued to follow her down the hall. "I don't think many of them will be going with us. They're all either pregnant or have small children."

"I had a feeling..."

Ella looked up as we entered. She nodded tersely at me.

"You all remember, Lowell's cousin, Lur," Anetta announced loudly. "She's in charge now."

A few of the young girls looked pained at Lowell's name. Anetta must have told them he died before she came to see me. Some of the girls looked angry, others seemed devastated by the news, while still others didn't care. They must not have been from Lowell's fold.

"Are you all okay?" I asked. "Can I do anything for you?"

"Let us fight," one girl sat up in her bed.

"You're not fighting," I cut off the discussion as I surveyed her bulging stomach. "Nice try."

"She's in charge and you will listen," Anetta declared.

It took me a moment to work out that she had just placed herself as my right hand. She was a much-less-deadly Shadoe to my Lowell. I realized I was always going to need back up with Lowell's people and having one of his favorite women by my side was a wise choice. They all knew Anetta was close with Lowell. They would respect her.

"Your jobs are to protect your children," I remind them. I couldn't help but feel like Reyla was having an easier time convincing the girls in her room to stay put.

"We'll only be taking those of you with us who are able to fight," I explained our plan to the girl, telling them how we would be taking on the Society from within.

"Lur, what about when it's all over? What will happen to us?" a girl I vaguely recognized asked.

"We'll come back for you all. We'll move you into the towns and out of this camp.

"Once we bring down Canton and his men, we'll still have to take care of the people outside of the Wall. You'll all have your chance to participate then if that's what you want."

After answering a few questions, Anetta inserted herself back into the conversation, announcing that I had to go check on the children but would return later. I whispered a word of thanks under my breath as we slipped back into the hallway.

"You do better with the Baers' people," she said as she bumped into me with her hip.

"Did you *just* figure that out?"

"Figure what out?" Dov asked, nearly colliding with us.

"We're going to see the children," Anetta commandeered the conversation, "Want to come?"

She led the way down the stairs to where the children were housed. The noise grew with each step we took.

"Sorry, they're not usually this loud," an older woman greeted us at the bottom of the stairs. "They're usually required to be quiet, but their mothers wanted them to play, now that you have control of the camp."

"That's okay. They should be able to play." Dov

returned her smile. A few steps away, he pointed to a small girl, "That one looks like Jasleen."

"She does." I laughed. I missed that little girl.

Small children toddled around the room. A few grasped the hands of their mothers or nurses as they attempted to walk. I looked down when Dov suddenly tipped his face toward the ground. He smiled brilliantly as he scooped up the little boy clinging to his leg.

"Hello," he said softly. "Who might you be?"

The toddler reached out, lightly taping Dov's face. His fingers bounced over Dov's lips as he fearlessly explored his new friend. Dov shifted the child to sit on his hip as we walked around the room.

"Do you need anything? How can we help?" He took the time to speak to each woman in the room, making sure they were taken care of before continuing.

I finally sat down with a group of children to give the mothers a break. A few wandered off to walk around, but the majority of them stayed in the room, allowing me to watch their babies for them for a few moments.

I quietly sang a song my aunt had taught me long ago, hoping no one else could hear me. A few of the children stopped to listen, but most kept playing.

The noise ebbed and flowed as the toddlers and young children moved around the room. Occasionally one would burst into tears. The nurses ran over quicker than I could ever reach the child, after all their years of being forced to keep the facility a quiet place for the doctors and overseers of the camp.

Dov took a seat next to me after making the rounds.

"You're good with them." His voice made me quiver.

"So are you, I see."

He waved to the little girl who sat in my lap, pulling on my hair that surrounded her.

"Hi there, little girl," he cooed. Picking up a strand of my hair, he dangled it in front of her as she tried to catch it. The tiny girl giggled each time she missed it.

"Is this our future, Auluria?" he asked, dropping my hair in front of her again.

"What?" I asked, afraid to move.

"You and me and a little one. Is this our future?" Blue eyes glanced up at me. He smiled and winked before flicking his fingers to send my hair into my face.

His laugh was so deep and genuine when I closed my eyes to try to avoid being hit with my own mane, that everything inside of me jumped. Dov tipped my chin toward him.

"If this is what our life will be like then I will be a completely happy man." He paused. "I know we've needed to talk, Auluria, but this is what I want to talk about the most. What do you want for us?"

The small child squirmed in my arms, upset that Dov had stopped playing.

"Hey, little girl," he turned back to her for a moment,

dangling my hair once more. I had a moment to process. "I didn't forget about you."

I waited for him to pacify the little girl, giving her enough attention to satisfy her. My hand darted out, mimicking Dov's motions when he pulled my face to look at him, pulling his face back to me.

"Yes," I nodded, an inch from his lips. "This. I want this. I want *you*."

I was overwhelmed by the scent of him as he kissed me. No one else could ever wear that sweet, spicy scent as well as Dov could. The moment was quick, but it said more than any other kiss we had ever had.

He pulled back, holding my lower lip between his. My heart went into overdrive. When I opened my eyes, he was watching me, grinning around biting his lip.

"I was hoping you'd say that."

"How will your brother feel about this?" Nervousness took root in my stomach, shooting through my legs. The little girl looked at me, feeling the switch in my posture.

"He's coming around, Auluria, you know that."

The little girl's nurse came over, lifting her from my lap. She quickly thanked us and walked away. Dov stood, holding his hand out to pull me to my feet.

"What does this mean for us?" I asked as he escorted me to a room with the older children to check on them.

"It means we get through this, take down the Society,

and then...we make sure we don't get separated again." He lifted my hand to his lips. "I promise."

"Dov Baer?" a voice interrupted.

He lowered my hand, reluctantly looking away.

"You're the one everyone is talking about?" The boy looked about ten. I couldn't tell if he was impressed or skeptical.

"I suppose I am." Dov leaned down to be more on his eye level.

"What are those?" The boy nodded to Dov's arms. We both glanced down.

"Oh," Dov realized, pushing his sleeve up further. "Those are scars."

"Why?" he asked, crossing his arms.

"Why...do I have them?" Dov tried to figure out his question.

"Gregory, don't ask things like that," a woman scolded.

Dov and I looked at each other, trying not to laugh.

"I have a friend who has the same name as you," Dov was on the verge of breaking down. "He would ask a question like that too.

"I got these because some bad people didn't want me to help some good people."

"He got those saving us, Gregory. You should thank him. He took that pain so that we didn't have to," his mother said. She leaned over to me and added, "From what I hear, you did, too. Thank you."

"How did you get them?" the boy pushed.

"Trust me, you don't want to know. It was pretty painful," I tried to sway him away from that line of questioning.

"Gregory, go get your brother." His mother shooed him with a wave of her hand. She waited for him to walk away. "Some of the girls who were recently brought in arrived with stories of Goldilocks and the three Baers. I assume that's you?"

She picked up some of her son's skepticism. The woman waited for us to explain our glorious past.

"A recent nickname," I shrugged.

"No tales of unrealistic heroics?" She placed a hand on her hip.

"Afraid not," Dov chuckled.

"No shiny promises of riches for all?" She wasn't going to let us off easy.

"None whatsoever," Dov replied. "All we want is to get out from under the rule of the Society and then help our allies over the Wall get their freedom as well. We're willing to fight for that."

"The scars are proof of that," I added.

"So the stories aren't true?" She asked, almost looking disappointed.

"We haven't heard any of the stories, so we don't know," I confided in her. "What I *do* know is that we're going to take down the Society and end these camps."

"What's your plan for us when this is all over?"

"You can go wherever you like. Home...or you can make a new home."

"Well, with a future like that looming ahead, I guess you'd better win. I think they're looking for you." She nodded behind us before walking off to catch up to her son.

"You'd better come upstairs," Reyla announced, latching onto my arm. She dragged me across the room.

"What's going on?"

"Anetta and Ella are going at it," Reyla's voice was high-pitched as she moved us faster than a normal walking pace.

"The*y're fighting*? Why?" Dov asked, wrapping his hand in mine temporarily.

"I have an idea..." I quickly explained what had happened earlier when Anetta had sided with me over Ella.

"Great, are we going to face this when we get back too?" Dov shook his head.

"Haven't we been?" I gave him a frustrated look.

"You're in charge; Ella is not. Time to handle this," Reyla didn't bother to hide the exasperation in her voice.

Something slammed ahead. We ran faster.

Chapter 7

"This doesn't concern you, Baer." Nikko's voice was dangerously low and rough.

"You can't kick us out," I challenged him.

"No one said *you* had to go, *your majesty*," Locust scoffed. "But this has nothing to do with *them.*"

He jutted his chin out at Dov and Reyla.

"We're not just going to leave, Locust," Reyla snipped, her fierce side coming out. "You don't get a say in this any more then you had a say in what happened before we all decided to work together."

"You, *little girl*, have *no idea* what I did or did not do when Lowell was still alive." He took a menacing step toward Reyla as Ella took another swing at Anetta. "But you're right. I had no say in joining forces with *you.*"

"That's because *she's* in charge." Reyla pointed to me. "And Shadoe. Not you."

"We did what *Shadoe* said," Ella glared at Anetta.

"Auluria is just as much responsible for Lowell's people as Shadoe is," Anetta challenged her. "You answer to her too."

"Do you honestly think once this is all over that we'll answer to anyone but Shadoe?" Ella circled the blonde.

"Back off, Locust," Dov said sharply as Locust stepped dangerously close to Reyla. She stood her ground, but I could see the panic in her eyes.

I connected with Dov long enough to indicate that I'd handle the girls and he could deal with Locust. Dov turned to take on Locust at Reyla's side. Nikko followed me.

"Leave it alone, Lur. You know this is how Lowell handled things." Nikko warned me, to prove myself worthy of taking my cousin's place.

"You so quickly turned your back on Lowell?" Ella shouted hysterically. "You know he despised her."

"He only turned on her when she decided not to obey his every command." Anetta threw back at her, blocking a punch. She missed the kick and cried out in pain as Ella connected.

"You followed his every command, but so suddenly you're willing to walk away?" Ella pushed harder, lashing out again with her foot. Had she been coming after me, I would have used that move against her the way Shadoe had trained me to...but she also wouldn't have been able to walk back to the mansion.

The room filled with noise as Ella and Anetta shouted at each other. Nikko chimed in, cheering Ella on. Reyla's voice mixed into the sound in the room, but even through the chaos, I heard Dov's voice above them all. I shut it out, forcing myself to listen to the girls in front of me. When they didn't relent, I attempted to control the situation.

"Stop," I said, mustering as much of my cousin as I could, keeping my voice low and even. When they didn't break apart, I tried again. "Enough."

Anetta ducked a punch, her movements far more agile than I remembered her to be. Furious, Ella attempted another attack, this time landing a kick to Anetta's hip. She crumpled on the floor before kicking back, sending Ella staggering several feet.

"Let them be," Nikko said, reminding me of Shadoe.

"Enough!" I shouted louder.

Anetta was on her feet again. She held her hands up to yield to my angry intrusion. Ella didn't stop.

"Fine, we'll do this the hard way."

I stepped forward, ready for a fight. Gripping her elbow, I spun her to face me.

"I said enough," I gave her one more warning. Ella didn't take the hint.

She threw a punch at my face, anger sizzling off her. I

was prepared for her outburst and ducked, taking her foot out in the process. She hit the ground and rolled, bouncing back up.

Ella moved to try to hit me again, but I moved faster. It was easy to block her move. She wasn't expecting the elbow to the face and she went down.

"Really?" Nikko criticized. He reached down to help Ella up, but pulled away at the last second, attempting to backhand me.

I reared back, kicking him as hard as I could, anger overtaking me.

"What is going on here?" Justin shrieked as he ran to my side. I nearly turned to him to defend myself, but I realized who he was in time.

Nikko stumbled over Ella, crashing into the floor. She stood up, ready to take me on again. Furious, I circled her.

"You want a hand, Goldilocks?" Justin asked, laughter in his voice.

Dov's shouting distracted me, allowing Ella to strike. My lip broke open as she connected.

Anetta glowered, moving in to help me. Nikko recovered, ready to side with Ella. I wanted desperately to turn around so I could see what Dov's scuffle was about.

"He's fine," Justin murmured, knowing where my head was at. "Can I help now?"

"Stay out of this," Anetta and I both responded as if it had been planned.

"You did *what*?" Dov's voice broke my concentration again. A loud thud sounded, but Shadoe's training snapped me back to the fight where I was already engaged. Dov could hold his own, and with competition like Locust, I doubted the fight would last long.

I maneuvered my body to flip Nikko when he launched himself at me, using the proximity to my advantage. Anetta took on Ella again, slamming the bottom of her boot into Ella's shin. Justin snorted in amusement.

"Enough, Ella," Nikko finally said. "Shadoe's not going to like this."

"I'm still in charge here, Nikko. If you had done this to Lowell, he would have destroyed you." My shoulders moved rapidly as I tried to control my breathing.

"You're not Lowell," he sneered. He used his wrist to wipe the blood trickling down his forehead.

Justin deftly stepped forward. He grabbed Nikko's shoulders and spun him around, slamming him into a wall face first as he threw me a playful wink. He mouthed, "I got you."

Nikko bounced off the wall, new blood trickling down his face. He sputtered at Justin as Justin arranged a scowl on his face.

"*She's* Lowell," he bellowed, pointing to me. "*I'm* Shadoe. *You* are *nothing* but an underling.

"You come at her, and you come at me. For as easily as she could take you down, I can do a lot more damage, a lot faster than she can. Don't try me and don't test her." Justin growled, making Nikko blanch.

"Don't forget, Nikko, not only did I train directly under Lowell and Shadoe, but I also trained under the Baers *and* Brittella. In case you've forgotten, I started a war and escaped death more times than you've ever even seen it." I matched Justin's ferocity. "When this is all over, I have the power to decide if you go or stay. More importantly, I have the power to decide your position within this leadership structure. I suggest you choose wisely."

I played into Justin's attempts to position me in authority over them.

"*Dov!*" Reyla screamed, making us all turn.

Locust brandished a knife, playing by Lowell's handbook. Reyla looked terrified as Dov prepared himself to disarm the man, tugging up his sleeve so it wouldn't get in the way.

The last thing we needed was for Dov to be hurt before we returned to Canton's mansion. Tension rolled off of them. Justin flinched just enough to let me know he was going to involve himself in the confrontation, risking another of our top men. I inserted myself into the situation before he could.

"Locust." I dropped my voice seductively as I called

his name. It set him off balance. I stepped toward him to further distract him.

Dov rushed forward, wrenching the knife from his hand. Locust looked around, shocked.

"If you *ever*," I continued speaking the way Brittella had taught me, taking slow, deliberate steps forward to upset him, "try to hurt my boyfriend again, I will make you suffer a worse fate than *anything* my cousin could have dreamed up for you.

"If you are incredibly fortunate enough *to earn your way back* into my good graces before we get back to the mansion, I *might* consider not telling Shadoe. But you *will* suffer whatever consequences *I* deem appropriate for an offense like this.

"Dov is your leader. *I* am your leader. To try to hurt either of us is treason, and you know what happens to traitors in the Society.

"You have no Shadoe to cut you down at the last second, Locust. You only have me. I am your judge, jury, and executioner, and you have made me *very* angry."

The closer I got, the wider his eyes became.

"You will pay for trying to hurt your leader, Locust, mark my words. Before the end of the day, you will pay for your actions. Nikko can't save you. Ella can't save you. No one but I can save you."

Locust looked cornered as I moved closer. Everyone but Dov had already started inching away from me as I revealed a side they didn't know I had. Locust took it as his cue to move away too, stepping back each time I took a step until he reached the wall. His throat bobbed when he realized he couldn't move away any farther.

"I suggest you come up with a very compelling apology and a plan for making this up to us before I give you my verdict, Locust. I suggest you think very, very hard."

My tone took an icy edge by the end of my speech; another tactic Brittella had taught me during my time with her. I hadn't realized it until that moment, but she had trained me to be Lowell's successor. She knew I would never be like him, but she gave me the ability to *sound* like him when I needed to protect myself with his people. I could practically feel Lowell's words breathing down my neck.

"Get out of sight and be back here in one hour for your sentencing, Locust," I commanded him. "If you try to run, I'll have Nikko hunt you down, and I promise you, he won't be kind. We tolerate deserters almost as well as we do traitors."

Locust scampered out of the room as quickly as possible. I turned, drawing on everything Brittella had taught me to do. I summoned a knowing smile as I found Nikko in the crowd.

"If he runs, you will hunt him down and bring him back to me. He will stand trial, and I don't care if we're in the middle of a war with the Society, he will live by Lowell's law. Do you understand?"

"Maybe you *do* have a little of Lowell in you after all," he commented. Blood still dripped down his forehead.

"Watch him." I jerked my head toward the door. "Help him make the right decision."

I waited for Nikko to nod. He and Ella followed Locust through the door.

"You want to explain that?" Dov looked as if he had never seen me before.

I dropped the look, relaxing my body.

"Brittella," I shook my head. "She knew one day I'd need to sound like Lowell to be effective with his people, so she taught me. I didn't realize it until just now, but she was smart enough to have the foresight to protect me, even back then. She might have recently reminded me."

"So that was all just an act?" Justin asked, looking slightly concerned.

"I'm not really going to have them hurt him," I rolled my eyes. "But now Locust fears me and Nikko respects me. I don't think Ella will ever care about me, but Nikko will keep her in check."

I paused, looking at each of them. Anetta shook her head slightly when I glanced at her, arranging a softer look over her features. She had known Lowell better than Dov had. For a second, she looked as if she had seen his ghost. Maybe I took it too far.

"At least they'll listen to me until we get back to the mansion now," I smiled, looking away from her.

"I'm going to have to talk to Brittella," Anetta teased, adding a grin as she re-joined the land of the living.

"I've seen you in action, *honey.*" Brittella posed in the doorway, having slipped in unnoticed. "I have nothing to teach you. I *do,* however, have some things to teach the young ladies here."

"Brittella," I tried not to gasp. "How long have you been here?"

She smiled coyly, ignoring my question.

"I believe you wanted a report, Auluria." She nodded for Anetta and me to follow. "You too."

"I did. Just a moment." I turned to Dov, needing answers before I left. "What was that all about?"

"He found out that lecherous Lowell-devotee tried to get too touchy with you before your mission," Brittella answered for him. "*Don't give me that look*, Auluria. Of *course,* I heard everything. How else do you think I got so good at my job?"

Brittella traded in secrets. I had always assumed she acquired them by way of her influence over people, but a smart woman also knows how to find answers without the help of man or minion.

I turned back to Dov, sliding my hand from his elbow, to his wrist, down to his hand where I entwined our fingers. I wanted a moment with him, but, surrounded by people, that was the best I could get.

"Thank you for defending me," I said, appreciating his effort to protect me. "Locust never touched me."

"Shadoe wouldn't let him," Dov mumbled.

"No. Well, yes. Neither would Lowell. Actually, Lowell saw pretty quickly to that when he pronounced my engagement. But even so, do you honestly think I couldn't hold my own against *that*?"

"I only faced off against him for a few minutes," Dov chuckled, "Just imagine what *you* would have done to him."

"Oh, I think you did a pretty good number on him from the looks of things. Did you hit him with a bag of rocks?"

Locust looked like he had gone a few rounds against Arin in the interrogation room.

"Too much?" He winced.

"We probably could have done without the facial injuries. Might be a little hard to sneak him back into the mansion." I laughed.

"I can fix that," Brittella said with a wave of her hand. She stepped closer as if she was about to approach Dov. "As for *you*, kiss your girlfriend goodbye and go check on your little friend down the hall; she's been moping around about not being able to go help her sister... Foolish girl."

She turned on her heels to face Justin, shocking him. Her hand darted up to his chest as she eyed the length of him. Her lips quirked up into a gentle smile meant only for him as she dropped her hand. Finishing her examination, she let out a small *hmm* before walking away. She paused at the door.

"Ladies," Brittella grimaced when I approached, noting my split lip. "You should clean that up."

Reyla attached herself to my side, even though she hadn't been invited. She giggled at the look of terror that seemed permanently etched across Justin's face. I had a feeling that's the look all of Brittella's contacts had when she started grooming them to work for her. I turned back and shrugged, offering him a playful wink that made Dov snort as he tried to hold in his laughter. I'm sure he was grateful that it wasn't him.

I had to force myself to keep walking. Reyla looped her arm through mine, knowing I wanted to turn back and take my place at Dov's side. It was beginning to seem like every time something big happened, Dov and I were ripped apart.

"I've managed to find a few girls that I believe will work well on your team," Brittella noted as we walked. "They're the more recent girls who have no responsibilities around here yet, nor do they appear to be carrying a child.

"Here we are," she said, turning left into a small room. Seven girls stood as we walked in.

"Of course, you'll have to see for yourselves, but I'd certainly take them on for training were we not fighting a war." Her eyes sparkled as she spoke. "They have many of your talents, my dear, but they still need work. Perhaps you could train them."

"Perhaps we need to reevaluate where we place Brittella," I whispered to Reyla. "I think she might need to come with us and teach our spies."

"Do you think she'd do more good here or there?" Anetta whispered.

"I really have no taste for war, ladies," Brittella interjected. "I see I was misguided in thinking I had nothing to teach you, Anetta. Clearly, the art of a gentle whisper is not among your talents. You should pay more attention to Auluria; her training is flawless. At least, my part of it, anyway."

The girls looked wary of the conversation, fidgeting across the room. I could already tell which one of them was Brittella's favorite. She stood straight, balancing her weight on one foot, the other stretched lightly across her knee, giving her a graceful curve. Her face was soft as she gave the appearance of having a light touch. She would be a perfect student for Brittella.

"Have any of you been trained to fight?" I waited as all seven nodded. "Good, time to see what you can do."

I had never seen Brittella look out of sorts before, but standing near the wall in the nearly empty room we occupied, she looked more uncomfortable than Justin had half an hour earlier. She swallowed hard, attempting to stifle a gasp.

I refocused my attention, watching the young girl face off against Anetta. The blonde easily stalked around the young girl while she held her ground.

"Not bad," I mumbled.

"I think it's time you and I had a little talk, Reyla. Come along." Brittella tugged at Reyla's sleeve.

"Umm, okay..." Reyla tripped after her, caught in Brittella's death grip.

"Have fun," I said, unsure of what Brittella had in store for my friend.

Knowing it was time to change the game, I silently slipped up behind the girl we were testing as the other girls watched. Anetta saw my approach and held a swing, giving me an opportunity to surprise the girl.

She whipped around, sensing my presence and tried to take me on. Dov, Silas, and Devin stood near the door, watching quietly as we tested the girls to make sure they would survive when we attacked the Society.

The girl was vicious; Wallace's men had trained her well. She growled as she threw her full weight at me, taking her aggression out. The girl claimed she had no allegiance to Wallace's men because they hadn't rescued her. Based on her reaction when we told her about Wallace's death, I believed her.

My name was muttered a few times by the men near the door, but the pounding of blood in my ears prevented me from hearing more. I angled myself to see them over the girl's shoulder and found them all grinning at me.

Justin timidly stepped inside. He relaxed when he realized Brittella was no longer in the room. He nodded for us to join them.

"He's back," he informed us quietly.

Anetta and I had a silent conversation with our eyes before we both nodded in agreement. I turned to the girls, wishing Talley had been there to help test them.

"Congratulations, we're confident that you all will be great assets to us. We'll give you instructions in the morning. Be prepared to leave early with us." I dismissed them. The girls filed out of the room, pleased with themselves.

"Have you decided what to do yet?" Dov asked.

"Yes." I took a breath to steady myself.

Locust stood in the middle of the room when we arrived looking like a man about to be hung. Under Lowell's reign, he might have been. Nikko, having weighed his options, stood with his arms crossed as he faced me. He nodded to show he would cooperate. Ella was nowhere to be seen.

Dov, Silas, Anetta, Reyla, Raselin, Fitch, Devin, Justin, Talley, and a few others filed in and stood next to me, creating a line of judges for Locust to face.

"Do you have anything to say, young man?" Raselin asked.

Locust looked like he was about to be sick.

"I'm sorry for my actions," Locust mumbled. "I felt threatened and my reaction was to defend myself and I should have made a different choice because I know you weren't going to escalate the fight like that."

His eyes were focused on the floor in front of our feet, hands behind his back. He shifted as if he were twisting his fingers.

"How do we know we can trust you not to pull a knife on one of us again?" Talley asked, staring him down. Locust looked up, surprised to hear her voice.

"I won't," he stated.

"You shouldn't have the first time," Talley countered.

Raselin nodded to me, giving me the floor. I took a few paces forward, putting myself between Locust and the group.

"I am not my cousin, Locust, but I can be if I need to. I don't like being like Lowell, so the fact that you've made me step into his shoes isn't helping your case.

"That said, I've come up with something that I can live with."

I stepped back toward the group as Locust watched me, trying to figure out my angle. My eyes never left him.

"Locust, because of your actions, you will never be allowed to rise in the ranks. You will never achieve a position higher than the one you have now. Once we return, after we're done handling the Society, Shadoe will be responsible for deciding if you can stay or if you will be dismissed from our command."

"You're telling Shadoe?" Concern made his voice lift higher than usual.

"He needs to know. We have to be able to trust you and I can't be impartial on that. Shadoe will be the one who decides if you stay or leave, but I won't tell him until after we bring down the Society. That way you'll have a fair chance to prove yourself valuable to him."

"I suggest you thank her for her benevolence, young man," Raselin added quickly, crossing his arms defensively. "That could have been much worse."

He remained silent, looking down. No one spoke, waiting for him to summon the ability to speak again.

"Thank you for giving me another chance, Lur. I'm sorry." He looked at me on the last sentence.

"Nikko will be responsible for overseeing you until we get back. Don't do anything to make me regret this second chance."

Everyone turned to watch him as he walked out of the room, Nikko in his wake. The group turned to me as if it were my job to tell them what to do next.

"You should go say goodbye to Hannah," I waved to Reyla, Dov, and Silas. "You probably won't see her in the morning before we leave."

"Do you want to come?" Dov asked, holding his hand out to me.

"No, you go ahead. I'm sure I'll get to know her later on, but this should be for her friends." He gave me an understanding smile before following his best friend and Reyla.

Raselin led the others out to get them set up for the night, but the Hershs lingered.

"You okay, Goldilocks?" Justin asked, sidling up next to me.

"Yeah, I'm okay."

"What are you thinking about?" Devin asked. He blinked as he looked at me.

"I'm not sure," I answered, suddenly feeling exhausted.

"Want to sit with us for a few minutes?" Talley suggested, motioning to the floor. When I nodded, she slipped down to the floor across from me.

"Sharone's going to be so excited to hear her sister is okay..." Devin started.

"I'm sure she will," Talley's head bobbed as she spoke.

"It would be like getting one of you back...although I doubt Hannah is a monster like you two."

"Hey!" the boys protested together.

"Hannah is older than Sharone, so really, it would be like *us* getting *you* back." Justin corrected her.

"Well, in that case, Hannah might want to rethink going back," Talley teased.

"You couldn't leave us if you tried, sis." Devin wrinkled his nose at her.

I watched their playful banter, fiercely jealous of them. Justin noticed and stopped laughing.

"What?"

"Nothing, I was just thinking about how nice it must be to have siblings."

"Aww, Auluria," Justin gave me a sad smile. "Haven't you figured it out by now?"

"Figured what out?" I frowned, waiting for him to turn it into a joke.

"You're one of us now, Auluria," Devin grinned as Justin leaned over and slung his arm over my shoulders.

"Auluria, please. We adopted you almost from the moment we met you," Talley said from across the circle. "Why do you think we keep hanging around with you?"

My heart swelled.

"You don't think we stayed in that storehouse with you all that time because it was our *job*, did you?" Devin asked. "You realize there were much more productive uses for our talents at that point in time, don't you?"

"We had to talk them into letting us watch over you. They wanted us out scouting and surveying the towns." Talley informed me, reaching out to rest her hand on my knee.

"Like it or not, you're stuck with us, Goldilocks." Justin pulled me in for a side hug. "And don't you forget that when it comes to who gets to walk you down the aisle in this upcoming wedding of yours."

"Yeah, me," Devin announced.

"Wedding?" I felt the color drain from my face.

"Oh, don't try to deny it, Auluria," Talley laughed. "We *all* know it's coming."

"I feel like I'm always the last to know these things," I said, letting out a nervous laugh.

"Don't be so naïve, Goldilocks," Justin winked at me, scooting closer. "And the answer is me. I'm the one walking you down the aisle."

"No," Devin protested, prompting a full argument over what their roles would be.

"Don't worry about trying to explain this to Dov," Talley leaned in and quietly said over her brothers' fight. "We've already had this conversation with him."

Justin and Devin bolted to their feet, upsetting the conversation. The two moved behind me, arguing loudly, arms in the air. Justin lunged at Devin, locking him in a chokehold. The two wrestled until they were in a heap on the ground.

"This is your one and only chance to get out, Auluria," Talley whispered. "Take it or leave it."

"I'm good," I replied.

Our attention was pulled in the direction of the two men yelping on the floor, alternating between threats and laughter.

"And tomorrow, we go back to the mansion."

"Here's hoping it's how we left it," Talley added.

Chapter 8

The hooded man turned, revealing his face, as our small group approached the mansion. Arin shook his head, warning us off. We changed directions, moving to the right as we entered the building, not acknowledging him. A few minutes later, he joined us in a small room we had quietly snuck into.

"We have to be careful getting everyone in," he said gruffly. "The other magistrates are here and will know if something is off."

"Why are they here?" Silas asked, brow furrowed.

"They must have figured out something was up. They've been asking a lot of questions." Arin replied, looking over his shoulder at the door.

"Has Shadoe been able to keep Canton in check?" I asked, praying he had.

"Canton's been behaving himself, but we're also keeping him away from the other magistrates. I'm sure they find it suspicious."

"Where's Berwyn?" Dov asked.

"I can go find him." Arin started to back away. "You should warn the others."

"I'll go," Ben volunteered, looking to Dov for approval.

"Thanks, Ben. Have Fitch help you sneak them in a few at a time and make sure Raselin knows to come right away. Tell him we'll meet in the study."

"On it," Ben said, slipping out behind Arin.

"Now we have to get to the study," Silas murmured. "I have a feeling that won't be as easy as it sounds."

"Doubtful," Dov said heavily. "This intrusion could really change the course of our plans. I hadn't anticipated the magistrates coming here. I thought we would take the fight to them."

"We'll adapt," Silas offered. "We always do."

"Gloria, can you—" Dov was cut off.

"Yes." She dashed off.

"Where did she go?" I asked, wondering how she knew what he wanted. Then I remembered my first mission with Dov. He and Gloria used to work well together before I appeared in his life.

"She's doing a little reconnaissance. She'll be back." Silas brushed his hair back. "You ready?"

"Let's go."

We followed behind Silas and Reed, walking two at a time in line. Silas nodded when we passed a group of our people moving in the opposite direction. I searched for Sharone in the crowd but didn't see her.

We took a back staircase, hoping to avoid the magistrates and their people. Distinguishing their people from our own team would be difficult while wearing the Society uniforms to blend in.

Berwyn was waiting in the study when we arrived, Eden, Shadoe, and Necesta by his side. He looked annoyed as we entered.

"Well?" he asked once the door was closed.

"The camps are ours," Dov reported. "Have any of the others returned?"

"Two of the teams are already back," Berwyn said, explaining what had happened. We had lost a number of men on one team but had been successful at capturing all of the camps. "The last teams should return any time now."

"What are we doing about the magistrates?" I asked out of turn.

Berwyn's icy gaze turned to me. I resisted the urge to shrink back.

"We need to take them out," Shadoe grumbled. He clenched his teeth when he looked at me.

"We can't; they brought soldiers with them," Berwyn protested.

"And now our men are back," Shadoe argued.

"You think at least of a few of them won't escape and warn the others?" Berwyn raised his voice for a moment, forgetting to be quiet. He immediately dropped it to a harsh whisper. "We're so close. We can't ruin this now. We will *not* risk this."

"You think they aren't going to figure this out while we're standing around, waiting, Baer?" Shadoe sneered. "You're a bigger fool than I thought.

"We need to strike *now* before they see it coming."

"Glad to see things haven't changed much," I muttered to Silas, who, for once, didn't laugh at my joke.

"Our priority right now needs to be to get our people back inside the mansion," Dov mediated. "How many soldiers did the magistrates bring?"

"Five hundred men and they're all asking questions."

"How many of the magistrates are here?" Silas asked, attempting to get a better view of the situation.

Dust floated in the air, sparkling in the late afternoon sunlight pouring in through the window, catching my eye. It changed direction in swirling clouds of sparkling matter each time someone spoke with their hands.

"Twelve magistrates and fourteen justices," Shadoe

informed us, looking as if it were taking all of his mental restraint to keep from snapping at us.

Necesta reached out and put her hand through Shadoe's elbow. He looked as if he wanted to turn and yell at her, but he held steady.

"We will work a plan out now that our people are back home, but they're right. Our first priority, dearie, needs to be to get them back inside the mansion. Goldilocks, where is Raselin?"

"He should be here soon, Necesta. He was in the second group." A thought occurred to me as I spoke, quickly adding, "How have none of the magistrates' soldiers found the soldiers in the cells yet?"

"We haven't let them downstairs. We've kept them very busy up here," Eden answered, finally speaking. "We've even sent some of them on missions just to get them away from the mansion."

"Any chance we can just swap some of the magistrates' men out for our people?" I ventured a guess at a plan.

"They're too familiar with the people in their own groups. They'll notice if someone goes missing and is replaced." Berwyn voiced my worry.

"Where are the new recruits?"

"Raselin," Necesta crooned, looking at the door. She released Shadoe and joined her friend. "You made it back in one piece."

"Most of us did," he replied sadly. "We met one of the other teams on the way in. There were losses."

He quickly explained what he had learned. Berwyn added in that he had made arrangements for the people who had joined our forces from the camps to be hidden in the town since the magistrates were already in place once they arrived.

"We'll send for them when we're ready," Eden added, giving a pointed look at Shadoe. She scowled at him, looking as if she were prepared to shred him on the spot, cutting bit by bit away until he was nothing.

A loud knock sounded at the door. The sharp sound made us all flinch.

"Sir, Magistrate Canton is asking for you." I recognized Sherman's voice on the other side of the door.

I grabbed hold of his arm as he brushed by me, apparently still behaving like my cousin. "Later," I mouthed to him. His face twitched with surprise as he wrenched himself away from me.

When I turned back, Eden was staring at me. I couldn't read her expression before she tore her gaze away, her curls bouncing with the motion.

"We need a plan," Raselin whispered, unsure if any soldiers lingered outside the door.

"Come with me," Berwyn waved his hand as he backed up.

He led us to the wall. Lifting a table, he set it a

few feet to the left. Berwyn turned back to the right, stepping over to a bookcase. He gently pulled on a board, moving it out just an inch. His other hand slipped behind it as a click sounded. The wall opened.

"Canton had a few security measures put in place. After a few days, he told Shadoe everything." He pushed the board back in place, grabbing the door so it wouldn't close. "Hurry."

Dov tugged at my hand as I stood motionless, worrying about what Shadoe had done to acquire that information. We all slipped into the crowded hallway behind the room, barely big enough for one person to fit through.

"Keep going," Berwyn whispered loudly as we followed Eden.

She stopped at another door and placed her face against the wall, where I assumed there was a hole to check the room before entering. Her fingers climbed the side of the wall as she observed the room until she found what she was looking for. The door opened to reveal a dimly lit room.

Eden opened the curtains, letting in the muted reflection of light that came from the other side of the building. Books sat out on the tables. Maps littered the room. Knives and weapons were scattered about on the furniture and floor.

"As far as we can tell, this room isn't accessible any way but the hallway," Eden said softly.

I glanced around and realized there was no door.

"Is it wise to be in here if *that's* the only way out?" I asked. *Shadoe couldn't have approved this meeting place.*

"Probably not, but it's the only place we're sure the magistrates' men can't hear us." Berwyn shook his head.

The other team leaders who had returned joined us and we recounted the takeover of the camps, going over our losses and gains. The boys from the camps waited in the towns, hidden with the people who had sided with us thanks to Dov's efforts before Canton's men caught us.

We talked until evening, coming up with a plan to get the magistrates to leave. We would send our teams ahead, to each of their districts to wait for their arrival. The idea was to strike as they arrived, not giving them time to prepare.

The wind howled against the outside wall, but without windows, we couldn't see if it was storming or if it was just blustery. The walls creaked each time the noise crept up, crackling through the ceiling.

"Auluria, walk with me," Necesta said, pulling me from the table. "You too, Dov."

Berwyn waved us off, wrapping up the meeting. We followed Necesta to the wall, stepping into the narrow hallway where she released my elbow. She clutched my hand, guiding me.

"You need to have a conversation with your friend," she said flatly.

"Which friend?" I asked.

"Shadoe, of course." She glanced back at me over her shoulder. "You left him here for all this time without anyone to keep him in check. He barely managed."

"What do you mean?" Dov asked skeptically.

"I mean, he's managed to restrain himself, but it's only because he knew you were coming back. That, and your brother can be rather frightening when he wants to be," Necesta squeezed my hand as she glanced at Dov. "But, dearie, I can see the strands starting to snap, one by one. He's untethered. You are the one holding him in place. You're the one keeping him from ending up like your cousin. You need to talk to him."

"Did he do something while we were gone, Necesta?" My body tensed up as I asked the question, dreading the answer.

"Not that I know of, but it's only a matter of time." She stopped abruptly. Dov collided with me as I avoided crashing into the older woman in front of me.

She rapped on the wall once before opening the door. We stepped into Canton's chambers. A fire crackled in the fireplace along the far wall. Canton sat in a chair, slinking back into the cushions. Shadoe stood in front of him menacingly. He flashed the smallest smile at the man before turning to face us. Canton's skin blanched.

Necesta patted my back before exiting. Shadoe waited for me to address him. I eyed the magistrate as he carefully watched me.

"Go," Shadoe said, prompting Canton to stand and scurry into a large closet. He closed the door behind him. "He's fine."

"Why did you get called out of the meeting?" I asked.

"One of the magistrates wanted to speak to Canton. We'd been putting the conversation off since yesterday."

"What did they want?" I inquired.

"A plan," he straightened his shoulders. "They wanted to know how Canton was planning on finding you two and your brother. We gave them one."

That should have horrified me, but I knew it was meant to put the magistrates where we wanted them for battle.

"I take it they'll be helping Canton destroy us?" I offered, walking to sit on the settee at the end of Canton's grand bed. Shadoe took Canton's chair as Dov gently sat next to me.

"Are you going to tell me what happened out there?" Shadoe redirected.

"What do you mean?" I asked, trying not to sound confrontational as Dov put a hand on the small of my back, sending a shiver up my spine.

He raised an eyebrow at me, challenging me. I jutted my chin out, silently communicating with him.

"So you haven't completely changed, Lur." He smiled sarcastically at us. "I knew it would come back to you sooner or later.

"We need to talk about this stupid plan of your brother's. Striking now is the best option. We need to take them out while they're still here—"

"Enough, Shadoe," Dov intervened. "We've all agreed that we need to get control of them in their own districts. There's too much that could go wrong taking control of them here and having to transport them back."

"You aren't listening, Baer—" Shadoe protested.

"You've discussed this with Berwyn and the others?" Dov held up a hand to silence him.

"They don't understand," Shadoe insisted.

"Do you want to talk to Berwyn and Raselin one more time?" Dov shook his head but reluctantly offered Shadoe one last opportunity to make his case.

"Well you two certainly aren't going to listen to me, so why would they?"

"Present your case, Shadoe. It can't hurt." I shrugged. "You and Dov can go now. I'll watch Canton."

"Are you sure you shouldn't come with us?" Dov hedges.

"Go, I'll be fine."

"I'll send Sherman," Shadoe announced as he stood. "Keep him in the closet."

Shadoe stalked over to the door, preparing to throw it open.

"Shadoe," he paused at my words. "I brought Brittella back."

"Good for you," he muttered over his shoulder.

"Why did you send me for her?"

"We needed her. I assume she got the job done?" Without waiting for me to confirm that she had helped us, he added, "Then it was a successful mission."

He continued stalking toward the closet where Canton had taken refuge, refusing to say anything else on the topic. When he opened the door, we saw he had shackled himself in place. Shadoe had trained him well.

Canton was perched on a settee similar to the one I had just occupied. He gritted his teeth as Shadoe checked the chains on his wrists.

"Cooperate," he instructed the magistrate. Shadoe turned back to Dov. "Let's go."

Dov gave me one more look before following Shadoe through the hidden doorway. I sat back down, propping my elbow on my knee. My mind drifted to where I could feel my knife hidden in my boot, checking to make sure it was still there just in case I needed it.

"Hello again, Auluria," Canton said once he was sure the others were gone.

"I'm not talking to you." I glared at him, leaning forward, putting more of my weight on my knee.

"But you should," he crooned, shifting the way he held himself. The scared man faded away as the magistrate came forward. "You see, I know things you don't want me to know."

I refused to respond to him.

"Oh, Auluria, you don't think I didn't learn about you before hanging you, do you?" He smiled at me. "Don't be absurd. Your cousin told me all sorts of stories. But more than that, I know *you*, Auluria. I saw what you did."

That got my attention.

"What did I do?" I asked, hoping to sound uninterested.

"I saw you try to save my guard. You're not like the rest of them," he insisted, trying to use my actions against me. "You won't let them do this to me."

"Of course, I will." I blinked a few times, wondering why he thought he could leverage those particular actions.

"They're going to murder me, Auluria. You know you're going to help me, so why not use it to your advantage? We could help each other."

"Magistrate Canton, the last man who tried to use that line on me didn't like the end results of his efforts. I'd refer you to the bloody mess that was—*is*—Justice Kenton, but I don't think you really want to see that right now." I smirked at my intentional slip of words.

"You didn't." His face slipped.

"No," I quickly agree. "*I* didn't—of course not—I would never. Shadoe did. Just like Shadoe killed all of your men...but he already told you that."

"You won't just hand me over to him," Canton tried to remind me. "You don't have it in you."

"I already did," I snapped. "Who do you think left you under his charge?"

"The Baers," he snarled at me, beginning to lose hope that he could coerce me.

"Where do you think they got that idea from? Remember, Canton; I'm part of two groups. They all listen to *me*. I'm the one who left you with Shadoe, and I'll leave you there again if you don't prove useful."

He started to stand up, his red robes fluttering as he moved, only to be stopped by his chains. He growled in frustration.

"You're not like Lowell or Shadoe. You can't just do this."

"Magistrate, you tried to have me hanged. You tortured my boyfriend and friends. You're lucky you're alive at all." I answered him. "Isn't this all getting a little old? You've tried this before."

The secret door opened as Sherman stepped into the room. He stalked to the closet, raising his weapon. The hilt of his knife slammed into Canton's arm, making him crumple in pain.

"No talking," Sherman demanded. He turned and glared at me.

I sat in silence as Canton sniffled from the closet. Sherman glowered outside the closet door as he waited for Shadoe's return. I held still, watching as Sherman glowered.

Eventually, Shadoe stormed in alone, rage vibrating off his arms.

"I knew that was pointless," he said quietly.

I stood, walking to the hallway.

"I'm sorry. I think they're right though, Shadoe. I think it's the best course of action." I walked backward, letting him guide me.

"You're wrong this time, Lur, but that's never stopped you before."

"Can we talk about this?" I requested.

"Go to bed, Lur." He collided with me as he tried to brush past me.

"Shadoe," I tried calming him.

He slammed me against the wall and slipped past me.

"Not tonight, Lur."

Shadoe stormed off, leaving me to find my own way out of the hallway.

"**G**et up," his frightened voice startled me awake. I jolted upright, nearly colliding with him.

"We have a problem, Lur." Red flooded my vision as the boy came into focus in the soft light filtering in through the window.

"What is going on?" I breathed deeply, trying to get enough oxygen to fully wake up and process his words as he continued to shake my shoulders.

"It's Shadoe," he said, rendering me fully awake.

"What happened?" I pushed him away and jumped to my feet, looking for Dov. He sat up next to where I had been sleeping, looking tired.

"During the night," the red-haired boy panted, "he

left. He took a group of people and went to get the new recruits."

"He *what?*" Dov bellowed, fully conscious. He slammed his hand into Silas' sleeping form, startling him awake.

"Shadoe took us into the town," the boy clarified. "He found the boys from the camp and brought them here."

Berwyn sat up, wide-eyed.

"*What did he do?*" Berwyn growled. Eden placed a hand on his arm.

"Wait, I know you," I tried to process what was happening.

"Yes, I'm Louis. We've met before." He sounded annoyed as he tried to rush me.

Images of the boy Silas and I freed from the Society cells, then again when he helped me to free Dov from Canton's captivity flashed through my mind. He worked for Lowell, and now, for Shadoe.

"They're downstairs," Louis said. "You'd better come."

"Berwyn!" Nian shouted as he raced into the room. His moves were frantic. "Berwyn, Shadoe brought the recruits. It's a bloodbath, Berwyn."

We raced to the door, tripping over each other to get there.

"Wait, weapons," Dov reminded us, skidding to a stop.

"You won't need them," Nian turned back to us. "It's all over now."

The main floor was littered with bodies. Society guards lay in their own blood, mixed with a few boys from the camps. Carnage was everywhere.

"No," I breathed, ready to cry. Dov gripped my fingers tightly.

Raselin gasped behind us as he joined our group on the landing.

"How did this happen?" he asked.

"It doesn't matter," Berwyn cut him off. "We have to make sure we have everyone before they manage to escape."

"If anyone is still alive, take them prisoner," Dov instructed.

Eden leaned over to me, whispering, "They look just like their father when they stand together like that. Griz would be so proud of those two."

I wondered what Griz was like. I had heard stories from the brothers and Eden about him—even Reyla and the others had told me stories—but I wished I had been able to meet the leader of the Baers' group. It was just one more thing Canton had taken from us.

The sounds of a fight outside filtered into the room.

"We need to get help outside," Berwyn turned to direct people.

"I'll go," Raselin pointed for Berwyn to go down the hall. "You handle inside the mansion; I'll take reinforcements outside."

Berwyn nodded as Raselin bolted down the stairs, calling to our people to follow him as they spilled into the foyer. The oldest Baer turned back to us.

"Split up. Find all of the magistrates and justices," Berwyn shouted as he moved down the hall. "Be careful."

"Come on," Eden hissed at me, declaring me her partner. She brushed a piece of her hair back into her hood, tucking it behind her ear. Our opposition may be dead, but it was best to use our cover until we had the magistrates and justices in our custody.

The small group crept down the hall to the guest wing, lingering behind Berwyn, Silas, Dov, and the others. We each took a door, bursting into the rooms simultaneously. In the distance, I heard our people running outside, engaging with the enemy as they fought in the courtyard.

A fire quietly crackled, warming the drafty room. The embers glowed as the breeze from the door made the flames sway. Red curtains hung heavily over the window, blocking the muted early morning light from entering.

My eyes swept from the curtains, across the floor, following drops of blood. A hand sat motionless on the floor, palm up. The rest of the corpse was hidden by the bed. My body was drenched in a cold spark of nerves, but my eyes kept traveling up, over the comforter to where feet sat quietly below the blanket. It appeared undisturbed until it reached the man's waist. The comforter began to twist, as if in the middle of being ripped away and thrown to the side.

Blood soaked through the red color, staining it even darker. Hollow eyes stared up at the ceiling, grasping onto the man's last view. The magistrate was dead.

Eden stiffened next to me, lost somewhere between horror and happiness. She despised the Society for what they did to her and her people, but the tragedy of death wasn't lessened by her hatred of the men that hurt our people.

I forced myself around the bed, finding two other soldiers also dead on the ground. Shadoe's men had been thorough.

Taking in the scene, I realized how much trouble Shadoe would be in for going behind our backs. It was an errant tactical move on his part—one that Lowell would have made—and perhaps it *could have* worked. But going behind our backs and specifically working against the team's orders...I didn't know how Berwyn and Raselin would respond to that.

I also knew that we couldn't afford to lose someone as skilled as Shadoe. For as highly trained as the Baers were, Shadoe was better. His training had been harsher. His work was more punishing than theirs. No one could get the results Shadoe could get.

I needed to find him.

"Auluria," Eden's voice pulled me back into the

moment. She waved me out of the room.

In the hallway, Berwyn asked for a report.

"Dead," I responded. "The magistrate and three of his men."

Berwyn shook his head as everyone reported at least one death in the room they had checked. Several reported deaths from our own ranks as well.

Shadoe must have snuck the boys in and blitz attacked the sleeping Magistrates.

"We need reinforcements down here," Henry called from the foyer downstairs. We all rushed to the stairs.

I clung to the banister as I flew down the steps, moving far faster than I should have been going with a weapon in my hand. With each step, the noise grew louder.

The Magistrate's men raged against us, but unsure of who belonged to the resistance and who belonged to a different magistrate, they occasionally turned on themselves.

It was hard to see in the early morning hours, but the blood on the ground was distinctly darker than the stone beneath it. I tried to avoid stepping in it. A Society man ran at me, not noticing the liquid on the ground, and made my job easier as he fell before reaching me.

A second man charged at me. I lowered myself, flipping him over my back. Ben took him out for me.

"You okay?" He asked quickly. When I nodded, he

turned his attention back to the fight.

"Auluria," Dov called, warning me. I turned in time to plunge my knife into the stomach of a Society soldier. He crumpled, eyes wide, as I pulled my blade back. I kicked his weapon away, close enough that Dov could pick it up, before retreating.

I gritted my teeth, trying not to think about the way he fell after I struck him. My head felt light, but I didn't have time to waste thinking about it.

"Hey," I said lightly as I moved along side Dov.

"Hey," he said, offering an apologetic smile.

"Dov?" Berwyn yelled, his back to us as he and Eden fought side-by-side.

"We're fine," Dov shouted back.

"No, please!" a frightened voice was cut off behind us in the crowd. When I turned, I saw Shadoe.

I was accustomed to Shadoe looking smug when one of his missions succeeded, but his gaze infuriated me more than usual, the carnage he created in my peripheral vision. His arm lashed out, taking down another Society man, but he kept his eyes latched onto mine. He would see his mission through, even though it cost our men their lives.

Dov breathed deeply beside me. "Go help him," he said reluctantly.

"Are you sure?" I questioned.

"Yes."

I tentatively took a step. Shadoe *did* need me; Dov was right.

"I'm here," I announced, taking my place by his side.

"How bad?" he asked as he took on another soldier. Berwyn and Raselin were furious at him, but Shadoe was willing to take their anger for this victory.

"Pretty bad," I slashed at an approaching Society man.

A light mist danced into the courtyard, slowly filling the space as we fought. The light bounced off of it, making it brighter than it usually was that time of day. The toxic scent of spilled blood permeated the air, sharply piercing our senses.

At last, the fighting dwindled, leaving a handful of Society man alive and captured, and far too many of our own dead. I surveyed the area. Lowell would have been pleased.

"Shadoe, what did you do?" I asked, turning to him.

"I made sure of our place here, Lur. I handed us the victory. When this is all done, they can't cut us out."

"They wouldn't have done that, Shadoe." I couldn't believe his reasoning.

"Report," Shadoe yelled, making me jump out of my skin. His leaders ran toward us.

I tolerated them as they gave individualized reports to Shadoe as Berwyn and Dov looked on. Raselin had ended up inside after the battle ended and watched from a window, Justin and Talley at his side.

I stood, arms behind my back, feet apart, waiting for it to end. The death count was higher than I had anticipated.

"The magistrates and justices?" Shadoe pompously inquired to the group.

"We checked their rooms before we came down to the courtyard," I jumped in, finally speaking. "It was a massacre."

Shadoe forced a smile down, silently congratulating himself on winning over Berwyn and Raselin. I stood miserably, watching him gloat.

"Two magistrates escaped with a handful of their guards," Nikko supplied, attempting to prove he was loyal to me. It was smart thinking, considering how bad this was about to get for Shadoe.

My jaw fell.

Shadoe's smug look faltered as he realized his mistake and what it would likely cost him.

From the corner of my eye, I saw Berwyn, Dov, Eden, and Silas collectively straighten taller, leaning in at my expression. They knew something was wrong even from that distance. Raselin, still standing in the window, leaned forward, putting his palm on the glass. Talley stretched up, placing her hand on Justin's shoulder to try to see over her tall brother. Justin's jaw dropped, matching mine.

"What?" I breathed.

"We couldn't stop them," Nikko added, willing us to believe they had tried.

"Where did they go?" I growled. My hands flew to my sides as I dropped the soldier-like pose I had been maintaining.

I looked up, sharply jerking my head to indicate that the others should join Shadoe's celebratory party.

"Dismissed," I hissed at our people, sending them scattering away. Nikko stayed behind.

"What?" Berwyn's voice was dangerously deep.

Raselin raced through the foyer and out into the courtyard, skidding to a stop as he caught himself on Dov's shoulder, Justin right behind him.

"They escaped," I screeched, accidentally sounding more frantic than I meant to.

"Who?" Concern flooded Dov's voice.

"Three of the magistrates."

Everyone looked as if they might be sick. Raselin stumbled backward. Justin offered a hand to steady him.

Shadoe swallowed hard before locking his jaw. His eyes narrowed as he processed the news and tried to work out an escape plan.

"How could this happen?" Eden wailed, hands in her hair as she curled in on herself.

"They'll be coming for us now," Berwyn's voice wavered.

"It will take them time," Dov said, steadying himself

as much as steadying us. "It will take them time to return to their towns and then more time to return here. We have time."

"How could you do this, Shadoe?" Arin asked, having followed Berwyn over. He looked ready to kill Shadoe on the spot.

Shadoe remained quiet. I'd never seen him like that before; not even when Lowell lectured him. Not even when he nearly killed me on that cliff.

Necesta ambled into the courtyard, quickly making her way over to the group. She heard Arin's tirade and hurried to Shadoe's side.

"Now, you owe him," she urgently reminded us, wrapping a protective hand around Shadoe's arm. He was still in shock. "You owe him for helping to save Dov's life. Now is the time to repay him."

She glared defiantly at anyone who looked like they were going to question her.

"He is one of our leaders. He made a judgment call, albeit a poor one. He initiated a tactical strike and it failed. It was a mistake," she insisted. "You owe him."

"We owe him," I repeated, seeing my chance to keep him from suffering whatever retribution Arin would likely come up with *and* take away anything else we might owe Shadoe.

Color started returning to Shadoe's face.

"Berwyn," I said cautiously. "Berwyn, please."

The oldest Baer stared at Shadoe and I worried that he was seeing Lowell—the man who had killed his father—instead.

"He will be okay, Auluria," Dov promised. "But we need to get this handled."

He turned and motioned everyone over. They crowded around, stepping over bodies.

"How *could* you?" Eden suddenly screamed. She ran at Shadoe, slamming into him with her open hands as she pushed him.

Shadoe stumbled backward but didn't retaliate. Eden kicked him just below his knee. He grunted loudly, anger flashing across his face.

"How could you put us all at risk like that?" Eden screeched. Everyone was too stunned to stop her.

She swung her arm, attempting to slap him. Shadoe reached up, grabbing her wrist roughly. Eden used her other hand to connect with his face, the blow sounding so loudly that it echoed off of the mansion walls as the sun started to peek up over the landscape.

Eden's hair flew wildly as she continued her brutal attack. Shadoe blocked most of her efforts but allowed her to get a few good punches in.

"You nearly killed Berwyn," she dissolved into tears as she continued to fight against him. "You're going to get us all killed! You're as bad as Lowell!"

"Eden," Berwyn finally called his wife. She didn't react, continuing her outburst. He tried again. "Eden."

She summoned all of her strength, suddenly looking like the woman that had dragged Dov across the mansion courtyard the day we rescued him from Canton. It terrified me.

Letting out a war cry, she scratched at his face. Her foot slammed into his as she landed a punch to the gut. Shadoe was enraged but managed to control himself as he grabbed onto her shoulders and swung her around. He didn't say a word, but his eyes were murderous.

"Shadoe, let her go," I warned.

Eden spat every vicious accusation she could think of at him, calling him out on every infraction. Berwyn wrestled her away and she lit into Shadoe about nearly killing me on the cliff.

"Eden," her husband said softly, burying his face in her hair near her ear. It broke her. She settled back against his chest.

"How could you?" she whispered.

Dov squeezed my hand. I hadn't noticed he had picked it up. Looking down, I realized Silas held my elbow. The two of them had restrained me from interfering in Eden's moment. I was grateful they kept me from involving myself. I honestly wasn't sure which one I was hoping to protect—Shadoe or Eden.

Berwyn turned his wife to face him, running his hand over her back to soothe her.

"I'm okay," he murmured to her, reminding her that he had survived the poisoning. She calmed. She sniffled into his arms as he held her.

After a moment, she realized what she was doing and straightened her shoulders. Turning back, she glared at Shadoe. I couldn't remember if his lip was split open before Eden had gone after him or not.

He clenched his fist, glaring back. I knew Shadoe well enough to know in that moment he was reevaluating every decision he had made since Lowell died. His jaw ticked.

Necesta took her place at Shadoe's side again, lending him her allegiance. She wouldn't let anyone's feelings cloud the group's judgment on what should happen to Shadoe for picking the wrong battle.

"Have you had your say, dearie?" she asked Eden.

Eden tried to hide her shudder. She let out a forceful breath but didn't speak.

"Good," Necesta proclaimed, "Time to move on."

"We can't let this distract us from handling this situation," Raselin added.

Dov moved into action.

"Reed, Nian, Anetta, collect all of the weapons and take them inside. Henry, Ben, Carter, Gregory, Devin, Justin,

Fitch, Sherman, handle the bodies if you can." He turned to see who else was nearby. "Nikko, we need information about the magistrates that escaped. Go see what you can find."

Everyone rushed to start their assignments, working as quickly as they could.

"Reyla, get the girls and start preparing supplies. We don't know what we'll need yet, but collect everything you can." He paused as Reyla rushed off. He pointed at Louis before adding, "Help her."

"Canton," I murmured, reminding him.

"Sherman, get Brittella and take her to oversee Canton until we get this all worked out. Don't tell him what happened yet."

Sherman nodded and strode toward the entrance to the mansion to find Brittella. Next to Shadoe, she was likely our best chance at controlling the magistrate. She wasn't going to like it.

"Talley, go check on the prisoners downstairs—"

"Don't bother," Shadoe interjected, coming back to life.

"Why not?" Dov's voice trailed off as he realized Shadoe had slaughtered those men as well. He swallowed hard, trying to stay calm.

"Berwyn, Raselin, take Necesta and Talley and have a conversation with Shadoe. I have an idea. I'm going to take Auluria and Silas and try to work it out. Come meet us when you're through. Eden, you stay with us."

I trusted Necesta to keep the peace in Shadoe's hearing and Talley to follow through.

"Just go," I murmured to Shadoe. He moved forward rigidly, ready to accept his punishment like the good soldier Lowell had trained him to be.

Berwyn looked torn, divide between needing to come up with a solution to our new problem and wanting to destroy Shadoe.

"Berwyn, go. Let me handle this," Dov pushed gently. His brother finally nodded gruffly before kissing Eden's hand and spinning to walk into the mansion.

Eden shuffled over to us, looking drained. We paused long enough to let the others get inside before Dov turned to us.

"What's the plan?" Silas asked before Dov could speak.

"They know we're here," Dov started, thinking it through before he spoke. "If we stay here, they have the advantage, and they'll have us cornered."

"You want to take the fight to them..." Silas mused, processing his words.

"If we clear out now, we can hide in the towns. We can surprise them as they try to get through. It will be smaller groups for us to handle and they won't be expecting us."

"The towns are already with us," Silas added. "You saw to that before."

"We could set up strategic places within the towns

and create choke points," I continued, pushing the plan forward. "They'll never see it coming, especially if we do it immediately and meet them closer to their territory. If we move soon, we'd only be a few hours behind them."

"By the time they get there, rally their troops, and try to return, we'll already be waiting for them." Dov's eyes lit up as he spoke.

"We'll hit before they get organized," Silas concluded.

"You're sure we can do this?" I asked.

"I think it's our only chance, Auluria." Dov wrapped an arm around me, pulling me close.

"Are you okay?" I asked Eden. She nodded.

"I shouldn't have done that," she muttered under her breath.

"It was bound to happen," Silas gave her a half smile. "I'm surprised you held it in so long."

"I really don't like that guy." She glared at the mansion doors as if he were still standing there. "I don't know how you put up with him for so long."

"Just think," Dov snorted. "She was supposed to *marry* him. She would have had to endure him for her entire life."

Eden mimicked Dov's snort. "And instead, you get *this one*."

She dropped a hand on his head, messing up his hair like Talley occasionally did to Devin and Justin. He looked as shocked as I felt.

"Did you just give your approval, Eden?" Silas drawled.

Realizing what she had just said, Eden looked at me, wide-eyed.

"*Maybe*," she snapped. "Don't we need to look at some maps or something?"

"No," Dov chuckled as he shook his head.

"Don't think so," Silas shrugged, grinning so widely I thought his face might break.

"*I* don't need to," I shook my head, smiling at her.

She huffed, rolling her eyes.

"We need to leave the bodies," Eden said abruptly.

"What?" Silas questioned.

"If we're abandoning the mansion, we need to leave a message for anyone who approaches it. We don't want the Society taking it back and using it as a stronghold against us.

"If we leave the bodies out, it's a warning. At the very least, it creates too much of a problem for them to be able to easily use the mansion. We can handle it when we get back...assuming we make it back."

"Let's talk to Fitch," Dov agreed. "I don't like it, but it's a good plan."

"We need to get moving if we're going to abandon this place by this afternoon," Silas commented, motioning us back to the mansion. "This won't be easy."

Chapter 10

My skirt brushed against my legs as I walked hand-in-hand with Dov. He casually strode next to me, acting as if he were examining the wares on a table in the market on the outskirts of town.

I relished being in a dress again. It had been far too long.

Eden, along with Berwyn, mingled with the crowd. Her voice floated over the hum of people talking as she bartered for a loaf of bread. Reyla slipped her arm through Justin's as they walked down the street.

Dov did most of the talking, drawing people's attention and quietly telling them about the plan, while I looked for anyone I could identify. He chuckled merrily with a man selling gloves in preparation for the impending winter.

"And is this your lovely bride?" The man's voice we deep and warm.

"Not just yet, but we're getting there," Dov flashed him a mischievous smile as I looked back to the conversation. The man grinned at me, laughing heartily.

"We're working on that one," Silas strolled by, Gloria at his side. She made a face and pulled him along.

"You can't be serious?" Devin raised his voice, arguing over the price of boots at a table on the other side of the street. Talley glanced around, acting embarrassed by her brother.

Our contact had told us the entire town was willing to support us in our mission to rid the Society of the magistrates and their soldiers. All we had to do was quickly inform them of our plans.

We had been welcomed into many homes over the past two days, staying only long enough to rest and move on. There was one town between us and our final destination.

A woman gasped loudly behind us. I turned to find her several tables down, standing across a makeshift table from Berwyn. Her husband was engaged in conversation with the Baers, looking like they were talking to long-lost friends.

Her gaze traveled beyond Berwyn and Eden, falling

first on Dov, then on me. He waved just as the woman's face fell. Tears welled up in her eyes as she grabbed her skirt and maneuvered herself around the table. It wasn't until she was halfway to us that I recognized her.

"Oh no," I breathed.

"Auluria?" Dov asked.

Silas skidded out of the way to avoid being run over by the woman. Gloria looked horrified as he crashed into her.

"It's you," she said, coming up to me. "It's you, isn't it?"

Everything spun, like my world unraveling before me. Dov steadied me.

"Auluria? You know her?" Dov whispered.

My eyes felt wild. I tried desperately to tame them, but I knew I failed. My hands groped for something to ground me, finding Dov's forearm. He knew something was wrong.

He turned to me, placing his hands on my elbows.

"What's going on?" he demanded.

"I..." I stumbled.

I couldn't tell them. I *had* to tell them.

"Hello," I said to the woman, my voice shaking. "Yes, it's me."

"Whatever is wrong?" The woman looked nervous.

Her husband trailed behind her, Berwyn and Eden looking over his shoulder.

"Is this...?" He gaped at me. "It is, isn't? You're that girl."

"What girl?" Berwyn growled.

"We took her in for a night once," the wife explained. "She hurt herself outside our home and she spent the night with us."

"She tried to run away a few times, but we finally convinced her to stay," the husband added.

Berwyn and Eden slowly turned to me with exaggerated looks of accusation. Dov's gaze was one of shock and curiosity.

"You should know that I've been working with the Baers all this time," I tried to preface what I was about to admit, hoping it would soften their reaction. "I'm so sorry."

They watched me, eagerly awaiting an explanation.

"My cousin sent me to you," I looked down at the ground, wishing I could melt into it. "You were so kind to me and I'm so sorry."

Berwyn cleared his throat as I babbled.

"My cousin knew you worked with...I'm assuming the Baers," I glanced at Berwyn for confirmation. "I didn't know that then, nor did I know what my cousin had planned."

"She's Lowell's cousin," Berwyn supplied, evoking shock and outrage from the couple. They didn't say anything though.

"I'm so sorry; I didn't know," I begged them to forgive me. "Lowell sent me to you—"

"Why?" the husband asked.

"Papers." I looked down again.

"You weren't hurt?" the wife sounded wounded. "You stole from us?"

"I'm so sorry." I tried reaching out to her, but she pulled back.

"What were the papers?" Dov asked gently, trying to help.

"I don't know," I admitted.

"They were your location," the husband said. "It was the only thing we had that she could have found."

"So," Dov's face morphed into a grin. "You brought Auluria to us...to *me*." He took my hand, placing it over his heart. "I owe you a great debt of gratitude, in that case."

The couple looked shocked for a moment.

"We can't thank you enough for the kindness you showed Auluria that day," Dov praised them. "Without you, she never would have come to us, and without her, we'd still be under the control of the Society."

"We still *are* under the control of the Society," Berwyn reminded him.

"Not for much longer," Dov beamed. "We're almost free."

"I know what I did was wrong, and I'm so sorry for

betraying you," I tried one more time. "But I hope you can forgive me."

They hesitated for a moment.

"It all worked out in the end," the wife said. "And if it got you away from that vicious Lowell, then it was worth it."

The husband looked at his wife, willing to agree with anything she said. He nodded to me, accepting my apology.

"Thank you," I sighed.

"When this is all over," the husband said, turning to his wife, "We need to figure out how we were compromised."

"Lowell had many resources," I recalled, "but we're all on the same side now."

"So we see," the wife smiled politely.

Dov's fingers flinched over mine where it still rested on his chest. He smiled at me when our eyes connected.

"The good news is that we have one more bit of information for you," the husband smiled.

I huddled against Dov, wishing the cold away. The wind swept a piece of my hair up, tossing it into Reyla's face as she curled against my shoulder.

"Do you mind?" she teased playfully.

Dov reached up for me, pulling the stray piece back down. He tucked it between us as he kissed the tip of my nose.

"I know we wanted you two back together, but do you think you could cut back on the lack of public awareness?" Silas groaned.

"Be quiet, Silas," Reyla shook her head at him, "They are adorable. Don't be jealous."

"He's very jealous," Dov grinned at his friend.

Shadoe grumbled from his place alongside Raselin at the next fire over.

"Remind me why we didn't stay in the town?" I mumbled, shivering as the wind picked up again.

I heard the log behind us creak. Using my hair to block my face from onlookers, I mouthed his brother's name to Dov. He nodded slightly and I made a face, pretending I hadn't spoken. The log creaked again, letting me know Berwyn had turned back around as he monitored Shadoe. Canton sat on the ground far enough away to not be able to hear us, under constant supervision. The trainer from the camp sat far enough away that they couldn't communicate, also under guard.

"We're only staying for a little while," Dov whispered.

"And it's safer to move through the woods than the town at this time of night," I whispered in a nagging voice. "I know, I know."

"Are you okay, Rey?" Silas squinted to see her across the flames. "You look like you might shiver right off that log."

"I'm freezing, Silas," she admitted.

He pouted at her, making me laugh.

"So helpful, aren't you, Silas?"

"Usually," he grinned. "Want an extra shoulder, Rey?"

She nodded and he stood up, walking around the flames to join her. We all moved down, barely fitting on the overturned tree trunk. He wrapped an arm around her shoulders, bumping into me with his hand.

"How come *I* wasn't invited to the party?" Justin pouted as he walked over with a piece of bread in his hand.

Reyla batted her eyelashes. "*I couldn't say,*" she taunted.

"Don't look at me," I added. I tried to hold a hand up in innocence, but it was tangled in Dov's, and I inadvertently raised our hands together.

"Thanks a lot, *Auluria.* See if I invite *you* to the next family outing." Justin teased, taking Silas' seat.

"You have to—it's mandatory now," I reminded him.

"Have the scouts come back yet?" Justin asked, changing the direction of the conversation. I wanted to see if the information the couple had given us had helped.

"No, not that I know of," Dov replied. He tucked my hand between his to warm it for me.

"I hate having to wait around for Devin," Justin mumbled, biting into the bread. "Oh, this is amazing."

"I just have this feeling that tomorrow is going to be the day," I said, my thumb tracing circles on Dov's skin with the hand he wasn't holding. I wasn't sure if I was prepared for what we would find.

"I have that same feeling," Raselin said from behind where he sat by Shadoe. "Shadoe?"

"It's likely," Shadoe replied. "By now, I'm sure they've made it back and have rallied their troops. If it were me, I'd already have my men on the move."

"Should we leave earlier than we had planned?" Eden asked begrudgingly. She was still angry that Shadoe had been allowed to not only stay, but also participate.

"That might be wise," Berwyn nodded.

"That *would* be wise," Devin announced, joining the group. "It sounds like tomorrow is the day."

He dropped down next to Justin, stealing the last of his bread.

"Hey," Justin protested, looking shocked.

"*Hey nothing.*" Devin popped a piece of bread in his mouth. "I've been out all night while you sat around here. Go get me more food, little brother."

The two argued until I stood up. "I'll go," I said, walking away.

With the warmth of Dov's body gone, my body went into an extra cold state as I wove my way through the different fires. Necesta fell into step beside me.

"Now you listen here, Goldilocks," she started, matching my movements. "You need to be careful when we take on the Society. Do you still have your necklace?"

I pulled it out from under my collar to show her.

"Good, good," she crooned. "Get Devin some food—the poor boy—and then you're coming with me. We have to refill that before the fight."

"You can refill it?" I questioned, fingering the necklace.

"Well, part of it, anyway. I found a few ingredients along the way, but I need your help."

She steered me toward where the food was being cooked and warmed. I collected a few things for Devin and the others. Necesta walked me back to the group.

"Where are you going?" Dov asked, sounding a little desperate. I touched his cheek, cupping his jaw in my palm.

"I'll be back soon. Necesta just needs me for something."

He turned his face into my hand, kissing me. "Hurry back."

I followed Necesta to the edge of the fires, our shadows casting long, dark figures ahead of us. She sat down, patting the rock next to her.

"Can you see all right?" she asked gently.

"Yes." I watched her pull a small bowl from her satchel. "What are we doing?"

"Grind this." She forced the bowl into my hands.

She retrieved a second bowl, adding in more ingredients. We worked in silence as the wind tugged at our hoods and whipped our skirts around our ankles.

"Oh, Goldilocks," she sighed. "You've come so far."

"Have I?" The corners of my mouth tugged up.

"I imagine even more than I know," she grinned at me. "I've only been with you on part of this journey. Are you the same little girl your cousin took in all those years ago?"

"No," I laughed, shaking my head. "I most certainly am not."

"Are you the same girl engaged to your handler?"

"Definitely not," I shook my head rapidly.

"I should hope not." She winked.

"You're not the same girl sent to seduce a Baer, nor are you the girl who had to choose between your family and your people. Goldilocks," she stopped her work to turn to me. "You have changed the face of your reality, but not only that—you've also changed each and every person here.

"Without you, dearie, none of this would be happening. The Baers would still be living their quiet existence in the woods, simply trying to survive. Your cousin would have done something stupid and you would likely be dead. Shadoe wouldn't have the slightest conscience—though I'm not sure how much of one he has now—and we most certainly wouldn't have come over the Wall to find our freedom. You're the key here, Auluria."

She set her bowl down, motioning for me to do the same, and took my hands in hers. She smiled a toothy grin.

"I knew the girl I met that day in the market was special," she praised me. "I knew you would do great things. I want to thank you, Auluria, for bringing this old woman *home*."

"Don't sound so grim, Necesta," Brittella's voice floated over to us. She flounced over, taking a seat behind me. "You sound like you're dying and trying to say goodbye."

"Who knows what tomorrow will bring, Brittella," Necesta chastised good-naturedly.

Brittella chuckled, picking up my bowl.

"What are we making, my darlings?"

"Oh, just a few things for tomorrow," Necesta quickly explained each one. "Now, Goldilocks. Should you need any of this, I've been teaching Maylin. You can ask her if you ever need something done quickly and I'm not around to do it for you."

"I'll keep that in mind."

"Dearie," Necesta continued, "I've given the girl all of

my notes. I knew she would stay at the camps to help and I wanted her to be prepared. She's been a good student. Sharone too, though I'm sure she'll be preoccupied now that she knows her sister is alive and she's about to become an aunt."

She glanced at Brittella, adding, "Like this, dearie."

We worked in silence for a few moments, letting the wind whisper secrets to us. The two women watched each other, one magnificently dressed, the other looking like a quiet grandmother, and polar opposites. Brittella finally paused.

"I think we're going to be good friends, Necesta."

"Perhaps we shall," Necesta answered with a grin.

"By the way," Brittella murmured as she looked back down to her work. "I saw what you did back there."

"What was that, dearie?" she asked innocently.

Brittella's eyes sparkled as she looked back up, giving her the same knowing smile she frequently gave me. Necesta chuckled as she looked back down. They were both women of many secrets.

When we finished and Necesta had replenished my store of antidotes and medicines, she sent me back to the group so the two of them could talk alone—likely about me.

"Come on." His eyes were still fiercely blue, deep and intense, even in the shadows from the fire. I blinked, bringing him into focus.

"What's happening?" I murmured as he smiled.

"I'll explain, just come along," he whispered back.

"Are we leaving?" I stumbled along behind him. He practically sprinted around the fires and sleeping people.

"Not yet." He turned, glancing over his shoulder with a wicked smile.

His dark hair moved in the breeze as he tugged me forward. I fixated on it as we moved, reminding me of the day I woke up in his house, unsure of who he was. It fell over his eyes each time he looked back at me.

"Dov, what are we doing?" I had accepted his spontaneity, giggling by the time he slowed.

"We've only had a few dates, Auluria, and I will not go marching off to start a war tomorrow without at least one more."

"Oh," I blushed, giggling like little Jasleen when she got around a handsome man.

"Sit with me." Dov leaned against a tree, holding out his hand.

He wrapped his legs around me as I leaned against him, my back against his chest. Heat radiated off of him, warming me as I curled into his embrace. Together, we stared up through the trees in silence, watching the stars.

Each time a wicked wind rose up, he pulled me tighter to his chest, protecting me from it.

"Have you ever doubted me, Auluria?" Dov murmured in my ear.

"What do you mean?"

"I don't want you to ever doubt my feelings for you," Dov said softly. "I know it's been hard for us. It started out as a deception, and then I kept us apart because I didn't trust you. When we finally found our way back together, Canton ripped us apart, and I sent you off with Shadoe—and then he nearly killed you—"

"And *you* nearly died," I reminded him.

"That too," he nodded into my hair. "I just want to make sure you feel like you can trust me and that you know I'll always be here for you."

"What, no more cold shoulder?" I teased. "I was kind of getting used to the silence...and Silas' interference."

"You hated Silas' interference," he reminded me. Dov paused before adding, "Do you honestly not know who he likes?"

"Everyone in this world knows who he likes except for me," I grumbled.

Dov leaned forward, whispering a name in my ear.

"No," I whispered in disbelief.

"Yep," Dov leaned back against the tree, dragging me back with him.

"I can work with that," I finally said, trying to keep from glowing at how simple my job would be.

"It won't be that easy," he smirked, knowing what I was thinking.

"Of course it will be," I grinned back at him as the leaves jumped to life overhead. A shower of dying leaves cascaded around us, swarming our vision as if they had been fireflies in the summer. The pieces swirled around us, more beautiful than I had ever seen fallen leaves before.

"I love you, Auluria," Dov whispered, reaching an arm around in front of me to tangle in my hair, reaching across my chest. I turned to him, catching his lips with the side of mine.

Kissing backward was no easy task. I turned to the side, trying to make it easier on us. Finally, he scooped up my legs, lifting them over his knee so that they sat between his raised leg and hip. Dov cradled me in his embrace, pulling my hair as he tangled his fingers in my mane.

"I promise I won't lock you out again," he murmured between kisses.

"I promise I won't deceive you," I responded, my hand running up and down his chest, making his breath catch.

"I promise to always listen and believe you," he continued, using his feet to pull my body closer.

"I'll never try to manipulate you again," I committed as

he kissed me again.

"Oh, you can manipulate me into doing your bidding anytime you want," he panted as the kissing grew more intense. His left hand wrapped around my waist, pulling at my hip.

I freed my arm from where it was pinned between our bodies and caressed his chin, guiding him back to me each time our lips broke apart.

"I will spend the rest of my life making sure you are safe and taken care of," he opened his eyes, watching me as I leaned in to kiss him. He moaned softly as I touched his lips, begging me not to pull away.

I leaned back, trying to get a different angle as I wrapped my arms around his neck. Every muscle in his shoulders was pulled taut. His arms went under mine, lifting me into a more comfortable position as I settled onto his abdomen and upper leg, forming a wedge for me to sit on.

"I'll always be there to take care of you too," I promised my allegiance to him.

He brushed my hair with his hand, pulling it back and forth over my shoulder as we stared at each other's lips, trying to catch our breath.

I relaxed my body, realizing how rigid I had gone while kissing him. Sliding down, I curled up against him, nestling into his neck. I didn't mind when my breath moved his hair, tickling him. My heart jumped as his eyes fluttered shut, trying to keep them from rolling back at the sensation.

"This is an interesting date," I commented, barely able to move my cheek to smile from resting it so hard against Dov's shoulder.

"I didn't even get to the best part yet," Dov murmured.

"*That* wasn't the best part?" I looked up, shocked.

"Oh, my dear Auluria," he grinned at me, "No, no it wasn't."

He reached into his pocket, nearly tipping me over. He withdrew his hand, carefully hiding something.

"I have something for you," he smiled at me.

"I can see that," I crooned, waiting.

The wind shook the trees above us again, showering us once more in leaves. They danced in brilliant oranges and reds in the muted firelight from the camp just close enough to still give us light.

"I know this hasn't always been easy for either of us, and I didn't want to do this until after, just in case, but I can't wait any longer." His eyes glittered even more than the stars in the sky above us. "Auluria, I fell hard for you the moment I met you. I got so caught up in you that I couldn't see anything else but you, but you wouldn't let me get away with that.

"You made sure that I not only saw you, but I saw myself and everyone else around me. You made me into such a better man than I ever thought I could be—"

"You were perfect," I interjected, jumping forward to kiss his nose. "You took care of everyone Dov. I, in no way, could have *ever* made you a better man than the one I met, who ran into fires and took beatings for people. You've always been the best man, my love."

"I'm not finished, ma'am." His eyes were soft as he gazed at me. "I love you with the very depths of my being and I'd be lost without you.

"You've taught me something very important, Auluria."

"Hmm?" I watched him carefully.

"One spark can light the entire universe on fire. One choice, one action, one word can give permission to change the way a life is lived. You've irrevocably changed me, Auluria. You set my world on fire—literally, once or twice—" he smirked, eyes sparkling, "and you've completely changed the way I'm living my life. I'll always be grateful for that.

"Berwyn gave our mother's ring to Eden when they were married, so I want to give you this." He unfolded his hand, revealing a silver medallion on a black cord.

"I thought the Society had this," I gasped, fingering the paw that rested in his hands.

"They turned it over to Canton," he smiled slyly. "We may have found it and reallocated it."

"Well, you *do* like reallocating things," I smirked.

"I want you to have this, Auluria," he whispered

earnestly. For a moment, I thought to insist he keep his father's medallion, but I knew what this meant to him. "Marry me."

He said it like a statement, for there was never any question.

I touched it one more time before looking at him. Tipping my head sideways, feeling like I was in a dream, I pursed my lips.

"Yes." I teared up.

Dov reached through my hair, securing the medallion around my neck, before crashing against my lips once more. My fingers wove their way through his hair, as my lips became more swollen from kissing him.

Our movements were happy and frenzied, colliding with each other again and again. When they finally slowed, I found myself standing, pinned against a tree. I had no memory of moving, but I didn't need one. All I needed was Dov's arms wrapped around me. I whimpered when he pulled away to gaze at me.

My hair caught in the bark as I leaned forward, pieces dragging behind me. Dov brushed them down, leaning around me to rest his arm on the trunk of the tree as he had done before.

"Auluria," he breathed gently, making me shudder.

I sighed, enjoying the moment.

"Dov!" a piercing voice shouted, echoing in the forest, jolting us both into action.

Chapter 11

"Dov!" Berwyn yelled again as we crashed toward the campsite.

"What happened?" Dov asked as we skidded to a stop in front of Berwyn and Eden.

"We have to move," Berwyn looked frantic. "Now. They're coming."

"They're moving already?" Dov looked shocked as he brushed his hair back, reminding me for a moment of Nian.

"They must not have wanted to wait until morning." Berwyn turned, guiding us through the camp. "Whatever they have planned, they must think it's important to enact it sooner rather than later."

Eden eyed the necklace around my neck.

"Better put that away for now," she mumbled. I tucked the medallion inside my dress alongside Necesta's.

Everyone was quickly packing their bags. Justin tossed me my pack as he pulled on an extra layer of clothing. Silas doused the fire, making sure the embers no longer glowed as Reyla quickly tamed her hair back into a braid that she could quickly release if she needed to, should the enemy try to use it against her.

Berwyn paced, checking to see if anyone needed help. It reminded me of those first few days in the Baers' cabin as he stalked about. Eden kept a watchful eye on him as she gathered supplies and hid extra weapons in her boots.

"Reyla," I whispered as I sidled up next to her, adding weapons to my own boots."

"Hmm?" She looked down to where I was bent over.

"I have something to tell you."

"Already?" Silas yelped a few feet away. Reyla and I both looked over to find him grinning wildly at Dov. Dov nodded enthusiastically before they both looked at me.

I shot straight up, knowing I needed to tell Reyla before they gave it away. My hands flew to my neckline, fishing out the medallion. I held it between my fingers to show her.

It took her a moment to realize what it was, then to register that I was wearing it, and finally, her jaw dropped as she realized *why* I was wearing it. Reyla slammed her jaw closed, swallowed her words—hard—and tried to suppress a squeal.

My best friend bit back a grin, nodding sharply once, before turning away.

"Good," she said in a clipped voice, trying to contain her joy. "But we're celebrating this later."

"Celebrating what?" Justin asked.

I quickly tucked the medallion away. "Nothing."

Justin looked back and forth between Reyla and me. When he turned to catch sight of Dov and Silas, he figured it out.

"You weren't going to tell me?" he yelped.

"We're about to go into battle, Justin. We don't need distractions," I chastised.

"Who said anything about distractions, Goldilocks? This is something to fight *for*!" He smiled as his eyes darted around to find his brother, ready to hold it over him that he knew first.

"Justin, now is not the time," I reminded him.

"You're not going to tell Talley and Devin?" he looked disappointed.

"I will...but *quietly*," I relented.

"Move out," Berwyn instructed loudly.

The last of the fires were put out as we turned to go. I couldn't help feeling like I was back with Lowell's people, moving from one campsite to the next. Sherman and Nikko's presence didn't help the feeling as they walked along next to Shadoe. Nikko carefully aligned himself closer to me.

We hurried toward the town, quickly leaving the trees behind. We sprinted down the streets, warning people as we went. They grumbled as we roused them from their beds, but quickly made arrangements for those that couldn't stay behind to fight, to go to the storehouses.

The half town emptied of people, leaving only our fighters to take their place. Moving into houses, we took on the look of residents. We prepared to go out into the towns and run the market as they would normally do, our goal to corral them in one central location only hours away.

"We're out of time," Ben shouted, running toward us from where he had gone to scout ahead. "Here we go!"

It was still dark, the sun behind the town line as we scrambled into empty houses. We would no longer be able to turn on them in the market. I bumped into Berwyn as we closed the door behind us, thirty people crammed into the tiny house.

"You'd better not do anything stupid out there, Auluria," he grumbled harshly into my ear.

"Not planning on it," I snapped, annoyed.

"Dov won't survive it if you die out there, especially now."

"What do you—" I cut off my words, realizing he knew Dov had proposed. He probably had to get

Berwyn's permission anyway, so it shouldn't have surprised me.

My hand rested on the wooden door, waiting to push it open on Berwyn's signal. Dov peered out the window, watching for our opening. Berwyn kept his eyes focused on his brother, waiting for his mark.

Society soldiers marched through the streets, their footsteps falling so loud that we could hear them several streets away. In the dark of early morning, everything reverberated off the buildings much louder than in the brightness of day.

Each approaching step brought me closer and closer to the day of my hanging. A tightness grew in my chest, and I had the overwhelming feeling that we wouldn't make it through this battle.

Faces flashed through my mind; my parents, my aunt, little Jasleen, even Lowell. I looked nervously around the room at the people who had become my family. Silas stood at Dov's side, ready to fight to the death for his people. Reyla waited by my side, Anetta watching me intently. My future brother and sister loomed near the door, tenseness holding their bodies captive. My former handler looked ready to murder. Nikko, Sherman, Ella, Locust and a few of his spies stood by his side. The Hersh siblings hovered by another window, watching from the other side. Necesta quietly waited by them, insisting on fighting with us. Gregory stood by Maylin and Carter, while Henry wrapped an arm around Katarina's waist, murmuring soft words into her ear. The room was filled with people I knew and cared about, while my love prepared to give the signal to attack.

I saw Dov tense up and knew they were drawing near. Terror washed over me. Not everyone would survive this. It might be a miracle if *any* of us did.

Focusing on the door, I calmed my thundering heart down as my cousin had taught me to do. I watched one spot on the wood, tracing the grain of the door with my eye just enough to form a repetitive pattern. Over and over, one circle after the next. Up, down, up down. Calm. Breathe...in, out.

Everything fell into an overwhelming hush despite the boots colliding with the street outside. My breathing filled my senses, in, out. It flooded my ears leaving only the sound of air and my heartbeats.

Cutting off the inner dialogue running through my head telling me what to do, I switched my focus, picking one sole breath out of the masses. Dov breathed in and out, short and quick. I focused on him, followed his moves, watching every tiny thing he did. I would fight for him.

His eyes latched on to Berwyn's, and he gave a slight nod, looking worried. Berwyn swallowed, turned, and dropped his hand. I collided with the door, pushing it open.

We spilled out into the street, the entire legion of Society soldiers turning in surprise. The house across the street opened as well, more of our men pouring into the open with loud yells.

The houses were immediately set on fire by the soldiers, but our people had more than enough time to exit and join the fight. The soldiers closest to us never had a chance. Shadoe ripped into them as fiercely as Berwyn did, using the claw he had once slashed Dov's brother with once again.

Raselin ran toward us from the other house, trying to identify the leaders of the Society soldiers, knife dripping blood as he yelled. Talley stayed by Necesta's side, attempting to protect her.

My knife came out bloody as the first soldier fell at my feet. Droplets covered the back of my hand and wrist. He squinted his eyes at me, dragging his knife across the top of my wrist, leaving a trail of my own blood to pool at my feet. The sharp sting brought me back to reality.

Turning, I threw my elbow at a soldier, crashing into his nose. It broke with a ferocious shattering noise. He screamed in pain, both hands flying to his face. Twisting my body, I used my other elbow to slam into his stomach. He doubled over, allowing me to deliver a clean hook to his face, sending him reeling backward.

Another soldier ran at me, giving me just enough time to flip him over my back. I brought my boot down on his face, praying I had only knocked him out and not snapped his neck.

One of the boys from the camp ran past me at full speed, colliding with a Society man. He grunted as they toppled to the ground. The boy got the upper hand and the fight grew louder around us. He didn't stop punching the man's face until he was unrecognizable, a bloody mass in the middle of the road.

The fire crackled from the homes the soldiers had lit up the moment they realized it was an ambush, giving a harsh orange glow to the area. Ashes fluttered in the sky like snow, or a million gray and black butterflies come to collect what was theirs; their life-pollen the blood spilled across the dirt and stone.

I whipped around, my hair trailing behind me in my signature move. It slapped into my side before falling to rest for the briefest moment before I started running.

The soldiers moved back, running around the houses to find a new angle to attack from. I wasn't about to let them escape or get the upper hand on us. Our only hope of survival was to take them out there—in that moment —as we took them by surprise.

The house we had vacated began to crumble as the man I was chasing suddenly fell. A wound in his temple opened up, draining red into the street, though I hadn't touched him and no one else was in sight.

"Go," a voice called from high above. A man from the

town stood in the window, fire filling the room behind him. He lifted his slingshot again, taking aim at another man I likely would not catch.

The rock struck the soldier, silencing him, as the man in the window cried out in pain. He stood, hanging out of the window as the fire licked at him. He burned as he took down my opponents one at a time as I battled them on my own. His shrieks filled my head and he crumbled under the searing flames, sacrificing himself so that I could live to fight.

The remaining two soldiers turned to take me on, but they didn't expect me to be able to fight for myself. I shattered them, breaking bones and drawing blood. The man on the left fell first; the soldier on the right going down at nearly the same time as Dov pulled his knife from the man's back.

"Let's go," he said grimly. "More escaped that way.

A loud explosion sounded, rocking the area. I fell to my knees, pitching forward. I narrowly avoided slamming my face off of the ground. Dov scooped me up, forcing me to run. We rounded the structure to find more building pieces fluttering to the ground.

"Reyla!" I shrieked, alerting Silas to the impending danger. He turned, pushing Reyla behind him.

I gasped as Dov matched Silas' movements, pushing me around him. Devin ran at us, taking out the man Dov was trying to protect me from. They toppled onto the ground, wrestling for control of the situation. Dov jumped forward to help him as I sprinted toward Silas to lend my assistance.

I kicked the man, knocking him off balance enough for Silas to take him out. Reyla had turned, engaging another soldier. She pulled his feet out from under him as I slashed at his throat. I felt like my insides had crawled out of me when the nasty red line scratched across his skin.

"No!" Lydia screamed, forcing us to whip around to her. She was barreling at a soldier but never stood a chance of reaching him in time. Chester was on the ground before Lydia crashed into his murderer. She sprawled on the ground, tumbling over the Society man. She slammed into his shoulder with her knife, ripping the muscles so viciously I don't know how she didn't amputate his arm.

Chester lay on his back, facing the glowing sky, as ashes rained down on his face. The pieces covered his clothing. Reyla reached him first, slapping the embers that burned tiny holes into his wardrobe.

He gagged, fighting to speak as blood began to pool in his mouth.

"Tell Barone...I'm sorry I failed him..." he managed around the blood. It dripped from the corners of his mouth.

"You didn't," we both shook our heads violently as the life faded from him.

He choked, coughing weakly, sending tiny droplets of blood into the air. For a moment, he looked peaceful, then his eyes dulled.

I looked the length of him, discovering a gaping wound in his abdomen. It wouldn't have saved him even if we had held pressure on it. Reyla held his hand to her chest and I couldn't help but picture her hovering over Peter's body had she been there the day he had died to save me.

"We have to go," Lydia instructed, dragging herself over to us.

"Lydia, you're hurt," I felt my face drain of its color.

"It's mostly his," she nodded to the soldier she had maimed. "I'm okay. Just tie this around my arm."

I quickly reached for the strip of fabric and tied it securely over the hole in her arm. She nodded, watching for soldiers.

"We have to go," she repeated herself.

"Ladies, time to move," Fitch exclaimed, reaching around his wife to guide her away. He noticed her arm, giving her a concerned look.

"I'm fine," she assured him, offering a weak smile.

I grabbed Reyla's hand, running behind them, as Chester's shell continued to watch the ashy butterflies in the sky.

Dov paused, waiting for me to catch up to him. Berwyn and Eden were at my heels as we followed the youngest Baer around the corner, following the sounds of a large group of soldiers. Reinforcements were coming.

The clouds looked darker than the sky itself, a mix of purple with hints of orange sparkling through them as the fires sizzled. We slowed at the edge of the buildings, knowing we were about to meet a new group of Society men. Silas slinked forward, creeping around the corner of the building to check. He darted back quickly.

He leaned to look around us, realizing more of our people had joined our team. I glanced back, seeing a large following. Silas held up a hand and nodded. Quietly counting down, he gave us the signal to move.

We ambushed them, hitting them hard before they saw us coming. The inevitable battle cry went up, surrounding us in chaos once more. Fists slammed into flesh, making people cry out. Knives cut, etching the battle lines into our very beings.

"Babe," Dov said gently to let me know he was there, taking up a place beside me.

"Good timing," I yelped, ducking under a blade. I lifted my hands up as the man's hand passed over me, jerking his arm up. His knife skittered to the ground. Dov slammed his heel into it, bending it unnaturally, as I twisted the man's arm enough to flip him.

Another explosion rocked the earth where we had left

the rest of the group. It sent tremors along the ground we stood on. The Society soldier groaned on the ground, his shoulder painfully out of place. I left him, knowing I was needed elsewhere. I was desperately trying to kill as few people as possible.

"You okay?" Reed asked, sidling up next to me. His hand crashed into a man who thought he could take us on.

"I'm fine," I tossed a grin at him. "You?"

"I'd rather climb over a wall any day," he grinned, thinking about helping his people across the Wall. "You realize that hair isn't doing you any favors, don't you?"

I raised my eyebrow at him, nearly crossing my arms in challenge during our reprieve from the fight as he knocked the man out.

"They're targeting you, Auluria. Might want to tuck that back."

"Isn't that the point?" I asked.

"The point is to get yourself killed?" he joked, rolling his eyes.

"My hair is still less likely to get me killed than Nian's." I protested.

"That is a very good point," he laughed.

A cloud of smoke from the explosions and burning buildings floated toward us, hovering over our fight. It reflected the orange glow from the distance, creating a strange look to the sky. I sneezed as the scent of the smoke hit my nose.

"Now!" a voice yelled. I turned to find Locust running down the street, Martin chasing behind him. Cupping his hand, Locust lifted Martin into the air. He crashed into a large board the soldiers had erected near one of the buildings, knocking it over.

Martin rolled as he hit the ground. The soldiers descended on him as Locust fought off two of them. Reed ran to help them, taking out soldiers along the way.

"Behind you," Nian said, nearly making me jump out of my skin. He flipped his hair and grinned. "You okay?"

"I'm fine, what are you doing?" I asked, arms up and ready to take on another attack.

"There!" he shouted, darting toward the building. He paused for a moment before squatting to the ground. He stuck his leg out just in time to trip a line of soldiers. The first man fell over him, the others tripping over the tangled heap of a man on the ground. They crashed hard on top of each other.

I screamed as Sherman appeared out of nowhere with an ax, eliminating the problem in a pile at his feet. Nian backed away as quickly as he could, retching as the men screamed for mercy.

I fixated on the pool of blood forming around the bodies, slowly leaking further away from its origin point. The smoke above us shifted, revealing the beginnings of a beautiful morning sky. A new orange color filled the sky beyond the clouds as the sun started to rise. Just as quickly, the smoke moved, covering it again.

I started to move to Nian to help him up when shouting broke out.

"No!" Locust screamed. It was the most terrifying noise I had ever heard come from a person, including the torture I had suffered at the hands of Canton's men.

I froze and followed his gaze to a set of nearby trees. Ropes had been strung over the branches. Four soldiers held onto two of our men as a swarm of Society men grabbed hold of the free ends of the ropes wrapped around Martin and Reed's necks.

Locust tried to free himself, desperate to reach them in time. I screamed louder than I had when Canton's man had burned me, tears clouding my eyes. The soldiers threw themselves to the ground, jerking the ropes up, snapping Martin and Reed's necks.

"Reed!" I fought, but it was too late.

They were gone.

Sobbing, I felt Nian scoot over to me. He was trembling as he realized what had happened. We sat, shaking with tears and hatred until Dov launched himself at the man coming for us. They tumbled in front of us, snapping us awake.

When I looked up, Justin and Devin were taking on the men who had hung our friend. Dov wrestled the solider in front of us, slamming the man's skull into the ground.

"Go," he grunted.

I grabbed Nian's hand, pulling him to his feet. Once moving, he ran faster than me, reaching the fray long before I did. We dove into the middle of it, lashing out at anyone we could find.

I ran into a soldier, knocking him to the ground. I had no remorse when I beat him, still reeling from Reed's gruesome death. This man had murdered him—not to defend himself, but to prove a simple point: that he could.

"Auluria," Eden finally pulled me off of the man as he lay unconscious beneath my pounding fists.

I pointed to the bodies still hanging from the tree and watched the rage slip on like a mask. She turned, taking on a solider with a vicious cry. Somehow, Eden managed to get her hands on a set of the spiked claws that Shadoe had used on Berwyn. My blood ran cold thinking about what that might mean.

"Do you even know how to use that?" I shrieked at her, landing a punch to a Society man. He reared back in pain.

"Don't look at me like that, Auluria," she snarled. "I wasn't a complete idiot when I hung around Lowell. I picked a few things up."

The metal piece left angry lines down the side of the man's face and I prayed it wasn't laced with poison.

"Where did you get that?" I begged for information.

"Never you mind, Goldilocks. Pay attention to your own fight." She kicked at the man, sending him into a tree. For a moment, I was jealous I didn't have one as well. I wouldn't have minded marking up the soldiers who had hung my friend.

My throat burned, though whether it was from the smoke or a not-so-distant reminder of my own almost-hanging, I couldn't be sure. I felt as if the rope was wrapped around my neck, tightening, squeezing out all the air, leaving me dark.

By the time it was over, the soldiers lay in a messy heap on the ground. Silas, Dov, and Berwyn had finished off the men who hadn't been a part of the hanging.

Justin and Devin quietly worked to take Reed down out of the tree. Nian and I helped guide his feet to the ground, silently laying him out. Nian stayed with Reed and the Hersh brothers and I untangled Martin's body from the rope. Tears burned against my eyes.

"We can't stay," Dov whispered as we all surrounded Reed's body.

Reyla cried into Silas' shoulder as he held her. I sat on the ground with Justin and Devin. Dov stood beside me, holding my hand in the air for so long that it started to tingle. Nikko stood over Martin, mourning the loss of his friend silently as he brooded.

I leaned forward, kissing Reed on the cheek. He was

one of the first people to welcome when I started training people over the Wall.

"We have to go," I whispered to him and the others. "We have to go."

I sniffed, gathering myself and forcing my tears in check. I pulled on Dov's hand, using him to lift myself. I was grateful for his constant balance when I didn't topple him and myself.

"We're not done yet," I said as another outburst from a street over filled the air.

Chapter 12

Using my sleeve, I wiped the tears and soot off my face, clearing my sight. We slowed as we approached the source of the sound. Someone cried so strongly it turned into a wail.

Soldiers and men lay in agony in the middle of the street, begging for mercy; begging for an ending. We branched off, helping our people when we could.

I saw her before the others did. Her leg was missing, torn off in the explosion. Bits of paper littered her brown hair. Her lip quivered as I knelt down.

She cringed when I brushed her hair back out of her eyes.

"Go away," Ella murmured, trying to turn her head from me.

"Take my hand, Ella," I tried to comfort her.

"Where is Shadoe?" she asked, her voice sounding like a child whining.

"I don't know," I apologized quietly.

"Ella?" Nikko's shock hit us before he made it to her side. He threw himself on the ground, taking her hand from me. "Ella."

"Where is Shadoe?" she insisted. Her leg bled more fiercely than the other wounds on her body.

"Get Shadoe," Nikko begged.

I nodded, running. A street over, I found him, clawing at his enemy. When I screamed his name, he plunged the claw into the man, raking it through his body.

"It's Ella," I informed him. "Come quickly."

He stared at me, not moving.

"Shadoe, you can't just stand here; Ella's been hurt. She's dying, Shadoe, and she's asking for you." Hysteria rose in my voice, making Shadoe shrink back. "Don't you dare do this. She needs you, now come on."

I pulled him down the street and around the corner, instructing him on how to behave. He knelt down next to her, taking her hand. I swallowed, giving him one final glare to force him into taking care of the girl before I sprinted off, knowing she didn't want me there. We hadn't been friends, but I never wanted to see her die like this.

I watched carefully, looking for signs of life among

the corpses in the street. None appeared to be clinging to life, but I checked anyway.

Arin raced past me, several of our men following him. I spun, watching them run, but didn't join them. Instead, I looked for Dov, Silas, Reyla, Justin...anyone I loved.

"Auluria," he called to me. Dov waved me forward.

I ran down the street, only to be followed by Shadoe, Sherman, and a very distraught Nikko. The buildings loomed over us, starting to sparkle in the early morning sun as it worked its way through the smoke. It glinted and glared, making it a horrific sight as we tried to avoid it while running.

We passed a large building surrounded by patterned rocks. A small garden sat out front, and, though dead, it sparked something in me.

I knew this place.

The further we ran, the more I recognized. It had changed since I was last there, long before I ever met the Baers, but I would know it anywhere. I was home.

A group of soldiers appeared, looking like they hadn't seen any of our battle. Their uniforms looked crisp and clean, no blood in sight. They spotted us and took off in our direction.

"Dov, go left," I instructed. I bolted to reach him as the others followed behind me.

"We'll hold them off," Shadoe said, realizing my plan.

"No, Shadoe—" I protested.

"Just go; we'll be right behind you." He spun, taking Sherman with him. Nikko stayed by my side. I wondered if Shadoe was trying to earn his way back into our favor.

I sprinted as fast as I could, guiding the large group down the road. Justin and Devin aligned themselves with me as we ran, only giving enough space for Dov to run at my side. Silas kept a watchful arm around Reyla and Maylin, while Henry guarded Katarina. Ben ran with Sharone and Gloria, sheltering Sharone as they ran.

Berwyn called to me, asking me what I was doing.

"Going home, Berwyn," I shouted back.

"It can't be," Eden yelped when she too recognized the neighborhood. "It's her aunt's house."

"We're going to *Lowell's* house?" Berwyn sounded shocked.

"It's the best place for us right now, Berwyn," I yelled over my shoulder. "Trust me."

I crashed through the yard, up the walk to the house. We fought to open the door, but quickly enough, we were inside.

"Here," I shouted, rushing to the trap door Lowell had hidden in the house. When I threw the door open, I was hit with the familiar damp scent.

"Go," I yelped, pointing down.

"What is it?" Justin grimaced.

"It's safety, now move," I lectured. "There's a door to escape. You can escape and reach the other side."

"We're not just going to leave you," Justin argued.

"I don't expect you to," I said, knowing he'd never leave without us. "But you have to go down there. Once you're sure the others are safe, this will give you a way to take the soldiers by surprise. Once you're down there, they can't get to you, but you can get back to us up here."

He nodded, understanding my plan.

"Hurry," I willed them to move faster as everyone quickly jumped down into the hidden room under the house.

"What's the plan for us, Auluria?" Dov asked.

I handed off responsibility of the door to Silas as he forced Reyla to climb down. Racing through the house, I checked as many of Lowell's hiding places as possible in case he had added any weapons since the last time I was in the house. Dov watched me in amazement as I flew through the steps to access the secret recesses.

To my dismay, Lowell hadn't hidden anything, though my first hint should have been the intense layer of dust and cobwebs scattered over the modest home. My knife, however, was just where I had left it the last time I had been there, long before I met the Baers.

"Lowell sure liked his secrets, didn't he?" Dov asked.

"This one is mine," I said in a flat voice, making him nod once. "Are you ready for this?"

He took a deep breath, "I am. But first, before we mess

up this nice house, do you want to show me around your home?"

He smirked, but I knew he was serious. This was my only link to my past, and he wanted to be let into it before it was gone.

"Quickly," Berwyn instructed as he and Eden took up positions at the windows.

I grabbed Dov's hand and quickly showed him my aunt's house, pointing out important things I wanted him to take notice of for the stories I would tell him later. His eyes raked over every inch, committing it to memory.

When we were out of sight of everyone, he pushed me against the wall, into the shadows.

"I'm sorry this is about to happen," he said sadly, kissing me. "I promise I'll give you a home even better than this one when this is all over. If there's anything you want from here, now is the time to get it."

"I took all I wanted before I left the first time, Dov. I'll be sad to see it go, but I'll be okay," I promised him.

"They're here," Eden's voice sounded calm. Silas tapped on the floor, letting Justin know.

Dov and I walked into the main room, ready to face the Society once and for all...or at least until we had to handle the other magistrates. Everyone tucked themselves away where it would be harder to find us.

Silence filled the room. It stretched on so long I thought they might have gone, ignoring the tiny, dark house. The door cracking against the heel of a man's boot sent my heart into overdrive. Dov squeezed my hand.

Four men entered the house, dressed in Society uniforms, weapons ready. They crept in slowly, investigating the scene. Seeing nothing, they relaxed. Moments ticked by, slowly dragging out before us.

One man gasped as he came face-to-face with Berwyn Baer, son of the great Griz Baer. Berwyn stepped menacingly from the shadows, covered in darkness. It dripped off of him as he stepped into the light; a truly terrifying sight.

Berwyn towered over the short soldier. The Society man quivered as Berwyn took another silent step toward him. The man's eyes grew so wide, I thought it might break his face. Berwyn lifted his arm, taking care of it for him as he backhanded him so hard, the man collapsed on the ground and didn't get back up.

The other three turned as the man hit the floor. We moved, ripping ourselves away from our hiding places in the dark corners of the house. Lowell had known what he was doing when he added in places to watch and hide, changing the existing structure of his mother's home.

When the soldiers didn't return outside, they sent in reinforcements. One by one, we took them out, silencing them before they could scream a warning. It wasn't until we heard the commotion out in my aunt's yard that we knew Shadoe had arrived.

Soldiers poured into the house, weapons ready, as their counterparts clashed with Shadoe and his men outside. Vicious growls mixed with dying whimpers as people from both sides suffered in agony.

"This is like old times," Eden said sarcastically, backing up to me. "Seems like we were just here, doesn't it?" She nodded to the window and my gaze fell on the yard where I had seen her for the first time when I was much younger, long before I knew who she or any of the Baers were or would become.

"Did you see me back then?" I grunted as a soldier kicked me, attempting to pull my leg out from under me.

"No," she responded. "I would have remembered the hair and put it all together."

Her point was not lost on me. The best-laid plans could unravel if even one thing slipped out of place.

Berwyn slammed a soldier against the wall, choking him until he passed out. The man slid to the floor with a thud. Dov elbowed a man, reaching behind him and bringing him over his shoulder in a calculated throw.

I was attacked from the side. My body spun away from the safety of Eden's back. The soldier picked me up from behind, lifting my feet off the ground.

My hair slammed into my face as I struggled to free myself. I gathered all of my strength, lifted my feet in the air, and brought them down, slamming into the man's knees. He dropped me, and I crashed into the floor, a sharp pain radiating through my wrist.

Acting on its own, my body twisted around so that I was on my side. I kicked at the man who had dropped me. His bone cracked as he fell to the floor. I tried not to smile. The kick Berwyn sent to the man's head stopped the screaming. I looked up at him in horror.

"You okay?" he asked, reaching down his hand to me. I set my uninjured hand in his and allowed him to pull me to my feet.

He pulled me to his chest, wrapping me in his arms as a soldier lashed out at me. I could feel the raised scars beneath his shirt. He had far less than Dov did, but they were still there.

Berwyn grimaced, using his arm to push the man away before releasing me. "To the right," he said, alerting me to turn.

The noise outside the window caught the soldier's attention. I used the opportunity to push him through the glass. He toppled out, face first. I pushed his feet for good measure, making sure he couldn't catch himself.

Beyond the yard, I saw our people, fighting against the Society men. They had gone around through the secret door and doubled back to aid our fight. Reyla, Katarina, and Henry stood just beyond my aunt's laundry line where we used to hang sheets and quilts out to dry in the warmer months.

"They're outside, we have to go," I yelled to the Baers.

"Auluria," Justin yelled, opening up the secret door.

I whipped around to face him, not realizing he was still there.

"I have an idea," he added, climbing into the room. "I had them block off the entrance before coming back. If we can get them in here, we can trap them."

"How do you plan on doing that?" Berwyn asked, join the conversation now that the soldiers were all incapacitated inside the house.

"Lure them in," Justin said. "It doesn't matter how. Stand in the doorway and wave for all I care. Just get them in here. If we can get them close to the trap door, we can open it up, push them all inside, and move the furniture in the house over the door. No getting in or out."

"Not bad," Eden mused. "Berwyn?"

"It could work." He turned to his brother. "Handle this. Eden and I will help everyone outside."

Dov nodded as his brother and sister-in-law bolted out the door toward the fight. He watched them for a moment before turning back to us.

"How are we going to do this?"

I stood outside of the house, creeping around the

corner. Dov waited just inside the front door, listening for me, while Justin hid down inside the secret hiding space under the house. When the soldiers chased me, I would know enough to jump over the trapdoor as Justin flung it open, but the soldiers wouldn't have enough time to process what was happening. Justin could easily swing around the ladder and climb up before the Society men had enough time to pick themselves up off the floor once they tumbled in.

Knowing I had to engage at least one of the men, I steeled myself to pull away from the safety of the building. The noise rushed around me, intensifying as I jogged into the yard, quickly drawing attention to myself.

The wind blew, sending an icy chill down my spine as my hair wrapped around in front of me. Swallowing, I shook my hair, demanding attention.

"It's her," one man shouted, pointing. "The girl the magistrates are looking for!"

I bit back my smile, turning to run toward the front of the house where Dov waited behind the door. They followed as I charged into the house. I felt my fiancé's presence behind me, quietly hiding.

Justin timed it perfectly, throwing the door open just before I darted to the side. The soldiers fell in, cursing as they toppled at awkward angles. They piled on top of each other as Justin lurched around the steps, climbing them as quickly as he could. The top soldier was just starting to climb off the others when I slammed the door, missing Justin's ankle by a mere breath.

"Cutting it a little close there, aren't we?" He looked at me with wide eyes.

"A little on the slow side today, aren't we, Justin?" I mimicked his expression.

"I didn't have to lift a finger," Dov mused with a shrug, looking at his hand. "This is my kind of mission."

I jerked upward as the men tried to open the door beneath me. Justin and Dov paled before rushing to move the couch. Once situated, we piled as much loose furniture as possible over the couch and door, trapping the men below. They pounded against it, wailing to be set free. We didn't relent.

"Devin," Justin dodged around us, launching himself toward the door. My mind flashed to Reed hanging in the tree, feet dangling in the air. We followed Justin, leaving the accusatory voices behind.

Only a few soldiers remained upright when we appraised the scene before us. Shadoe's men—*my* men— had been vicious, brutally attacking the Society men.

I slide down along the house, watching the end of the battle play out. Justin moved quickly to his brother's side as Dov hovered between me and the fight, eyeing me cautiously.

"I'm fine," I waved him off. Hesitantly, he went to help finish the fight.

I rested my head in my hands, pulling my knees close. My skirt had ripped at some point. If I angled the hole right, I could see one of the scars I had endured on Canton's torture table. My skin tingled at the sight of it. I would have traded more of my blood to have seen less of others' blood.

Dov had been right. One spark *could* light the entire universe on fire—it was playing out before me. My choices, my actions, my words all lead to this moment. Dov's had too...and Justin's, Silas', Reyla's, Berwyn's and Eden's. Each and every one of us made choices that led to this.

"It's time to find the magistrates," I whispered to myself.

It took a full minute before I stood up, brushing off my skirt. I walked slowly, intentionally, straight toward the man Dov had cornered. The soldier looked over Dov's shoulder, wary of my approach. His expression made Dov pause.

I made a noise so Dov would know it was me before I reached over his shoulder, pushing the soldier back.

"Where are the magistrates?" I asked in an even, controlled voice.

"What?" he stumbled.

"Where are the magistrates?" I asked, slower and more deliberately. "Do you know where they are?"

I began pushing him faster, nearly tripping him as I backed him up at knifepoint.

"I...I..." he stammered.

"You know; I can see it in your eyes." I held the knife up to his eye. "Take us."

He was one of their leaders.

I smiled sweetly, meaning it to scare him. I made my point. He nodded fiercely.

"Take him over there. Have the boys round up the rest. We need to go see the magistrates." I told Dov, exerting my leadership in front of the scared soldier.

Dov nodded, grabbing the man's collar. He shoved him toward the crowd.

"This is your chance, gentlemen, to surrender," he yelled loudly, using the man as an example. "Work with us now, and you can have a life after we take down the magistrates."

Several men surrendered, making Shadoe sneer. Dov accepted their abdications of their posts as they knelt on the ground. We rounded them up, sequestering them where they couldn't do any more damage.

We left Shadoe and Nikko in charge as we looked for survivors from our team on the other streets. The fighting had died down, leaving fires raging and blue skies peering through the smoke and clouds hovering above us.

"We need to find Talley." Justin sounded nervous. His

eyes darted back and forth, sweeping the area for his sister.

"We'll find her," Devin sounded grim, his voice tight as he spoke.

The pressure in my chest grew the further we walked from my aunt's house. It was taking too long to find people. Silas and Dov stopped each time they saw one of our team, checking for signs of life. We moved on when they found none.

She sat against the crumbled remains of a stand in the former market. Ashes still floated in the air as the orange glow of the fire died down. Tears streamed down her face.

Talley looked up at us. When she saw us, she began sobbing uncontrollably, jerking the woman lying in her lap. Necesta's hair lolled over her vacant face with the violent movements.

Justin and Devin looked sick as they lowered themselves next to their sister. I froze, staring at the scene. One heartbeat, two heartbeats.

"Reed," Devin whispered to Talley, making her shake even more fiercely.

Dov and Silas wrapped their arms around me, catching me before I even had the impulse to fall to my knees. I let them support me, giving into gravity.

Necesta looked so quiet. Her hand rested over her chest casually. I waited for her to take her next breath, but it never came. My fingers found their way to the necklace she had given me. It wouldn't help her now.

I wasn't sure if I wanted to touch her or not. I wanted to say goodbye—to hold her hand one last time—but I didn't know if I could bear to say goodbye to anyone else. Certainly not to Necesta.

Raselin stumbled over, appearing out of nowhere. He sank down next to Devin and watched Talley cry. Eventually, he ran his fingers through a strand of her hair before wiping his silent tears.

"You were a good woman, Necesta," he choked out. "You were brave and strong and smarter than any of us. If it weren't for you, we never would have made it this far. Thank you."

He lifted her hand to his lips, quietly kissing the back of her wrist. Raselin set his friend's hand back down on her chest, pulling away.

"We'll honor her sacrifice," he announced, standing.

"We will," Dov echoed, gently pushing me forward. It was my turn.

"I'm sorry," I croaked into her ear, knowing she wasn't there to hear me. I felt as if I were losing my aunt all over again. Sorrow ripped at my insides, eating me alive.

I don't know how long I sat there, but when I finally ripped myself away, I threw my tired body into Dov's arms. I apologized for the way I was acting as he brushed my hair back with his hand.

"I'm here to love you in your hardest times, Auluria."

His words echoed in my head as we trudged away, leaving the wreckage of our hearts on the streets of my aunt's town as we started toward the remaining magistrates.

Chapter 13

"You're sure they are there?" I asked Shadoe as he stalked around the corner.

"Are you actually questioning my work?" He glared at me.

"I just want to be sure," I snapped at him, losing patience.

"Auluria," Dov said softly, reminding me to be gentle with Shadoe. We couldn't afford to lose my influence over him; not now. We still needed him.

"How do we get in?" I asked, tempering my voice.

"We've already taken down most of their men. They'll have left a contingency to protect themselves, but they're hiding in a safe house. There can't be that many men there." Shadoe's footsteps fell heavy as he picked up the pace.

I worried that Shadoe may turn on us now that he had lost his rank. When the fight was over, he would no longer oversee our people. He would be allowed to train our fighters, but he would never plan another battle again. I wasn't sure if that would be enough for him, especially if he tried to live up to Lowell's standards for him.

When I had told him that we had lost Necesta, he flinched. Shadoe didn't even flinch when we talked about Lowell's death. He had been leery of her when we first met, but she had grown on him, especially when she stood up for him. He was probably worried no one would stand for him now, but I always would. Despite everything he had done.

I was also willing to let him do whatever needed to be done to end this war. I followed him around the building.

"There," he said, pointing. "That's where they said it would be. Nikko and Sherman watched it all day. They're definitely there."

"What do you suggest?" Dov asked authoritatively.

"I think it's not my job anymore, Baer." Shadoe straightened his shoulders.

Fitch shifted behind me, trying to get a better view.

"I think we should do a blitz attack. We should move in at once," he eyed the innocuous door. "I think we need to surround it and let a smaller group breach.

When they try to run, there will be nowhere to go. We'll have a few teams waiting by the tunnels we found, so even if they make it to the escape, they'll walk right to us."

"That could work," Dov mused, turning to Silas. "We'll go."

Silas nodded. "We can take the guys."

"Why is it *always* the same ones that go into every fight?" I asked, annoyed.

"I'll go too," Fitch jumped in. "Shadoe, you can bring Canton along. I imagine we'll be able to use him against the other magistrates."

"We're putting on a show now?" Shadoe scoffed.

"You *like* shows," I reminded him. "Bring the trainer from the camp, too."

"So, what do you want me to do, Lur, rough Canton up?" Shadoe glared at me.

It wasn't a bad idea. It would add an extra layer of fear when the magistrates saw us. Shadoe's intimidation tactics were far from my liking, but a few bruises and cuts wouldn't hurt.

"Why don't you let me handle that," I said, hoping he'd let me. We didn't need a repeat of what happened to Justice Kenton.

"We don't want him looking like Kenton," Fitch added, echoing my thoughts.

"So I'll leave his fingers in place," Shadoe shrugged,

ready to take some of his aggression out on the man who had destroyed our lives for so many years.

"Shadoe," I scolded, trying to keep my eyes from growing large enough to take up my entire face.

He narrowed his eyes at me.

"What are you going to do, seduce him?"

"When have I ever needed to resort to that?" I shot back.

He nodded at Dov, raising an eyebrow in challenge.

"She didn't need to seduce me, Shadoe," Dov corrected him. "She had me from the moment I met her. Unlike you."

Shadoe's next step fell heavy, lurching him forward just enough to know the comment hurt. Dov kept his face even, never flinching. A lesser man would have gloated.

"I'll handle Canton," Silas suggested, turning to lead us back. "We should get moving. We know they're here. They're not going anywhere. Leave your scouts, Shadoe, and let's go get Canton."

The walk back was filled with details for our plan. Dov, Silas, Shadoe, and Sherman would take the front entrance. Ben, Gregory, Henry, and Carter would take the back entrance. Fitch and a few of his men would be the second wave, entering through the front entrance after Dov's team entered. The rest of us would surround the building with a few fringe teams further out to cover the escape routes we had located.

I would work with Nikko, Locust, Justin, and Talley near one of the escapes that we found during our intelligence-gathering mission. We had located two others and placed Arin and Berwyn, and Raselin and Devin's teams near those posts.

When we arrived back to the main group, I was greeted by the girls from the camp we had liberated. They stood, quietly waiting for me, looking annoyed.

"Ladies," I approached them cautiously while Silas slipped away to handle Canton, Dov at his heels.

"We want to do more than hang out in the background," one of them said.

"You've been fighting alongside everyone else," I reminded them.

"Give us a job," she insisted. "We need to do something more than this."

In the distance, Eden walked by, stomping through the dying grass, still wet from where the frost had melted in the sun. She ignored us.

"Eden!" I waved her over. She begrudgingly walked over to us.

"Eden, you've met the girls from the camp," I grinned, knowing Eden was about to temporarily hate me. She'd forgive me in time though. "They're a little bored just fighting with the rest of us. They want something else to do."

"And?" Eden shook her head, her voice flat.

"And," I paused before rushing on. "You're in charge. Good luck."

I raced away as Eden shouted at me. We both knew she needed a job and training these girls after the takeover was finished would give her something more productive to do than sulk and plan her revenge on the men that had kidnapped her and tried to sell her on the underground market.

Her screeching followed me all the way until I reached Berwyn.

"What did you do?" he asked, eyes wide.

"I gave her a job," I met his gaze, refusing to flinch. "She needs something productive to do so I told her to train the girls. She'll hate it for a while, but give it a few months and see how good she becomes."

He watched me, thinking over my words.

"Do you honestly think she won't have the most effective team of spies this group has ever seen when she's done? Match her up with Brittella and the two of them will be unstoppable." I planted the idea in his head.

"What about me?" Brittella asked, looking up from where she was packing her bag.

"Eden is about to train the girls to be spies. I thought you could help," I said before Berwyn could speak.

She would need a new friend after losing Necesta so quickly. Eden and Brittella wouldn't ordinarily mix, but if they worked together, I imagined they'd learn to like each other.

"I—" Berwyn started.

"Brilliant idea, Auluria. I'll do it." She smiled and sauntered over to Eden who was still furious. Her hands waved in the air as Brittella approached her and told her that they'd be working together.

Eden swerved around to look at me where I stood with Berwyn. I raised my hand to wave, plastering a smile on my face.

"Now or never, Berwyn. Give her a job or watch her slowly lose herself every single day from this point on." I paused. "Give her a reason to keep going once we take the Society down."

Berwyn grunted next to me but nodded to his wife who turned a brilliant shade of red. I smiled bigger, angering her even more.

"You'll pay for that," Berwyn smirked, sounding like his brother.

"Yeah, but only for a few months and it will be worth it in the end," I replied, walking away.

"You're more like him than you know," Berwyn called. I paused, turning to look back, wondering what he meant. "You're selfless. Like Dov."

I blinked at him, processing his words.

"Good luck dealing with her wrath." He smiled sarcastically. "You know how she gets..."

He sauntered off, leaving me to think through all of the vicious torment Eden Baer would put me through, assuming I survived the attack on the magistrates. Maybe I should switch places with Shadoe and go in head-first to the danger. Death couldn't be that bad.

The girls hovered around Eden as we spread out to take our places for the siege. She looked like a mother duck with her goslings. Every step she took, they also took, backing up whenever she turned around.

The closer we came to the attack, the more focused Eden became and the less she cared about the younger girls following her. Brittella watched from a distance, giving me a smug look each time she made eye contact with me.

Nikko branched off as we entered the edge of the woods, just far enough out of sight to make a decently-covered escape. Justin stayed by my side, Talley following right behind us.

"Over here," Shadoe grumbled.

We waited by the covered entrance Shadoe had found the day before. The sun cast dark shadows through the tree branches. I angled myself with my back to the sun, attempting to stand in the bits of light between the branches. It warmed my legs and back where it kissed my clothing. I was grateful for the dark colors I was wearing, absorbing more of the warmth.

A crow flew overhead, landing in the tree above me. It's shadow left a cold streak across my neck for a moment, making me shudder when the sun left my skin. It sat silently in the tree, watching us curiously. It flinched as the wind kicked up.

Locust leaned against a tree, the lowest branches higher than his head. Crossing his arms, he surveyed the scene. A few times, he glanced at me with a questioning look. I hadn't told Shadoe what he had done, but it didn't matter. Shadoe would no longer be making the decisions after he went behind our backs. Locust's fate rested in my hands now.

Talley sighed quietly, trying not to distract us. I leaned toward her as the wind gusted again.

"You okay?" she mumbled under her breath.

"Yeah, you?" I replied, running my hands over my arms to warm them up as I turned to put my left side in the sun.

"It's far too cold out to be doing this," she muttered. I agreed.

"They're here," Nikko said quietly as he stood from where he had been kneeling near the hidden entrance, listening.

We straightened, preparing to stop their flight. The

group moved so that the men wouldn't see us immediately when they exited the tunnel in hopes that we could easily surround them.

Two guards burst through the door. Shadoe and Sherman grabbed hold of them, pulling them away, out of sight.

When the others didn't immediately follow, I stepped in front of the entrance.

"Gentlemen," I glanced inside, seeing two men in red robes surrounded by four other soldiers. "I suggest you do not make us come in there to get you. If we have to come into that tunnel, you won't make it out. But if you come out now, you'll see the other side of this battle."

"We give you our word," Justin added. "But you have to decide now."

The magistrate was the first to concede, pushing a soldier in front of him. The man exited, blinking in the brightness of day.

"Magistrate Markel," Shadoe sounded impressed. "I suppose I shouldn't be surprised *you* survived."

"Do I know you?" Markel glared at Shadoe, blinking in the light even though his hand blocked his eyes from the sun.

"Not yet," Shadoe sneered, voice dark and dangerous. Markel swallowed hard. Shadoe turned to face the second man in red. "Justice Hollis, you've made it too. *You* and *I* have a bit of a connection."

Hollis looked up at him, trying not to cower. I watched Shadoe stare him down, trying to figure out the connection.

"You worked for my boss, Lowell," Shadoe grinned deviously.

Of course he did. Lowell had connections everywhere. I wondered if Hollis was the reason Lowell was able to get an audience with me in Canton's cells before our hanging took place.

Justin, Sherman, Talley, and Nikko bound the soldiers, leaving the magistrate and justice to face us alone.

"Lowell is dead," Hollis said cautiously.

"Oh, we know," Shadoe glowered. "This is his cousin, you remember her..."

He motioned to me as the men in red turned toward me. I threw my shoulders back, trying to look striking and intimidating. At just the right moment, my hair blew in front of me in a glorious curtain of gold, making me grin.

"Oh, so I have *you* to thank for that," I said, trying to show as much detest for Hollis as possible. The color in his eyes dulled as they grew wide.

"Him?" Talley asked, walking over, finger pointing. She decided to get in on the fun. "This man?"

"Apparently," I crooned, playing along.

"Tsk, tsk," Talley sighed, walking closer as she pushed

her charge closer. "You should have played nicer, justice."

Magistrate Markel looked horrified as we closed in on the man. One of the soldiers took it as an opportunity to save his magistrate and attacked, throwing himself back toward Locust.

He fell to the ground, bringing Locust with him. They grappled, but the young soldier knew what he was doing. He slipped his feet through his hands where they were bound, bringing them in front of him.

Talley and I launched ourselves at Hollis and Markel, wrestling them to the ground as Justin and Shadoe tried to keep order among the other soldiers. Nikko threw his charge to the ground—kicking him hard enough to knock him out—before rushing to help Locust.

Hollis fought against me as I tried to subdue him. He pushed me, nearly knocking me off of him. I clawed at his face, hoping each line I left would remind him of the price of working for my cousin.

I should have known a surrender could never be that easy.

Talley held Markel down. He wasn't a small man, but she was tall enough to win in a battle of wills against him.

Hollis batted at me. I kneed his hip, making him shudder. He doubled over on himself as I flipped him over and restrained him. He calmed, knowing he couldn't get away. Once he stopped struggling, I tuned back into the scene around me.

Two of the soldiers were dead, Shadoe and Nikko stood over the remaining soldiers, wiping the blood off their knives. The soldiers huddled on the ground, making it very clear that they surrendered.

Sherman knelt next to Locust as he struggled for breath. A nasty line ripped through his stomach. I clenched my teeth, preparing to lose another teammate.

"Oh dear," Talley said when she realized what was happening. "This never gets easier."

"No, it doesn't." I sighed, tightening my grip on Justice Hollis. I would hold him accountable for Locust's death in the trials we would hold after we controlled the Society.

I rushed to Locust's side, fiddling with the necklace, hoping for a solution. Its answers failed me. I couldn't save him. His eyes fixated on the sky, watching the branches sway back and forth.

"Auluria," Shadoe called to me. I moved back, following orders.

Nikko stayed with Locust until he has passed, allowing the rest of us to take our prisoners back to where the team waited. I prayed the other groups hadn't lost men.

When we arrived back at the main entrance to the hiding place, Dov and Silas waited for us, surrounded by what was left of our people. They held the other justices and magistrates captive. The men looked terrified.

When we had upset their plans, the remaining magistrates and justices had fled to the one place they felt they could survive—the safe house. They hadn't anticipated that Canton had survived, nor that he had told us about the existence of the safe house.

Several of our people guarded the trainer from the camp off to the side. We wouldn't need him for the surrender.

Shadoe dragged Canton out in front of the group, covered in enough cuts and bruises to worry his contemporaries. He didn't resist as Shadoe propelled him forward.

"We are here to initiate a conversation on the terms of your surrender," Berwyn led the conversation. He crossed in front of the men.

Raselin met him halfway, taking up the discussion as if they had planned it.

"We will offer you leniency if you cooperate," he said gently, but firmly. "Surrender now, and you will stand trial. Don't surrender and we'll do this the hard way."

"We want to make this transition easy for the people," Berwyn continued. "We want everyone to be aligned with this transition of power."

Dov pushed me forward. "You're up."

Now that Shadoe had been removed from power, I was left in charge of Lowell's people. Anetta hovered by me, ready to back me up.

"If you step down now and allow us to take over your places without a fight, we won't need to have a conversation with your families...your people," I crossed my arms as I walked toward them. "I know you gentlemen are rather self-centered, but there have to be people you care about...people you don't want to die on your behalf because they assume you don't support this and try to fight against us."

"But more than that," Dov stepped in, "if *any* of your people die on *your* behalf, we will hold you accountable for that as well."

Gregory smirked from where he stood behind Magistrate Markel. Carter elbowed Henry; Dov had to force himself not to grin at the looks on the magistrate's faces.

"You will all be held accountable for your actions and will sit through trials, but those of you who cooperate will be given a certain amount of grace when the time comes to face your charges." Berwyn paced in front of them.

"All we ask is that you step down, take responsibility for your actions, and turn the rest of your soldiers over to us," I added. "In exchange for a little leniency. I suppose we don't need all of you to agree though."

I planted the idea that whoever cooperated first,

would benefit the most, hoping it would spur them into agreeing.

"Now, who would like to talk about peaceful terms for your surrender?" Raselin asked in a certain voice.

Hollis—knowing he had aligned himself with too many people—looked around nervously. The magistrates would turn on him when they found out how many people had been bribing him. If he worked with Lowell, I assumed there had to be more. Markel glared at him, fully prepared to hand Hollis over to save himself. All of the magistrates looked ready to make deals and betray the others.

A few of the men nodded, prepared to throw themselves on our temporary mercy. A sudden movement caught my attention as Hollis jumped out of his seat, throwing himself backward, trying to escape—or at least make his death less drawn out.

"You will not turn on me," he shrieked, holding something to Ben's throat. Ben attempted to bring his hands up to defend himself, but Hollis pinned them against his sides with his free hand. I instantly regretted giving them the respect of removing their bindings for this meeting. "Don't move."

He looked around nervously.

"Back," he hissed in Ben's ear. Hollis dragged him back, trying to escape as the magistrates turned on him, shouting out every transgression he had committed.

Markel jumped to his feet, but Silas slammed him down so hard that the entire group froze.

"They did this," Hollis shouted, jutting his chin out at the magistrates and justices. "They're responsible for the atrocities you suffered."

The men argued back.

"Everyone will be held accountable for what they have done. No one will take the entire blame," Raselin tried to reason with him.

"I won't go down for this!" He tripped as he stepped back, nicking Ben's throat. A small drip of blood spilled from his neck, forming a red path to his collarbone.

"Justice Hollis, please, no one is going to put all the blame on you," I tried to calm him.

"Lowell warned me about you," his voice rose. "He told me you couldn't be trusted, that you'd try to pin everything on other people, including him. You got him killed, and you're going to do the same to me because I worked with him."

Fear sparked in his eyes as his nostrils flared. He breathed deeply, his jolts of breath forcing Ben's hair to move back and forth.

"Lowell said you're the ultimate manipulator," he glared at me, "but I won't go down for this."

Dov had carefully worked his way out of Hollis' line of sight as he had been shouting to us. Dov lunged at the man, knocking into him in an effort to stop him and free

Ben. Hollis panicked when he realized what was happening.

The justice dragged his hand across Ben, slitting his throat.

Chapter 14

Air filled my lungs as I swung my legs out of the bed. Red still filled the room, but not as much as it had the last time I was inside the mansion.

"Babe, are you ready?" Dov knocked at my door.

"Almost," I scrambled to get dressed. Reyla bolted out of the bed we were temporarily sharing and rushed for her things.

"We shouldn't have stayed up so late," she grumbled.

Outside the door, Silas asked Dov what was taking so long. I picked up a pillow and threw it at the door. They jump on the other side as Reyla snickered.

When I swung the door open, both men were standing in white shirts and dark pants, looking far better rested than they had since we returned to the mansion a week ago. With the Society men cleaned out of the magistrate buildings and the remaining leadership in custody, we were all breathing easier.

Canton had played his part beautifully, orchestrating a surrender on behalf of the other magistrates, with Shadoe acting as his oversight. The magistrates and justices had given us everything we asked from them. When we paraded them in front of the towns, they gave full power over to us.

"Time to go," Dov offered his arm to me. I slipped my hand through his elbow and let him lead me down the hall.

"Looks like it's you and me, my lady," Silas said behind us.

"Why thank you, good sir," Reyla replied, playing along.

"Don't they look so adorable together?" Silas asked. I could hear him grinning at us.

"Indeed, they do. They should get married or something," Reyla laughed.

"Working on it," Dov called over his shoulder without looking at me. He kept his eyes straight ahead, grinning smugly.

"We have other matters to attend to first," I said loudly, shaking my head.

The room was larger without the moveable walls

creating cells on the side of the room. This time, Magistrate Canton sat in modest clothing on a simple chair. His colorful robes were gone, stripping him of his power. He waited for his sentencing.

He caught my eye when I walked into the room, silently begging me to stand for him against the masses. His eyes accused me when I shook my head, but I hadn't tried to save his soldiers from everything, only from death. I wanted him—and all of his men—to take responsibility for their actions, but I never believed they should die at the hands of an angry man bent on revenge. With our leadership presiding over the trials, they would receive a fair hearing and would atone for their sins.

We had time before the foreign nations figured out that the men under their power we no longer in leadership of the Society.

Mornings were spent sorting through the trials and gathering information from the former leadership during their hearings. Afternoons were spent working on a plan to truly liberate our society.

Canton—having caused the most trouble—would be sentenced first. We stood, taking turns questioning him. Raselin opened the floor, followed by Berwyn. Canton didn't have much new information for us—Shadoe had already found out everything we needed before we went after the other magistrates—but he answered our questions for the rest of our people to hear.

Dov, Berwyn, Eden, Raselin, Fitch, Talley, Silas, Anetta, and I were overseeing the trials until the towns could select representatives. We would remain on as leadership, representing our groups in the new Society and work alongside the new representatives.

"This is getting old, really fast," Silas leaned over to me from the long table we sat behind.

"Find something nice to look at," Brittella leaned forward, whispering. "Focus on that and it will make it easier."

I nudged him under the table, prompting a curious look from him. I tapped the flower tucked away in my hair, mostly hidden by my long mane, and batted my eyelashes. His face dropped.

"You know?" Silas hissed.

"I had to find out at some point." I grinned at him.

"You'll pay for this, Baer," he leaned in front of me, pretending to glare at my fiancé.

"I'm doing you a favor, buddy, now pay attention—Canton is saying something about being the wealthiest man in the Society or something equally as pretentious," Dov smirked.

"I knew he was working with him," Canton confirmed. "I allowed Hollis to take bribes from him, knowing I'd be able to use the information he fed me."

My stomach dropped.

"Wait, who is he talking about?"

Talley leaned around Silas. "They're talking about your cousin."

Canton knew what Lowell was doing all along. He had always known.

"Lowell surpassed his usefulness to us. He didn't know we were watching him as closely as we did, but he was always so willing to believe that he could bribe whomever he wanted and be given complete allegiance."

"Lowell was a fool," Eden muttered loud enough for everyone at the table to hear her. Canton wasn't phased.

"He had no idea we were watching him," Canton continued, puffing up his chest.

"Don't be absurd," Brittella whispered behind me. "Lowell knew exactly what Canton was doing. He played him. Your cousin told me all about Hollis running off to Canton. He manipulated the situation for a very long time."

"Which would explain how he was able to frame us," Dov mumbled with a sigh. "I wonder if he had all these connections when he framed my father."

"I doubt we'll ever know," I said sadly. "Lowell wasn't one to confide in people. I doubt even Shadoe's father knew the extent of Lowell's plans back then. Shadoe certainly didn't when he took over."

One of the girls Eden was training walked into the room. Still new to what Eden and Brittella were teaching her, she was more obvious than she tried to be. She bent down, whispering in Eden's ear.

Eden nodded, sending the girl off before she circled something on a map and pushed it down the table. When it reached us, I realized it was the site of another small pocket of soldiers. They worked for the richer men in the society—the men who didn't want the power structure to change. They were attempting to save their own power when they withheld the soldiers that worked for them.

Berwyn held his hand up as he stood, silencing Canton in the middle of his unending speech. He waved Nian over, quietly giving him instructions to send a group of our people to handle the situation. Nian brushed his hair back before taking care of his assignment, having jostled his locks when he nodded.

After a few hours, we ended the hearing for the day. Shadoe returned Canton to his cell while Berwyn and Raselin called our spies in for a meeting about what they had learned.

"There are more people outside," Nikko informed me as I exited the room. He followed behind me.

"Are we really going to let him follow us around all the time?" Anetta asked in desperation.

"Would you rather *not* know where he is?" I countered.

"Couldn't we send him down to the cells to deal with

Marty and Jake? I'm sure there are still body parts we could cut off?" she scoffed.

"There will be no more body parts removed," I reminded her, exasperated. "Not even for Marjorie. Speaking of, have you been down there yet?"

"No and I don't intend to." She shook her head.

"Hello, ladies," Lydia said, walking past us. Her arm was healing nicely. "Have you seen my husband?"

"He's in the meeting with the spies," I replied. "We're on our way outside to see the new group of people if you want to join us."

"Sure." Lydia changed course, stepping in line with the group walking outside.

The doors opened, letting the bright sun spill across the floor of the foyer. It sparkled off the tapestries we had yet to remove. It was cold outside, making me wish I had dressed warmer. Dov shuffled closer to me, keeping me warm.

"What do we have today, Louis?" I asked the red-haired boy as he stood at his post.

"I have a feeling it will be more appealing to the Baer's group than Lowell's," he commented, nodding toward the crowd.

Young faces flooded the courtyard.

"Eli," I was surprised to see him. "How did you get here so fast?"

"We heard you had control. We moved everyone that we could."

"Reyla!" a voice shouted from the crowd. Hannah sat in a cart, cradling her new baby.

"Get Sharone," I ordered loudly, hoping someone would listen.

We rushed forward to help Hannah up. She handed her baby to me, wrapped in so many blankets, you could hardly see her face. Dov and Silas pulled her up. Reyla wrapped her in an embrace as soon as she was standing. We fussed over the baby until Sharone arrived.

"What is going on?" Sharone grumbled.

"Just come on," Henry said, Katarina trailing behind him. The two girls gasped as they saw Hannah.

Sharone ran to her sister, throwing her arms around her as she sobbed. The second Hannah pulled back, I shoved the baby into Sharone's arms and let Hannah introduce her sister to her new niece.

"That's so sweet," Lydia said, tears in her eyes.

"A mother's love," Brittella crooned behind me. She latched on to Lydia's gaze.

"Oh, do you have to know *everything* before_*everyone*, Brittella?" Lydia growled.

"Necesta told me," Brittella snipped. "She also wanted you to have this."

She slipped her hand into her pocket and pulled

something out. She dropped it into Lydia's hand before sauntering away. "For the little one."

All eyes turned on Lydia.

"We were going to tell you later," she sighed. She shouted as we jostled her in a group hug, "Careful!"

We laughed together at her good news, enjoying the moment.

"I have no idea how Necesta knew; I didn't even know." Lydia smiled. She ran a finger over her gift from Necesta.

"I'd like to talk about my position here," Eli interrupted.

"The others are in a meeting now, Eli, but come sit with us for dinner and we'll talk about what might suit you," I promised. "Thank you for bringing the girls home."

"All right, let's get these people inside," Dov raised his voice to be heard. "It's freezing out here.

Everyone shuffled inside. They would stay with us in the mansion for a few days until we were able to return them to their families or find places for them to stay. The children happily ran around, playing between their mothers as they walked inside.

"Well, hello there, Goldilocks," a gentle voice said behind me.

I turned back around to find myself staring into the eyes of Barone.

"You made it," I grinned, hugging him.

"This young lady made sure of it." Maylin stepped out from behind him.

"I knew you wouldn't want me to leave without him. He's been...interesting company," she teased. "I left the doctors with a few of the girls who couldn't travel. They'll be along when they can. I thought I could be of more use to you here."

"I'm glad you're back Maylin. I didn't think you'd keep your promise so soon, but I'm glad you did. Come inside, you must be dying for a warm place to sit by now." I wrapped my arm around her and led her inside.

"Look who's back!" I cheered as Katarina rushed to us. I left the two to catch up.

Barone limped behind them, nodding when he saw Dov slow his steps. I would have to tell him about Chester later. The look on his face told me he already knew of his cousin's fate.

Dov wrapped his arm around my shoulder as we walked away.

"We're finally free," he said softly.

"We're finally free," I repeated, leaning my head on his shoulder.

"The last of Wallace's men have been rounded up," Justin said, nearly colliding with us as we rounded the corner. "Marty is still downstairs demanding to speak with you. I told him I'd give him a hand, but only if he twisted my arm."

"Callous," I said in a deadpan voice. I managed to hold the sincerity of it only a second longer than it took for my face to morph into a laugh.

"We should probably handle this," Dov sighed. "Want to come along?"

Justin fell into step behind us. We waved Reyla, Silas, and Eden over when we saw them along the way. Together, we took the steps down to the cells.

Miraculously, it was warmer in the cells than it had been in the foyer. We moved into the wing where Marty was being held. Dov nodded to Sherman, explaining that we would speak with Marty.

We waited inside an interrogation room. Dov was seated at the table, while the rest of us leaned against the back wall. It was dark, but not nearly as terrifying as when Canton's men had put me in one of the interrogation rooms with Lowell.

One of Sherman's men brought Marty in, pointing him toward a chair. With only one hand left to restrain, he remained with his hand free. He watched us warily.

"What is it, Marty?" Dov asked diplomatically.

"You take my hand and that's how you treat me?" He sounded unimpressed. If he still had both hands, I imagine he would have been picking at his fingernails in distaste.

"I had nothing to do with that, and you know it." Dov countered, resting his wrists on the table.

I raised my eyebrow, daring him to continue to waste our time.

"You're the one who started all of this, golden boy," Marty sneered. "Whether it was Shadoe or it was you, it's because you stole the golden girl."

"You and Jake never could let go of a grudge," Dov mused.

Marty set his stump on the table, tugging off the bandage. A tangled mess of skin where his hand used to be looked back at us as he set the bandage a few inches away. He examined his amputation.

"Yeah, well, I can't hold on to much these days," he held up his hand, moving his fingers as if he were about to clutch something, "so it looks like grudges are all I've got. Heard Marjorie had it out with you."

He sneered at Dov. I wanted to smack the look off of his face. He looked up and smiled at me.

"I hear they've been calling you *Goldilocks*. Looks like I was right after all." His eyes traced the length of me. "Too bad Jake had to handle Marjorie's meltdown and couldn't take care of you, golden girl."

"Too bad," I murmured. "I would have liked to have put him through a wall...or a tree. You've had decent experiences with trees, right? I'm sure he wouldn't volunteer for that though.

"Speaking of, since you missed us so much, would you like me to go get Shadoe? He's upstairs somewhere and I'm sure he'd love to catch up."

"Well, if he's not here, it's probably a good time to remind you—" Marty grinned, leaning forward to move the bandage. His grin morphed into something dark and evil as he dropped his voice. "—the golden boy doesn't always win."

Marty used his wrist to hold the bandage down while his remaining hand pulled out a small-but-fierce looking weapon. He lunged across the table at Dov who immediately shot back, the chair tipping over behind him.

Marty skillfully leaped around the table, still going after Dov. I reached him first, stepping between them as Silas shouted and tried to pull Marty away.

Eden screamed, kicking at Marty to fend him off as Reyla screamed, reaching out to steady Dov before he could fall over the toppled chair.

The room was chaotic as I crashed to the ground.

My name was yelled, over and over. Silas threw Marty across the room, slamming him into the wall.

"Get Maylin," Reyla shrieked.

I blinked.

"Auluria?" Dov's voice called to me, forcing my eyes open. "Auluria, open your eyes. Open them. Come on now."

He cradled my head in his fingers, using them to keep me up off the floor.

"That's my girl, open those eyes," he said kindly, persistently keeping me awake.

"Keep her awake Dov," Reyla cautioned in the distance. "Eden, try to stop the bleeding."

A burning sensation crept through my chest.

Then everything went black.

Chapter 15

The first thing I smelled was sweet spices. A wave of warmth washed over me, coaxing me out of my sleep.

Someone was breathing on me.

When I opened my eyes, all I saw was blue. Blue so deep and so intense I had to blink to bring it into focus. Dark fringe fell over the blue color as it sparked and flashed, awakening me fully. Those were eyes. The most brilliant blue eyes I'd ever seen.

Then it hit me...and I relaxed.

"What happened?" I asked Dov.

"Marty attacked me and you jumped in the way," he smirked. "You hit your head when you fell. You've been in and out all afternoon."

My hand floated to my shoulder where I found bandages. I tried to catch my face before it fell into a frown, but wasn't fast enough.

"He cut you," Dov's lips turned down. "I'm sorry, babe. It will heal though."

"Oh great," I tried to laugh. "Now we'll have matching scars."

He erupted in laughter.

"Mine are on my back, but if you want us to match, I can handle one more."

"Don't you dare," I lectured him. "No more scars, Mr. Baer."

"You don't like them?" he asked, adjusting his collar. "I think they're rather becoming."

He grinned down at me.

"And here I thought you'd find them attractive. If I had known, I would have avoided all of those beatings. There's just no pleasing you, is there?"

"None whatsoever," I agreed. I reached out my hand, running it over the muscles on his arm. "At least this time I didn't fall off the bed when you woke me."

"I didn't make you fall off the bed the first time either," he teased. "You did that all on your own, Goldilocks."

"Yeah, yeah." I brushed him off as he leaned toward me. "Do we have a plan figured out yet?"

"You mean after the meeting this afternoon?" he questioned.

"Yes," I settled back against the pillow and waited.

"We do, but we should have you checked out first." Dov insisted, standing to walk to the door.

Just as he opened it, Berwyn stepped inside.

"Still haven't gotten rid of her, I see," he joked. "So close this time."

He took a seat at the table, leaning back in the chair.

"It's my fault. I never should have told you to let her stay that first morning," Eden said, slipping into the other chair at the small round table. "Here I thought it would be nice to have another girl around..."

She rolled her eyes but smiled at me.

"Are you okay?" she asked.

"Eden basically destroyed Marty for you, so you don't need to worry about him again," Dov informed me.

"You always pull the scary strength out when you're saving one of us, Eden. I'm pretty sure if we had just handed Berwyn over to Canton in the first place, this would have been over within the first hour."

She glared at me but softened at the idea that she could hold such strength.

"You have a point."

"I noticed you're warming up to the girls from the camp," I hinted, making her scowled at me.

"She's up," Silas grinned, walking into the room. "About time. Come on in, guys."

Justin and Devin pushed each other, both trying to enter at the same time. They tripped into the room, barely righting themselves before hitting the floor.

"That's right, children, keep pushing and see how that works for you," Talley mock scolded them. She turned to me

as she flopped onto the bed next to me. "Hey, little one."

"Hey, that's my spot," Reyla pouted, taking up a post at the end of the bed. Katarina and Sharone hurried around the bed, sitting at Dov's feet near me. Maylin started her examination of me quietly.

"Goldilocks!" Gregory shouted, noticing all of the activity in the room. "And here we thought you were gone forever!"

He dramatically took a seat by the girls on the floor. Henry kept a watchful eye on Ben as he lowered himself to the ground, the bandage still wrapped around his throat. Ben waved to me, honoring his promise to keep the talking to a minimum until his wound had healed.

"They're in there," Nikki said from the hallway. "They're *all* in there.

Raselin and Nian rounded the corner.

"Holding the meeting in here, are we?" Raselin winked at me, his step lighter than it had been since I agreed to train his people to fight. "We handled Marty—or what was left of him, anyway. Fitch and Lydia should be here momentarily."

As if on cue, Fitch guided Lydia into the room. They both asked how I was doing before Fitch leaned against the wall and Lydia found a spot next to Talley on the bed.

"All of the towns are choosing their representatives within the week," Silas started. "Carter just checked in an hour ago. He's getting some rest now, but all of our people are in place to help assist the towns with the transition."

"We opened the markets back up, so trade will continue as before," Berwyn added.

It had been a productive afternoon while I was unconscious.

"Speaking of the markets," Eden interrupted. "Do we have confirmation on the underground markets yet?"

"Yes, Eden. They're all closed down. We rescued fifty women. I just found out in the meeting and forgot to tell you when Auluria decided to get herself killed...again." He tossed me a look. I bit my tongue to keep from sticking it out. "They're on their way to Markel's mansion. There are a few doctors there that will look over them and then we'll get them reunited with their families."

"We caught a number of the traders as well," Raselin added. "They'll be going through their own trials soon enough.

Eden looked satisfied, though I wasn't sure how long

that would last. I assumed only until the sentencing when she decided their punishments weren't strong enough.

"Oh," Silas interrupted. "We found the camp trainer's family and reunited them. He still has a trial to get through, but I think he will cooperate now that he has his family back."

I was glad we had located them. At least something had gone as planned.

"Have you heard anything from home, Raselin?" I asked, hoping our spies had brought word of the country we had abandoned to cross back into the Society.

HE TOOK A DEEP BREATH. It was like the life was sucked out of the room.

"Things are getting worse there, just like we knew they would. It's becoming dangerously close to what it was like here, even on the outskirts. I think we're going to have trouble getting back in."

Maylin finished looking me over and sat down with her friends.

"We won't let that stop us," I promised. "I'm sure we'll find a way."

"Our priority needs to be here first," Raselin said diplomatically. "We have to stabilize the Society first. Once we have everyone settled here and the country back in working order, we can figure out a plan to stop the

Northwestern countries and free the rest of them to the east and south."

"What are our plans for fixing things here?" Reyla asked. "I mean, aside from waiting for the towns to send representatives?"

"Better yet, how long do we have to stay here?" Maylin asked, finding a sudden spring of bravery. "I'd like to go home."

"We'd all like to go home, Maylin," Eden said kindly. It was a little unnerving to hear the lack of harshness in her voice. "Once we get through this, we can go home."

"Who is going to stay here if we all go home? Katarina piped in.

"I'll be staying," Raselin said, surveying the group. "I don't have a place in the Society anymore, so I'm not losing anything by staying here. Anyone who would like to stay is welcome, but none of you are required to stay."

He looked at the Hersh siblings. Talley leaned toward me. They would be coming back to the forest with us when the time came. I took her hand in mine, letting her know I was excited not to lose her.

"I would say by this time next year, we'll all be home," Berwyn announced. "Assuming there *is* a home."

"You haven't heard yet?" I asked, astonished that we would have information about foreign countries but not the Baers' house.

"The storehouses are fine. We've checked on everyone

there and have already started moving them back to their homes and into the towns," Berwyn corrected himself. "We just didn't take the time to prioritize looking into things like the cabin."

"What does it matter to you, anyway, Auluria? It's not like you'll be living there." Eden scoffed. My heart started beating out of my chest. "As soon as you're married, you two will need your own place."

Everyone turned to me, wild grins plastered across their faces.

"We might need a little help building a house," Dov informed them. Something told me he had the perfect spot in mind.

"Do you have plans for the wedding yet?" Katarina asked, grinning wickedly.

"When would we have had time to discuss that?" I snapped, grinning to let her know I was teasing.

"I don't know, somewhere between you almost dying and him almost dying." She shrugged casually. She leaned back against Henry who looked like he was in heaven just being in her presence. "You'll have to work it in between all these near-death experiences somewhere since you two love those so much."

"Thank you, Katarina, that was helpful," I rolled my eyes playfully.

She looked up at me and batted her eyelashes. "That's

what I'm here for." She stroked Henry's arm making him blush.

I rubbed my finger over Dov's hand as it rested on the bed. I wanted to lean against him too, but he was too far away in the chair. He gave me a knowing look.

"Once we get everything settled here," Berwyn continued, getting us back on track, "and we move back home, we'll be having meetings every week or so. Long term, we're hoping to have the Society back on track within a year or two and then we can start working on helping the people over the Wall after that.

"That doesn't mean we won't do what we can to help them now, but we can't orchestrate a rebellion with their people until we're stable here first."

"They're going to need all the help they can get," Silas added. "It's best to make sure we're prepared before we take that on. We barely survived *this* war."

"This time, we'll have more of a chance to plan our attack out," I smirked, squeezing Dov's hand.

I looked around the room at my new family. I would die for these people if that's what it came to and I knew they'd do the same for me. We had all been willing to die to make the world a better place for our friends and family. Not everyone had made it, some made the ultimate sacrifice, but it took each and every one of us to get to this point.

"Canton is still being helpful, as are the others. We'll

know everything we need to know about outside the Wall soon enough," Dov assured us.

Anetta darted into the room.

"You're up," her voice was flat. She turned to Berwyn. "Shadoe would like a word. He said he has new information about the Wall."

Berwyn stood, pulled Eden to her feet.

"You'd better all come. No need to repeat this." They all slowly followed.

I started to get up, but Dov pushed me back down. "Not you, Goldilocks."

"I'm fine," I insisted. "We need to see what Shadoe found out."

With the room cleared of people, it suddenly felt cool and densely silent.

"You and I have been through the worst of this war, Auluria. Taking a few minutes to rest won't stop anything from happening. I promise the world will go on."

He stroked my hair. I tolerated it for a moment before kicking my legs over the side of the bed.

"Auluria," he begged.

"We're just going downstairs, darling, it will be fine." I smiled sweetly. "You didn't even make this big of a fuss the first time I hit my head."

"You hadn't been tortured and thrown off a cliff at that point," he protested with a smile.

"Really? You're going to bring *that* up again?"

"Someone obviously has to." He waited as I slipped on my boots. I pushed my skirt aside, trying to avoid tangling it inside of my footwear.

When I stood up, he was watching me quietly.

"What?" I asked.

"Nothing." He grinned devilishly. He shrugged as I waited for more.

"Dov Baer!" I demanded an answer.

"You're beautiful. And somehow your hair is even longer than the last time I pointed out how long it was."

"Yes, well, time will do that. Grow things, that is."

"Like us," he said it so casually I almost missed it. "It took a little time, but look at us now. Seems like just yesterday we were dancing in my living room."

"Pretty soon we'll have our own living room to dance in, from what I hear." I took his hand.

He pulled his fingers out of mine, slipping it underneath my palm so he could raise it to his chest. I stepped forward with him, lingering in his presence. Dov smiled.

"Yes, Auluria, we will. But first, we go downstairs and find out what this big break is."

He stepped to the side, holding out his hand, gesturing that I should go first. Dov wrapped an arm around my shoulder, holding my other hand in his. We walked together, neither one of us in the lead or following behind, just as we had done and would continue to do for as long as we knew each other.

Dov squeezed my hand.

"I love you, Auluria."

"I love you, Dov." My heart sang so many extra words, but I didn't need to say them out loud.

I let go of his hand, wrapping my arms around his waist, clinging to his body as we walked.

"Is this okay?" I asked, realizing it was a little hard to walk without tripping.

"It's all right," Dov responded with a little laugh.

"*Just* all right?" I looked up into his glittering deep blue eyes.

"It's *just right,* my darling," he said loudly as we stepped into the hallway. "It's absolutely perfect."

Epilogue

"Uncle Dov!" a voice cheered, shaking the entire bed.

"How are you up so early?" Dov grinned, grabbing his nephew by the waist and turning him upside down.

"Mommy told me to go see you!" he grinned devilishly.

"*Of course* she did." Dov messed up his hair. "Remind me to thank her for that later. Now go play."

Dov sent the boy off before turning back to me. I sighed, snuggling closer to him under the sheets.

"Good morning, wife," he smiled down at me.

"Good morning, my love." I inhaled his scent, drifting back to the first time I had met him all those years ago.

I kicked my legs out from under the sheets, wrapping them around him. His fingers traced over my legs.

"I still think these are beautiful," he murmured, brushing over my burn scars. I grimaced.

His scars were beautiful and etched across his body just for me. Mine were a constant reminder that I had listened to people like a fool and nearly gotten everyone killed.

"They are, Auluria," he buried his face in my hair as he lay back down next to me. "You took each one of these for me so that I didn't have to suffer. They're beautiful."

My hands automatically went to his arms, even stronger than they were the day he caught me in the woods and carried me to his home. He let me trace the marks on his arms and back before winking at me.

"Come on; we should handle them," Dov finally said. He tossed the covers back and stepped out of bed.

In the kitchen, we settled down to make breakfast. Dov started cooking while I stepped outside for fresh berries from our bushes. The pond glittered and I considered inviting Dov for an early morning swim when a little blonde girl raced past me.

"Now, you two get back inside," I pretended to lecture. "You're parents would be furious to know you were running around out here."

"Aunt Auluria," the little girl put her hands on her hips, "Mommy lets me go outside all the time."

"Yes, but that's when she's awake," I grinned, knowing I shouldn't. "Maybe you should go wake her up."

The two raced into the house to wake up Berwyn and Eden in the guest room where they had spent the evening in preparation for the meeting today. I hoped the fresh berries would make up for the rude wake up call.

"Did you really just do that?" Dov gave me a look when I walked inside.

I shrugged flirtatiously as I set the bowl down. "Maybe."

"What's the worst they can do?" Reyla asked, walking in the door. "They can't do anything to upset the baby, now can they?"

She bent down to talk to my stomach, gently brushing over the bump I carried. She gasped, grabbing her husband's hand.

"I felt her kick!" Reyla exclaimed as she pushed Silas' remaining fingers against my stomach. My heart broke every time I saw the place where his fingers had been just a year ago. He grinned up at me, hand tucked neatly under Reyla's.

"It's still a bit early for that, Rey." I teased.

"Well, it's not my fault you two had to beat us." She joked back, daring me to take her joy away.

"We're only a little behind," Silas beamed.

"What?" Dov said, nearly dropping the pan he was cooking with. He set it down and raced to his friend to congratulate him. When Reyla nodded, confirming her announcement, I threw myself into her arms.

"What is all of this noise?" Eden asked groggily, rubbing her eyes.

"Have you never heard of quiet?" Berwyn snapped.

"Not when there's a baby around," I realized too late that I sounded like a bird chirping first thing in the morning. "And I'm not talking about mine."

Eden's jaw dropped. Her children circled her, running around her feet.

"Kids, sit," she ordered, pointing them to the couch. They hurriedly sat, knowing how to obey their parents the first time they spoke. The two were more obedient than Eden's spies.

Berwyn clapped Silas on the back, the scars on his hand showing under his sleeve. We had all gained more scars than I cared to think about over the years, but each had been well earned and well worth it.

After a few moments, we sat to eat. The sun glittered off the pond, reflecting all the way to the house. After we ate, we would meet with Raselin and his team to discuss the next mission over the Wall. I felt confident that we would soon find our foothold into the nation to the northeast of the Society, though Talley still insisted we should free one of the southern countries because it would be easier. A promise was a promise though, and I wanted to honor our word to Necesta.

Tomorrow we would meet with Shadoe to see how the training was going for our new volunteers. He had quickly transformed our fighters into an army with skills unmatched by any of the surrounding countries. While he was no longer allowed to make tactical decisions, he seemed to be satisfied training the men and women who worked with us.

We looked up when a knock sounded on the door. Devin slipped inside.

"Morning," he waved, inviting himself to join us. He popped a berry into his mouth.

"Did you find anything?" Dov asked, standing to get Devin a plate.

"We did," Devin confirmed. "I have to make it quick though, Maylin needs help with some doctor stuff today."

"What does she have you doing today?" I questioned, reaching for more berries.

"Collecting supplies or something. Can you believe she's *still* going through Necesta's notes after all these years?"

"Who knew she brought so much which her when we crossed the Wall!" I laughed. "She was a tricky one, that's for sure."

Devin laughed at the nostalgia. He quickly filled us in on what he had learned in his brief time over the Wall to the South.

"Hey!" Justin said, slamming into the room. He glared at his brother. "I saw you come in. You didn't even have the decency to tell me you were back?"

He reached over and took food from my plate. I slapped him with my fork. "You would dare take food from your niece or nephew?"

"She won't mind sharing with Uncle Justin," he grinned.

"You don't know it's a girl," I insisted.

"It's a girl," Dov said. Eden and Berwyn echoed his response, making me shake my head.

Reyla tucked her hair behind her ear, highlighting the flower she wore. Just like every morning that she and Silas joined us for breakfast, she wore the flower that Silas gave her—a symbol of the flowers that had mysteriously shown up in the storehouse after she and I had been hurt and were recovering.

Dov reached over, pulling one from the small pot he had sitting on the window ledge. He tucked it in my hair —a reminder of his love for me. His hand floated to my lap where I placed mine in his. He picked my hand up and kissed it.

"It's a girl," he whispered, making me roll my eyes.

"At the rate we're going, we won't free the Northeast country until your kids are halfway grown," Justin said between a mouthful of food.

"That's not a bad thing," Reyla interjected. "Auluria and I can't exactly fight in our conditions, now can we?"

Justin and Devin's eyes grew wide as they realized her

announcement. They laughed, congratulating the happy couple.

"Relax," Eden called us back to attention. "We'll just have Jasleen or Hannah's girl watch the kids while we're out playing Goldilocks and the three Baers again."

My breath still hitched anytime someone used that silly story name. Necesta really had known what she was doing when she started that because the entire country had seemingly forgotten I had a name that wasn't attached to my hair color.

"We really need to find a new name," I quipped.

"Why? I like being able to say I know you four," Justin protested. He grinned. "It really helped me impress that girl last week."

"Oh yeah, how is she?" I asked. "Do we like her?"

"I didn't get a say in Dov, you don't get a say in this," he reminded me, threatening to throw a forkful of food at me.

"Hey!" Dov chuckled.

"Shut up, Baer, this is between me and the girl," Justin teased.

"*My* girl," Dov reminded him.

"*Girls*." I hissed the plural form of the word, realizing what I had said after it was too late.

"She admits it!" Berwyn cheered.

"I told you it was going to be a girl," Eden threw me a satisfied smirk.

"We still don't know," I argued.

"Ask Maylin, she knows everything," Devin added, leaning forward on his elbow.

"Aunt Goldilocks, are you having a girl?" my nephew asked in surprise.

"Oh!" Justin nearly choked on his laughter, tossing the boy a wink. "Nice one, little man."

It was chaos. It was madness. It was mine.

I had lost my only remaining relative to the Baers and the Society, but it had freed me to live my life as fearlessly as Dov Baer lived his. He fought for his people and taught me to do the same, even when it hurt, even when it meant I would lose.

This freedom gave me my new family, and they gave me the hope to keep going, to keep pushing forward, to keep living and helping others live.

Tomorrow would be a new day that would bring us one step closer to freeing our enemies. Tomorrow we would push forward and change lives. But today, we had each other and that was more than enough.

"Love you, Goldilocks," Dov winked at me, turning my chin toward him for a kiss.

"Love you too, Baby," I smiled.

Our daughter really did move this time.

ACKNOWLEDGMENTS

My incredible readers, thank you so much for going on this journey with me. Since the time I started The Golden Trilogy, we've been through so much together—including Golden becoming a bestseller. I couldn't be more thrilled!

I hope that you've enjoyed Dov and Auluria's story as much as I have. If you're like me, you're probably devastated that it has come to an end...or has it? All I'm saying is that you should keep a close eye out for something in the future. Mostly because I'm not ready to say goodbye yet and there's still so much story to tell! Anyone want to learn more about this Duluria baby? Who do you think she might be? I'm not giving out any hints...yet.

Special thanks to Sissy and Jess for all of your hard work proofing this book and your incredibly loyal support!

Thank you to my lovely editor, Jody Desroches for all of your hard work!

Alexis, I'm so grateful to have you in my life! Your artwork on the chapter headers for The Golden Trilogy has been so incredible! The fans all love finding the hidden pictures!

To Auluria and Dov, thank you for letting me tell your story. You two have been in my head since I was a little girl, and while it took a long time to figure you out, I'm so glad I did! Forever and always, my babies, I love you!

Special thanks to all of you fabulous fans. I could not have gone on this journey without you. Thank you for your unending support, love, and the fabulous emails and DMs you send. You make this all worth it!

Remember, you have the ability to change people's lives, so live in a way that is meaningful, do the right thing, even when it's hard, and be a light in the darkness. You're a spark that will change the world, baby. Believe it. Live it.

Keep reading for a bonus scene from Justin's perspective, the first chapter of the final book in the series, and to find out how to play interactive games to help Auluria get ready for her mission to see the Baers, get more bonus scenes, and even gain access to Golden filters for your photos and live broadcasts.

Stay inspired,

-K.M. Robinson

"Clear," Auluria whispered.

I move quickly down the hall to the next door to clear the room. Auluria walks behind me, sweeping the hall.

When I feel her tap my shoulder, I open the door to the room. The shock of seeing a man is enough to make me freeze while I quickly assess the situation. One of him, two of us.

He stood in front of the window, quietly watching us as we entered.

"I've been waiting for you," the Society man said, tipping his head to the side.

I didn't trust him. I trusted nothing about this scene. I watched him carefully.

"I take it this means we lost." He leaned back on the window ledge. "You know the magistrates won't take kindly to that."

"I do believe that's the point," I reply.

He sighed. I could sense he was going to fight us no matter what we said.

"You realize I'm supposed to put up a fight…"

Of course he was.

"Oh? Why is that?" I asked, already knowing my distraction wouldn't work.

"Part of the job description." He watched me intently. It made me nervous. "I have a family and I'm sure the magistrates would take it out on them."

"What if we could help them?" Auluria asked from behind me. I can feel her rise up on her toes to see around me.

"You can't." He was giving up. "What if—" I was cut off.

"No, this is how it has to be."

The man jolted toward me quickly, but I was ready for him. I backed up enough that Auluria would be safe and managed to catch the Society man as he toppled forward, unprepared for my sudden shift.

The man elbowed me, slamming into my shoulder. I tried not to yell out loud, not wanting to alert any others that might be in the hall, but I wasn't expecting the blow and yelped despite my best efforts.

When the Society man pulls a knife on me, Auluria launches herself into action, grabbing his wrist.

We grapple with him, trying to take him down to the ground so we can wrestle him into submission. I managed to get one of his hands clamped behind his back as Auluria fought with him. Knowing it was the only way, I kicked the backside of his knee, knocking him to the ground. All three of us crashed to the floor.

Anetta and Locust arrive just as Auluria cries out in pain. My head whips over to make sure she's okay. She winces, glancing down at her knee, but otherwise, she appears unharmed. Good thing, because I'd have to hurt the Society trainer if he had hurt her.

The man struggling under our grip demands I return my attention to him. He's stronger than he looks, but I get him under control. Auluria fights viciously to hold on to him.

"Want me to kick him?" Anetta asked, stepping toward the Society man. I wouldn't be opposed to her kicking him in the face.

"No!" Auluria shouted. She, on the other hand, didn't want to see the blood. I had always admired her regard for taking care of people—even her enemies.

"Let her, Lur." Locust kept an eye on the hallway, shouting over his

shoulder to us. "We need to keep going and don't have time to deal with him conscious."

"No," Auluria repeated.

I stared at the two girls locked in a battle of wills. I had no doubt Auluria would win out, but it was amusing to watch them stare each other down. Anetta finally backed down, moving toward the door.

"You better handle this," Anetta warned.

I had had enough of the man wriggling to get free, and I didn't want to

sit around and watch the ladies battle it out any longer, so I took the opportunity to knock the Society man out, his head slamming against the floor.

Refusing to take any risks, Auluria and I held on to him for another moment to make sure he really was out. Auluria looked relieved when he didn't stir.

I glanced at Anetta and Locust in the doorway, still watching us. I could see how that would get creepy. Those two worked well together.

"You okay?" I asked softly.

"I'm fine. Are you okay?" Auluria responded, clearly concerned about me.

"I'm good. What are we going to do with him?" I stand up, looking down at our captive. I tap the man with my boot, making his leg move.

Auluria shrugs casually but I can see her searching for a plan. I don't think either of us had thought through what to do if we came across a hostage. She looks so stressed—this has been hard on her. I tried to come up with an answer so she wouldn't have to.

"What if we put him in the room down the hall? We could block him in the closet." I suggested. "Put a chair in front of it and he won't be able to

get it open even if he *does* wake up before we get back to him."

She thinks it through as I explain my spur-of-the-moment plan. She

nods before quickly turning to the door.

"Locust! I need you to help Justin move him to the room down the

hall," she called to our partners.

Auluria temporarily works with Anetta while Locust and I lifted the

man. We dragged him out the door as the girls covered in case any Society men showed up.

Locust and I wrangled the man to the closet, forcing him inside. Knowing it wouldn't be fun when he woke up, I tried to adjust him so that it would be less painful. Unfortunately, there was only so much help I could give him while still folding him in enough that we could close and block the door.

We tied his wrists under his knees, preventing him from being able to untie himself when he woke up. Unless he felt like breaking his knees to get his hands around in front of him, he was stuck.

When I closed the door, Auluria brought the chair over for me so I could wedge it under the handles. Tipped on its back legs, it fit perfectly.

"Good luck getting out of there, buddy," I mumble, brushing off my hands.

"They're here," Anetta nodded from the doorway, deflating.

After a moment, Dov stepped into the room, walking quickly to Auluria's side.

"Should I ask?" he joked.

"Creative jail?" I leaned against the wall and shrugged, gesturing to the chair.

"I'm not going to ask," Dov smirked. "Everyone okay?"

"We're good. Are they sweeping the rest of the building?" I answered, joining Dov and Auluria.

"They are," Dov replied. He swept Auluria up in his arms. It's a good thing I like those two or that would get annoying very quickly. "The good news is that the rooms where they keep the boys all lock from the outside, so we can lock the trainers in there. We've got the boys partnered with our people and they're overseeing the Society trainers.

"The bad news is that we definitely have a few bodies."

"Any of ours?" Auluria asked, concern in her voice.

"No," Raselin said, entering the room. "A few injuries, but no deaths, thankfully." "Most of the bodies are from when the boys initially turned on the

trainers before we talked them down," Dov added, gaze moving back to his girlfriend. "We need to talk to them."

"There's a dining room downstairs," Auluria suggested, looking adoringly at Dov. "We could hold a meeting there."

"That's a good idea," Dov nodded. "Let's get all of the boys down there. Fitch can oversee watching the prisoners."

"Good idea. We don't need everyone in the meeting," Raselin put his hand on Dov's shoulder. "Go get your people, Dov. We'll meet in fifteen minutes."

Auluria scurried after Dov. I followed Raselin out.

hap!

I fell hard on my backside.

"Get up," his voice commanded.

I tried to sit up, but pain shot through my back.

"Get up, we have work to do," he demanded again.

"I'm trying," I said through gritted teeth.

Shadoe was quite possibly my least favorite person. It had only been a week since my aunt had died and my cousin, Lowell, had brought me into his group of fighters where he was working to end the corrupt Society we lived in. I was lucky I had a cousin to care for me at all. I had lost my parents and my aunt; Lowell was the only family I had left.

Shadoe reached down to me and pulled me to my feet. Stepping back, he paused as I took a breath of air. Before I could even gasp, he launched himself at me yet again, pummeling me to the ground.

I shrieked as I hit the dirt, brown dusty particles covering my forearms and hands. Lowell stood several yards away raising his eyebrow at me. *I was weak* and he didn't like it.

"*Lur,*" Shadoe said, using the name I so despised.

"That is *not* my name," I growled.

"Get it right." He scowled.

I hated him.

But Lowell would not save me.

He paired me with Shadoe; a man who had been born to work with Lowell. His father before him worked with my cousin, until his death a few years before, and now Shadoe was his right-hand man.

I rose to my feet, determined not to fall again. Raising a hand in front of me, I protected my face like Shadoe had shown me. He threw a punch and I blocked it with one hand, then swept my foot around the back of his leg and pulled his knee out.

He faltered and I slammed the heel of my hand into his jaw, forcing him back.

I knew Lowell was watching, so I continued my attack.

Punching him in the stomach, Shadoe fell to his knees. I took the opportunity to bring my knee up, connecting it with his face. As I did, he gripped my leg; I once again landed on the ground. I struggled for air as he wrapped his hands around my throat. It hurt, but he didn't cut off my air supply.

"Better," he said, releasing me.

"You're improving, Auluria," Lowell commented as he walked over to us. He motioned for me to follow him. I was grateful for the reprieve.

"I know this has not been an easy transition for you, Auluria, but I appreciate that you are making the effort. I know Shadoe is training you hard, but it's only because I want you to survive. This fight that we are in is not easy. I won't send you out there unprepared."

"I'm trying," I said weakly.

"I know you are." He nodded. "You just have to *keep* trying. You did better today. But now that you are doing better, he's going to push you harder. It won't seem like it's getting any easier, even though you are improving each day. Don't get discouraged."

We walked along through the field toward the trees.

I wished Lowell would spend more time with me. We were never close, but at least when I was a child, he'd spend time playing with me. Now he only spoke to me when necessary. He let Shadoe oversee everything I did.

"Auluria, you know what we're doing is the right thing, don't you?" Lowell asked, his words drawn out.

"I do," I said with measured breath.

We continued forward to his temporary shelter. Lowell's group had a transient nature to it. They were always moving from place to place. They never stayed still for long. All of the housing was short term. We lived in the woods, in fields, and, on occasion, we spent a few nights in an actual home.

I never did understand why Lowell chose this over his parents' home. It sat abandoned in town since Lowell had taken me in. I missed the walls and the protection the small house offered. I missed the privacy.

"The government needs to be destroyed and reestablished," Lowell continued, sitting down in front of a fire. "You are smart, Auluria; once you finish your training, I know you will be a great asset to our campaign. I can see you rising in the ranks quickly. Even as a child, you were very good at problem-solving."

His lips tugged up just a touch as he remembered our childhood games. My own followed suit as I stretched a hand out toward the fire. The evenings were cool, and as we sat in the twilight I could feel the sweat on my skin take a frosty turn. I shifted closer to the fire.

"I'll do my best, Lowell," I assured him.

I hated the idea of fighting. I didn't like that I needed to be trained. But I also wanted to be prepared. I knew what happened to girls like me if the Society caught us alone.

We lived in a place that was haunted by threats from foreign nations. Our government gave them our food and resources to secure safety and protection, but it wasn't enough. They demanded more, and the more they demanded, the more the Society took from its people. A wall was constructed around the nation to protect it, keeping invaders at bay. The people were left with barely enough to survive. Like the fire in front of me, the nations only grew, demanding everything in their paths. The government wanted an army to defeat our enemies. The boys were sent to training camps to learn to fight while the girls that were captured were sent to breeding camps to further populate the country. Orphans were taken first, then young people, then anyone the soldiers found alone that could be easily overtaken.

I knew learning to fight would give me the power to protect myself, so I tolerated my lessons with Shadoe. I also knew Lowell was protecting me and I needed to help him. I wanted to stop the government too; the government that had destroyed us all.

"Auluria, Shadoe is doing a good job training you. I know it isn't easy right now, but trust me, it's for the best."

"I know Lowell, I trust you."

I saw his eyes brighten, the skin on his face tightening as he suppressed a grin. "Good."

TEMPERED
THE DOV PREQUEL

"Get up," Berwyn sounded angry.

"I'm up," I mumbled, rolling over on the cot. I untangled myself from the sheets, setting my feet on the cold floor.

"We have places to be, baby brother, now let's move," Berwyn chides.

"How are you up before me?" I run my fingers through my hair, working out a couple of knots. "You're never up this early."

"Only when we have a mission."

"We're going on a mission?" I asked, now fully awake.

"Dad has somewhere for us to be today—now, let's go."

"Okay, I'm up, I'm up." I scrambled to get dressed and pull my boots on. "What's the mission?"

"We're going to town," Berwyn said, grabbing a few berries from the bowl on the table. "We have a contact to meet."

"Is Dad coming too?" I hurried to the table to grab something to eat before we left.

"Yes, he wants to introduce us to the contact so that we can run messages for him."

"Ready, boys?" Dad asked, strolling into the room with an easy smile.

We nodded and followed him outside. I grabbed a few berries to take along the way.

The trees were bathed in yellow light. I ducked under the low branches next to my dad as I walked beside him —I was quickly approaching his height. To be fair, neither Berwyn nor I would ever be as tall as Griz Baer was, but I was happy with catching up.

"Apple?" he asked, pulling one down from a branch as we passed.

Berwyn reached up, plucking his own from the tree. I bit into the one my father tossed to me, the flavor making my jaw tingle into my ears—it was *perfect*.

"Where are we headed?" I asked, crunching on another bite of the apple.

"I need to take you two to meet someone today," Dad says, glancing over at Berwyn. "He used to be one of Lowell's contacts, but now that he's taking a step back, I need you two to step up and fill the void."

He put Lowell's probation in a softer light than he should have.

"Have you talked to him recently?" Berwyn asked, looking at our father out of the corner of his eye.

"Yes, we've talked," Dad nodded. "He understands that he needs to stay on course if he wishes to continue working with us to bring down the Society and restore a more peaceful nation. He's been doing well accommodating his restrictions."

Berwyn ducked under a tree branch as we stepped out of the woods. The dirt road was packed down so hard that the dust didn't even kick up as we walk into the town.

People bustled by, trading goods and having conversations. I waved to a guy my age sitting in his father's shop as he worked. Peter and his father secretly worked with our family, acting as our lookouts in the town—one of many.

We wove our way around carts and tables, only stopping once or twice to pick a few supplies up. Berwyn kept a watchful eye on me as if I might wander off, but my father's wink softened the oversight.

"This is Lionel," Dad nodded ahead, waving his hand slightly. "He's your new contact."

Lionel greeted my father warmly as we approached.

"Griz," he said, smiling. "Glad you made it. Lowell still on probation?"

"He is," my father answered. "He's coming around though. I think he just needed to get it out of his system. For now, you're going to be working with my boys. You remember Berwyn and Dov, right?"

"I do. Hello, boys." He smiled politely at us. "It's been quite a while since I've seen either of you. You were both pretty young the last time I was out your way. It's nice to officially meet you again."

"Nice to meet you, Lionel," Berwyn greeted him.

"Let's take a little walk," Lionel said as he turned. "I'll show you our locations for meetings."

He guided us around the town to several places, telling us what signals to watch for at each location so we would know when it was safe to approach. It was nice that he included me as part of the team—usually Berwyn did most of the work because he was older and respected more.

"Dov," my dad pulled me back as Lionel showed Berwyn around. "I know you've been looking to take on more authority in the group. I'd like to expand some of your responsibilities, starting with this. You've been handling quite a bit of the lower-level work with our contacts, but now I want you to start taking on more of our crucial work. I've already started Berwyn, but now it's your turn."

"I'd like that," I answered.

"You've been doing a great job, son," he replied. "I think you have a real talent for this. Silas too. I'd like to give him more responsibility as well. I've already spoken to his father about it. You two make a great team, and I'd like to pair you together for a few missions."

Silas was like a brother to Berwyn and me. The only thing that truly separated us was having different parents. Silas had been with us for as long as I could remember— our mothers were good friends when they were younger.

"That would be great, Dad."

"I need you to pay close attention to this. Lionel will be your brother's contact, but you'll need to meet with him on occasion too. You and Silas are going to be doing more intelligence gathering for me rather than this type of work, but you'll still need to be familiar with it. Think you can handle that?"

"Absolutely," I confirmed. I was beginning to like this trip.

"Good. Pay attention—I'm sending you back here later," he warned me.

I watched everywhere we went, trying to commit it all to memory. *I'd be back soon.*

"Lionel," I greeted him quietly, slipping up next to the man at a stand. He looked at a pile of apples, examining each one before setting them back down.

"Dov, Silas," he responded without looking at us. "Do you have it?"

I took the bag off my shoulder, letting it rest in my hand. Lionel casually reached down and took it from me, shifting it onto his own shoulder after a minute.

"That one, please," he said, pointing to a small basket of apples. "Thanks."

He handed the man money for his purchase and turned to me.

"Well, it's been a few weeks, how do you boys think it's going?" he asked.

"I feel like I've learned a lot," Silas responded. "Griz has been sending us on a lot of missions—I think we've done well."

"I agree," I added. "I feel like I have a much better grasp on doing reconnaissance work. Yesterday, we helped Arin out with a mission."

"That's good," Lionel responded. "Have you seen Peter yet today?"

"We stopped there first. He's actually coming back with us for a few days."

"Dov!" We heard him before we saw him in the crowd.

"Speaking of..." Silas mumbled quietly.

"Dov," Peter was out of breath when he approached me. He breathed heavily as he rested a hand on my shoulder, bent over to try to regulate his oxygen intake. "There's a problem."

"What's wrong?" Lionel asked, taking over.

"Something happened in the next town over," Peter gasped. "I don't know what it is, but my father sent me to find you. They're blaming your father for something. You need to go warn him."

Silas' face matched my own. Lionel gripped my shoulder, turning me to face him.

"Now, listen, Dov. You go find your father, and then send Arin to meet me by the edge of town. I'm going to do some digging today to find out what happened." He turned to Peter. "I want you to go with them and make sure everyone is in a safe location until we know what is going on. I'll send your father after you—don't go back to him."

We nodded.

"Go quickly and don't come back until we know what's happened. Avoid the Society men at all costs," he added. Lionel pushed us down the street, away from the town. "Hurry and don't get caught."

We rushed through the streets as quickly as we could without running. Once we reached the woods, we took off, racing as fast as possible up hills and under low tree branches.

"How bad is this?" I asked when we were far enough away that we wouldn't be overheard.

"Bad," Peter shook his head. "I don't know what happened, but, Dov, they're coming for your dad. I don't think its safe."

I took a deep breath, forcing myself not to stop running to process his words. We'd figure something out —we always did.

"What do you think Griz is going to do?" Silas wondered, darting around a tangled mass of roots sticking out of the ground.

"I don't know, but I think it's a smart idea to get him where the Society can't find him," I replied, using my hand to lift a branch as I fly under it. It snapped back behind me when I let it go.

"That's probably a good idea," Silas commented.

"Where will he go?" Peter asked, trying to keep up with us. He spent most of his life in the town, leaving him without our strict training and physical conditioning. He had done some of it with us, just not to the extent we had been trained.

"We have a few safe houses that we keep for this reason. We've also got the storehouses if we need somewhere else to stay," I informed him. "We have options— Dad has always been prepared."

"I have a feeling you'll be staying with us for a while, Peter," Silas mused as he pulled forward just enough to make Peter work harder to keep up. We were trying to do our best to wait for him, but we needed to get back to the group.

"Can't say it would be the worst thing in the world," Peter tried to grin. "Almost there."

He lowered his head as he pushed forward, trying to make the last bit of the sprint to the storehouse where we would find my father. We burst through doors, causing everyone within a twenty-foot radius to turn to us.

I scanned the crowd, searching for my father and Berwyn. The great Griz Baer leans around Arin to look at me. When he saw the look on my face, he marched over to me, Arin and my brother close behind.

"Peter and his father sent word that there was an incident in the next town over," I reported. "We don't know what is it yet—Lionel was going to look into it—but the Society is blaming you. We were sent to tell you."

My father's face paled.

"We had a mission there today." His voice was low and gravelly, a sign that he was worried. "We need to check on our men."

He moved toward the door, but Silas and I blocked him.

"You can't," I protested. "They're looking for you."

"I'll go," Berwyn volunteered.

I shook my head.

"Lionel said to send Arin," I responded, turning to the tall man. "You need to meet him by the edge of town for a report."

Arin turned to look at my father. After a long pause, Dad released him to go investigate.

"We think you need to stay in a safe house," I proposed. "We can't have the Society catch you before we even know what is going on."

"Dov, I know your heart is in the right place, but I'm not just going to leave our men out there to face the Society on their own." He stooped down to place his hand on my shoulder and looked me in the eyes. "I'll be okay. You wait here with your brother and I'll be back soon."

"I think you need to stay," Berwyn objected. "*I just....*you need to stay."

Berwyn didn't often have trouble with words, so it got my father's attention.

"You really think so?"

"I do," Berwyn nodded emphatically.

"Sometimes our bodies know things our brains don't, boys. *Sometimes*, you need to listen to that intuition." He took a step back. "We'll wait for Arin to report back."

Relief flooded over me. I watched as he wandered over to a group of people to start informing them of what was going on. I knew he wouldn't take this sitting down—he'd start making a plan immediately.

"At least we got him to stay," Silas murmured next to me.

"*Berwyn* got him to stay," I corrected him, running my hand through my hair.

"Yeah, let's remember that trick next time," Silas smirked.

"Good call," I grin. "Hey, where did Peter go?"

"He's over there talking to the girls," Silas waved in their general direction.

"Oh," I replied, looking down. I shouldn't have been surprised Peter would be taking advantage of spending time with the girls while he was here—he doesn't get to see them often. "Maybe you should go and talk to them too."

He shrugged as if it didn't matter, but it did. I knew Silas had a fondness for one of the girls but hadn't said anything to her yet.

"Maybe *you* should, buddy. *You're* the one they all dote over."

"Yeah," I rolled my eyes. "That's only because I'm Berwyn's brother and Dad's son."

"Probably," he agreed. His face lit up mischievously. If we weren't inside, I would have pummeled him. Too bad he was aware of that too and played into it. "But we've got to find you a girl *somehow*, my friend. *Take what you can get.*"

"Did I just hear you say that you're available, Dov?" a soft voice interrupted the conversation.

"Hi, Kat," Silas greeted Katarina, swinging around. "Long time, no see."

"Hello, Silas," she purred, sidling up next to him. She waved her hand around at the various meetings happening in the room. "You want to tell me what's going on or do I have to flirt with Dov to get it out of you two?"

Silas grinned, having much more fun with the conversation than I was—he wiped the look off his face before answering.

"It looks like one of our missions went sideways, and the Society figured out we were involved. We're waiting to see what happens."

Katarina pulls an apple out of her bag.

"When was the last time you boys ate?" she asked, twisting the apple in her hand. "You two should eat something now, in case you don't have time later."

"What's going on?" Reyla demanded playfully as she approached.

"Something is up and the boys need to eat before they go running off to handle it," Katarina announced. Silas grew quiet.

"We'll be okay," I supplied, "but thank you, Katarina."

"Fine, be that way." She sashayed away. "But don't say I didn't warn you."

"Okay," I called after her, turning back to Silas. Reyla followed after her friend. "You know, she was probably right."

"So, we'll go find food. It's probably a wise choice for your father to eat too. Let's go grab something for him."

We spend the next hour foraging for food and information.

BONUS SCENES

Want to read bonus scenes from Golden? We're giving out exclusive bonus scenes over on the K.M. Robinson Facebook page where you can read scenes from Dov and Reyla's perspectives.

Get them by sending the page a direct message

We're constantly giving out additional bonus scenes for preorder swag, giveaways, and more, so watch the social media pages carefully for the next scene giveaway.

THE COMPLETE GOLDEN TRILOGY

Did you know the complete Golden Trilogy is now available with all three books and two prequel novellas?

THE EBOOK BOXSET and printed omnibus contains

Golden, Locked, and Edge, as well as the prequel novella, Forged, which tells the story of Auluria's training before Lowell sent her on that deadly mission to destroy the Baer family, *and* an exclusive bonus novella, Tempered, which tells the events in Dov's life before he met Auluria —including what happened to his father.

You can only access Tempered and an exclusive note from the author through the boxset/omnius.

For more information, please visit
goldentrilogy.kmrobinsonbooks.com

WORLD PORTALS

Ready to learn exclusive facts about The Golden Trilogy and other K.M. Robinson Series?

World Portals are now available on www. kmrobinsonbooks.com

Learn behind the scenes facts, watch videos, play games, check out our book filters, find out where to get bonus scenes, view fan art, and get access to other secrets we've hidden away inside the World Portals on the website.

The World Portals are constantly changing and information is being taken away and added all the time, so check back frequently for new content!

Auluria will meet with you few times for different missions over the course of a few days, with gaps of time in between so you can "complete the missions" and report back. She will be in touch!

Have fun running missions to help Auluria find Dov and Berwyn and then go back in the story to see how your choices directly affect them in the story.

BONUS FACEBOOK FILTERS

Want to get your hands on some incredible Facebook filters for Golden? Now you have the ability to get filters for the story, characters, etc right inside your phone.

You can use these on your photos, profile pictures, videos, and live broadcasts. All you have to do is like my author page and they will automatically show up in your filters!

I've even taken these clips and put them on Instagram Stories by saving them to my phone and uploading them to Instagram.

Visit www.facebook.com/kmrobinsonbooks to grab these filters for your photos, videos, and broadcasts! Bonus points for tagging me @kmrobinsonbooks so I can see how you're supporting The Golden Trilogy.

ABOUT THE AUTHOR

K.M. Robinson is a storyteller who creates new worlds both in her writing and in her fine arts conceptual photography. She is a marketing, branding and social media strategy educator who is recognized at first sight by her very long hair. She is a creative who focuses on photography, videography, couture dress making, and writing to express the stories she needs to tell. She almost always has a camera within reach. Visit her at her website: www.kmrobinsonbooks.com

CONNECT ON SOCIAL MEDIA

facebook.com/kmrobinsonbooks

instagram.com/kmrobinsonbooks

twitter.com/kmrobinsonbooks

Get free excerpts and full novels from K.M. Robinson at
excerpt.kmrobinsonbooks.com

ALSO BY K.M. ROBINSON

The Golden Trilogy

Book One: Golden

Forged: A Golden Novella

Book Two: Locked

Book Three: Edge

The Complete Series Boxset/Omnibus with Tempered: an exclusive bonus novella

The Jaded Duology

Book One: Jaded

Book Two: Risen

The Complete Series Boxset/Omnibus with exclusive epilogue

The Siren Wars Saga

Book One: The Siren Wars

Book Two: Darker Depths

Book Three: Beyond The Shores

Origins of the Siren Wars: Prequel Novella

Book Four: Forbidden Waters (coming soon)

The Legends Chronicles

Along Came A Spider: A Prequel Novelette

And They'll Come Home: A Prequel Novelette

The Archives of Jack Frost Series

The Revolution of Jack Frost

The Redemption of Jack Frost (coming soon)

Stealing Steam Series

Book One: Lions and Lamps

Book Two: Pistons and Prisoners

Book Three: Railcars and Rulers

Top Hats and Telegraphs: A Prequel Novella

The Complete Series Boxset/Omnibus with Vambraces and Victories: an exclusive bonus novella

Virtually Sleeping Beauty: A Novella Retelling

The Goose Girl and The Artificial: A Novella Retelling

The Sinking: A Little Mermaid Novella Retelling

Cindrill: A Cinderella Assassin Novella Retelling

Sugarcoated: A Hansel and Gretel's Witch Novella Retelling

Blood Is Silent: A Red Riding Hood Circus Retelling

JADED: BOOK ONE OF THE JADED DUOLOGY

If the only way to stay alive was to convince your new husband not to murder you and make it look like an accident, could you do it?

At eighteen, Jade shouldn't have to be forced to marry the son of her father's enemy as part of a revenge plot for a failed rebellion. When she's thrown into the life of being the wife of the Commander's son and heir, her only hope for survival is convincing Roan Diamond to actually fall in love with her so that he doesn't kill her on his father's wishes.

While a dutiful son, Roan shouldn't have to trick his new wife into believing his family accepts her, but as the only one in a position to make the country believe Jade is part of their family, he will do what he has to before his family murders his young bride and makes it look like an accident to get back at Jade's father.

With half the country trying to protect Jade and the other half oblivious to the atrocities committed at the Commander's hand, it's a race to see who will win at a deadly game of cat and mouse.

One chooses life. One chooses death. In the midst of chaos, only one will succeed.

Now available!
Learn more about The Jaded Duology at
jadedinfo.kmrobinsonbooks.com

THE SIREN WARS: BOOK ONE OF THE SIREN WARS SAGA

War has hovered around the kingdom of Scylla for generations ever since the original sirens left the mer collection generations ago after nearly drowning the human prince. Over the years, select mermaids from the royal bloodline have been trained as spies to work for the reigning kings and queens, keeping the collection safe from sirens and humans.

Celena and her partner, Merrick, work covertly for the royals—not even her twin brother knows. When they discover the sirens have broken through the barriers the mer set up to keep the sirens out, Celena and her friends must race to the old kingdom of Metten to stop them from starting a war within their borders.

When she's dragged to the surface, Celena realizes that the war above the waters is as deadly as the one below the waves—and sacrificing herself may be the only way to protect her family.

The Siren Wars have only just begun.

Available now!

Learn more about The Siren Wars Saga at sirenwarsinfo.

kmrobinsonbooks.com

LIONS AND LAMPS: BOOK ONE OF THE STEALING STEAM SERIES

All wishes require sacrifice...*are you willing to pay the price?*

Cyra spent the last seven years being trained to steal an airship in a brutal competition that leaves the victor with millions. Last year, she won.

Aladdin spent the past year fighting to get enough money to take his mother away from Horallen after his father was murdered. Now, his evil uncle Kacper wants to force him into the competition and straight to his death inside the Collection Cave.

When Aladdin discovers a genie said to have been banished a century ago, the competition becomes even deadlier, and he knows he can't trust the girl who snuck into the competition this year...but Cyra might not survive his ruthlessness either in a game where only the lion's heart can win.

All wishes require sacrifice, and someone is going to pay the price for the Stourbridge.

Available now!

Learn more about The Stealing Steam Series at lionsandlampsinfo.kmrobinsonbooks.com

ALONG CAME A SPIDER: THE FIRST PREQUEL NOVELETTE TO THE LEGENDS CHRONICLES

Little Hacker Muffet
sat on her tuffet
destroying her cords and Way.
Along came a hacker named Spider,
who sat down beside her
and frightened his opponent away.

When Fet, one of the most skilled hackers in the Legends, discovers her best friend and leader of her group has been abducted and held for ransom, she must escape unnoticed and find Peep before it's too late.

WHEN SPIDER, a new recruit training to join her hacker

ring, slips out with her and claims to have a plan to save her friend, Fet is forced to bring him along. As she discovers he's not who he claims to be, she faces grave danger and learns just how deadly a spider bite can be.

Now available!

Learn more about The Legends Chronicles at

acasinfo.kmrobinsonbooks.com

VIRTUALLY SLEEPING BEAUTY

To wake her up, he has to enter the game and help her beat it...

SURELY THE CLASS president wouldn't illegally over-juice to stay in the virtual reality game citizens are allowed to play for four hours a day, but when Royce's aunt calls in a panic because her goddaughter hasn't left the game yet, his only option is to go inside the game and drag the girl out.

THE GOLDEN KNIGHT quickly discovers the princess' absence in the real world isn't of her own doing—*she's trapped inside the game by unknown forces*—and if she can't escape soon, she could die for real outside of the game. He's even more shocked to discover that Rora outranks him inside of the game, which means she'll have to fight to *protect herself* from the evils locking her inside a dangerous world.

CAN Rora and Royce work together to outsmart a vicious queen and evil magician, and defeat digital dragons, or will Rora slowly fade away until there's nothing left but an empty shell and the game ranking she will leave behind?

Now available!

Learn more about Virtually Sleeping Beauty at vsbinfo.kmrobinsonbooks.com

THE REVOLUTION OF JACK FROST

No one inside the snow globe knows that Morozoko Industries is controlling their weather, testing them to form a stronger race that can survive the fall out from the bombs being dropped in the outside world—all they know is that they must survive the harsh Winter that lasts a month and use the few days of Spring, Summer, and Fall to gather enough supplies to survive.

When the seasons start shifting, Genesis and Jack know something is going on. As their team begins to find technology that they don't have access to inside their snow globe of a world, it begins to look more and more like one of their own is working against them.

. . .

GENESIS SOON DISCOVERS MOROZOKO INDUSTRIES, but when a foreign enemy tries to destroy their weather program to make sure their destructive life-altering bombs succeed in destroying the outside world, only one person can shut down the machine that is spinning out of control and save the lives of everyone inside the bunker —Jack.

Now available!
Learn more about The Revolution of Jack Frost at
jackfrostinfo.kmrobinsonbooks.com

THE GOOSE GIRL AND THE ARTIFICIAL

What would you do if your artificially intelligent handmaiden stole your identity?

THREATENED BY HER ARTIFICIAL, Arta, Princess Goselyn is forced to switch places and pretend she isn't human when she reaches Prince Corinth to negotiate a treaty they both need to be able to take their respective crowns one day. If she doesn't comply, her Artificial, controlled by her evil cousin, will not only kill Goselyn's mother, but Prince Corinth and his father as well.

CAN the quiet princess outsmart a machine created to be

more intelligent than she is, all while surviving the other Artificials and robots working against her in the foreign palace, or will Corinth and his father find out and destroy her chance to save them all?

Learn more about The Goose Girl and The Artificial at goosegirlinfo.kmrobinsonbooks.com

THE SINKING

The sea witch wants to silence her, but not for the reason you think.

When a quirky older woman pawns a fancy seashell necklace at her mother's antique shop on the pier, Cara doesn't think much about the story the woman spins about the wearer turning into a mermaid.

ON HER WAY HOME, she accidentally drops the necklace into the ocean and is swept out to sea where she meets— a merman who volunteers to take her to his mother, the sea queen, to help her get her legs back.

.   .   .

CARA SOON LEARNS that it's Quay's eighteen birthday—a day that has been a curse for his family—and is meant to be one for her too. Now she must fight to survive the sea with Quay at her side.

Fans of The Little Mermaid will love this twisted take on the beloved story.

Now available!
Learn more about The Sinking at
thesinkinginfo.kmrobinsonbooks.com

CINDRILL

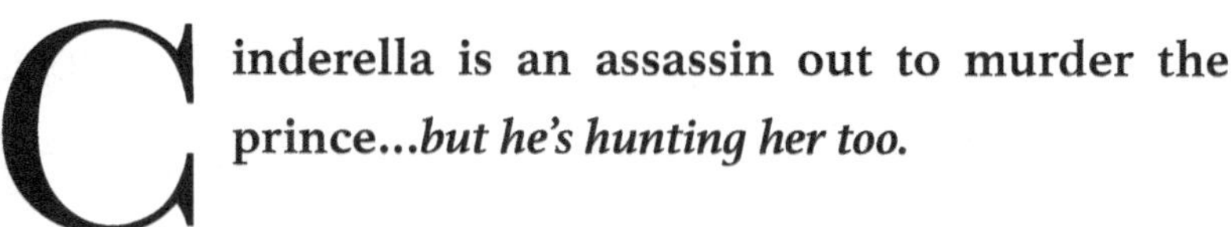

Cinderella is an assassin out to murder the prince...*but he's hunting her too.*

THE NANOBOTS CINDRILL'S master gives her to use as a mask allow her to slip into the ball wearing a face that isn't hers, but when the assassination attempt goes sideways, Prince Davin doesn't understand why her face changes when he injures her, slicing her foot open around a unique pair of shoes as she runs away.

WHEN CINDRILL RUNS into the prince the next day without her nanobot mask on, he doesn't recognize her, but immediately decides her skills will be useful on his hunt for the would-be-assassin woman who nearly killed his father and his fiancée the night before.

BOTH ARE TASKED with the job of murdering the other, but things don't quite go as they had planned when Cindrill's master and Davian's fiancée interfere as the two try to decide whether or not to kill the other.

IT'S hard to recognize a woman when she uses technology to change her appearance, but Cindrill is going to use that to her full advantage as she destroys the prince. ***Will either survive?***

Now available!

Learn more about Cindrill at
cindrillinfo.kmrobinsonbooks.com

SUGARCOATED

Hansel and Gretel's witch was actually on their side...

Annika's job is to create a cake to match the candy-colored rooftops, nightly firework shows, and daily parades ending in unexpected executions for the mad king's ball, but her true mission is to sneak a thirteen-year-old assassin into the palace using her gift of illusions.

Hansel's job is to protect his little sister, Gretel, once she assassinates King Levin and ends the destruction in Candestrachen, using his power over light to rescue the young girl from the chaos her influence over life and death will create.

. . .

WHEN THE ENTIRE forest reconstructs itself under Gretel's command while trying to save herself from a king's guard, Hansel and Annika must put their feelings aside and ensure their plan holds true—even if it means one of them has to sacrifice themselves to protect the mission.

Her illusions were meant to save her....but not everyone will survive the assassination attempt.

Learn more about Sugarcoated at
sugarcoatedinfo.kmrobinsonbooks.com

BLOOD IS SILENT

R*ed Riding Hood is a circus aerialist and the wolf is ready to cage her.*

SIENNA HAS GROWN up working for the circus, dangling off her signature red silks every night. Her grandmother has been known to wander off to train new acts for their boss, but when Sienna tries to find her to bring her back to the show, she doesn't expect the dashing and dangerous Elijah to join her.

WHEN they finally find Grandma Ida has been transformed deep in the heart of the woods, Sienna will stop at nothing to save her—but the wolf has her right where he wants her, and she won't be able to escape his claws.

SHE WAS TOLD NOT to go into the woods alone.

Now available!

Learn more about Blood Is Silent at
bloodissilentinfo.kmrobinsonbooks.com